"Why a

She eased away, thou . . . . waist.
"Because I've been afraid."

"Of what?"

He already knew the answer, she suspected. "Of finding love, only to lose it because   because of what I've done."

"Lark—" he began, but stopped.

Perhaps he intended to say more. Or perhaps he couldn't say anything. She only knew he intended to kiss her again. That she wanted him to. The anticipation built in her, and his arms tightened—

Thwap!

A jagged hole appeared in the trunk of the nearest cottonwood. Bits of bark flew. Lark cried out, Ross swore, and they both dove to the ground for cover.

* * *

Wanted!
Harlequin® Historical #813—August 2006

WANTED!
PAM CROOKS

My best to you.
Pam Crooks

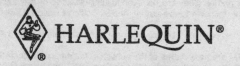

HARLEQUIN®

TORONTO • NEW YORK • LONDON
AMSTERDAM • PARIS • SYDNEY • HAMBURG
STOCKHOLM • ATHENS • TOKYO • MILAN • MADRID
PRAGUE • WARSAW • BUDAPEST • AUCKLAND

ISBN-13: 978-0-373-29413-8
ISBN-10:   0-373-29413-1

WANTED!

www.eHarlequin.com

Printed in U.S.A.

Available from Harlequin® Historical and
PAM CROOKS

The Mercenary's Kiss #718
Spring Brides #755
"McCord's Destiny"
Wanted! #813

DON'T MISS THESE OTHER
NOVELS AVAILABLE NOW:

#811 THE RUNAWAY HEIRESS
Anne O'Brien

#812 THE KNIGHT'S COURTSHIP
Joanne Rock

#814 THE BRIDEGROOM'S BARGAIN
Sylvia Andrew

Please address questions and book requests to:
Harlequin Reader Service
U.S.: 3010 Walden Ave., P.O. Box 1325, Buffalo, NY 14269
Canadian: P.O. Box 609, Fort Erie, Ont. L2A 5X3

To the Tuesday night sisterhood—
Marie Huggins, Marge Knudsen and Renee Spencer.

And to my editor across the Pond—Joanne Carr.
You're the best!

Prologue

Windsor, Canada, 1868

No one paid much attention to the old, nondescript buggy ambling down the road. But then again, no one dared. They might've been shot for their trouble.

Jack Friday drove the rig. His passengers knew him as "Catfish Jack" for his strange-looking eyes and reputation for being as ruthless as the cold-blooded, river-bottom dwellers of the same name. His crimes had chased him north across the border to hide out for a spell, leastways unless the law found him first.

Just like his passengers had.

They were all that were left of the Reno gang these days. With their leader, John Reno, incarcerated in the Missouri State Penitentiary, and brothers William and Simeon jailed in Indiana, only Frank was left to lead the others in crime—and keep them all alive.

"I'm telling you, I can feel 'em breathing down my neck, Frank," Charlie Anderson muttered. His uneasy gaze clawed the Canadian countryside. He kept his hand close to the Colt slung to his hip.

"Who?" Frank slouched in the seat across from him. The outlaw, known for his merciless train and stagecoach robberies, took a leisurely pull on his rolled cigarette.

"The Pinkertons. Conniving bastards. I can smell 'em coming."

"They can't touch us. They'd have to extradite us to the States first," Frank said with a cool smile. "And that ain't easy to do. Canada's the safest place to be right now."

"Them agents will find a way. Or maybe some crazy vigilantes will beat 'em to it."

"Or a damned bounty hunter."

The men's gazes swung to the youngest of their gang, a fiery-haired, pants-clad hellion known as "Wild Red."

Charlie scowled. "What're you worried about, Red?" he demanded. "You ain't got no one's blood on your hands."

"Don't need to kill a man to be wanted by the law," she said. Smoke curled from the cheroot between her fingers—slender and smooth and quick as lightning on a trigger. Her expression hardened. "Bounty hunters don't care what crime you did. Just the price on your head for it."

Frank grunted in agreement. "Red ain't no killer, Charlie. Just one of the best damn robbers there is. Ain't that right, Red?"

"Yep." What pride she might have felt from the rare compliment dissolved on a troubling thought. She studied the burning end of the cheroot. "I've been thinking a lot about the Muscatine loot, Frank."

"Reckon we all think of it now and again. None of us got our shares yet."

"Loot?" From the glint in Charlie's eyes, it was obvious his unease over Pinkerton agents and bounty hunters had slipped in importance. "What loot?"

"From the county treasury," she said, impatience giving a snap to the words. "Muscatine, Iowa. Last winter."

"You hadn't met up with us yet," Frank added. "You was still locked up in Missouri."

Charlie gave a quick nod now that he knew which heist they spoke of. "If you didn't split up the money, where the hell is it?"

Wild Red took her time replying. He expected her to spill more information, but she was cousin to the Reno brothers, and blood ran thick. She trusted no one but them.

"The money's just waiting for us, Frank," she said as if Charlie hadn't spoken. "All we got to do is get it."

"And how in blazes are we supposed to do that, bein's we ain't even in the same country anymore?"

"Borders can be crossed."

"Hell, Red, you got nerve," Frank said and shook his head in amusement. "Things are too hot right now. You know that."

She took a last drag on the cheroot, then flicked the stub into a scrap of weeds. "It's a waste, that's all. We can use the money to get your brothers out of jail, then hightail it to South America."

Over and over again, she'd thought of how they could live a normal life there. Without lawmen. Without the constant threat of a noose around their neck.

"In due time, cousin. In due time."

It'd been hard leaving thousands of dollars in gold, bank notes and sweet, green cash behind that night. Real hard. But John Reno had been emphatic in hiding the loot after they broke into the pretty new Muscatine Treasury office. He'd been unusually desperate, too. Wild Red suspected his growing list of robberies made him nervous. John figured the money would be their insurance to get them to South America. All they had to do was lay low for a while, then come back for it.

At the time, his plan made sense. Shortly after, though, he was arrested and thrown behind bars where he remained today. And there all that money sat. Waiting for them. Untouched.

Still, she made no further argument. Frank was right. In due time. She'd chosen the perfect hiding place for the loot. No one knew its location except for herself, John and Frank, and they'd sworn each other to secrecy.

"Turf Club just ahead," Catfish Jack said, twisting in the driver's seat and pointing to the cluster of wooden houses that loomed before them. "There's smoke comin' from Queenie's chimney. Looks like she's cookin' up one of her stews again."

There were few places fugitives could run to without retaliation, but the Turf Club was one of them. Men from all walks of life, guilty of crimes ranging from forgery to theft to murder, fled to Windsor and its Turf Club to hide out. Women came, too, if they were running from the law. Red had formed a friendship with Queenie, a sharp-tongued beauty from Mexico.

As the rig slowed, Charlie's hand found his Colt. The unease seemed to crawl up his spine again, even here at the Club, the one place he should've felt safe enough.

Odd that he didn't. His unease was catching, though Wild Red's slow, assessing gaze of the area revealed nothing out of the ordinary. Even so, she was glad for the weapons she kept strapped to her hips.

The rig stopped, and Frank and Charlie stepped out. Catfish Jack jumped down from the box, and when Wild

Red climbed from her seat, too, none of them offered their assistance. Not that she expected them to. Outlaws rarely afforded women like her the chivalry women in polite society enjoyed—and received.

They trailed into the house ahead of her. With the door closed and four walls to surround them, she allowed herself to relax. Sure enough. Queenie had a pot of stew simmering, and Wild Red's belly gurgled in hungry anticipation.

Frank strode to the kitchen. Dick Barry, a desperado who rumor claimed would coolly plug a man for two dollars—one, if he was drunk—sat at the table with a glass of whiskey in front of him. At their arrival, he rose and relinquished his seat to Frank, whose reputation and ability to elude arrest time and time again had earned him a high place in the hideout's outlaw hierarchy. Without greeting, Frank took it.

Something was on his mind. Wild Red could taste it. Charlie, too, seeing how he was watching Frank real close.

"Been thinking about what you said about the Pinks, Charlie," Frank said finally, reaching into his pocket for another rolled cigarette. "Maybe we ought to do something about 'em."

"Yeah?" Charlie leaned back in his chair. "Like what?"

"Knock off the old man. Allan Pinkerton. That should keep 'em off our tails for awhile."

Alarm filtered through Wild Red, but she took care not to show it. She'd never developed a liking for killing. "Damned crazy idea if you ask me."

Frank shot her a cold glance. "I'm not asking."

"Best thing I've heard all day," Charlie said and grinned.

"You got anyone in mind for the job?" Dick asked.

"As a matter of fact, I do."

Their gazes met, and an unspoken agreement filtered between the two men. Wild Red turned away in disgust. She caught Queenie's eye, and her friend gave her a quick warning shake of her head.

Wild Red kept her mouth shut. They lived in a man's world. Lawless men, at that. Nothing Wild Red could say or do would make Frank change his mind.

"What's the matter, Red?" Catfish Jack cooed. "You scared?"

He sat at her end of the table and didn't take part in the plans the other men made. He leered at her with those peculiar eyes of his, eyes that were shifty and cold. One had the unnerving way of looking in a slightly different direction than its mate.

"Leave me alone."

She needed a stiff drink. She rose to fetch herself a glass and partake in that bottle of whiskey the men were sharing.

From the window next to the shelf holding their dishes, a wagon moseyed into view. A wagon so oddly-built that the sight of it distracted her for a moment.

Catfish gripped her elbow and pulled her back down into the chair.

"Ol' Catfish'll take real good care of you, y'know that, don't you, Red?" he drawled. A grimy hand reached to smooth the wild wisps of hair that always escaped her hat.

Repulsed, she shoved against him with both fists and nearly sent him toppling from his seat, forcing him to scramble for balance.

"Don't touch me, you lousy son-of-a-bitch," she snarled.

Catfish spat an oath but Wild Red evaded his reach. Her gaze shot back to the window. The wagon was still out there, moving too slow to make much progress. It was built like a—a Trojan horse. All enclosed, strange-like, as if it was hiding something.

Or someone.

Wild Red leapt to her feet, both Colts in her hands.

"We got trouble, Frank!" she yelled and bolted toward Queenie, stirring the stew unaware at the stove. Red knocked her from view. "The law!"

Frank jumped up and swore viciously, his revolver swinging. "The law? Where?"

"Outside! They're right outside!"

Dick lunged for his Winchester rifle and took up position at the window. He smashed the barrel through the glass.

"Not yet!" Frank said, joining him. "Wait 'til you can get a good shot at 'em!"

But the whiskey Dick had imbibed all afternoon numbed all reason. "I'll get the driver first."

Just then, as if he'd heard every word of the plan, the driver dived over the side of the rig, out of view. The top of the wagon burst open.

"We'll shoot 'em crawling out, the bastards!" Charlie yelled. "Cover me, Catfish!"

Charlie ran toward the door. Catfish swung it open, his shotgun leveled. To Red's horror, the wagon bed belched out a horde of Pinkerton agents right along with a fusillade of deafening gunfire.

"The back door!" Queenie yelled over the roar, giving her a shove in that direction. *Thwap! Thwap!* Bullets pinged around them. *Thwap!* "Let's go!"

Red flew toward the only escape they had left, but before she could reach it, before either of them could, the door crashed open, and a tall, bloodthirsty bounty hunter stood waiting for them, his rifle cocked and ready.

Queenie swore. Wild Red aimed her revolver. Her finger moved over the trigger—

But the bounty hunter was faster. His bullet sliced through her, and Wild Red went down in a pool of blood.

Chapter One

❧❧❧

Five Years Later

Lark Renault pushed the Total key on her shiny new Victor adding machine, pulled the crank and compared the number which printed on the paper tape to the sum on her ledger page. She smiled and sat back in satisfaction.

Balanced to the penny.

She closed the ledger. The last of the quarterly reports Mr. Templeton, the Ida Grove Bank's president, had asked her to compile was finished. She took great pride in that he trusted her with the responsibility, especially since she'd only arrived in this western Iowa town barely six months ago and was his newest employee.

Not that the institution had a large number of people on the payroll. Still, he'd expanded her duties beyond that of a teller, even trusting her with managing the place by herself every day while the rest of the employees went to lunch.

Lark supposed it was her gift with numbers. She was amazingly accurate with them. Sums came quickly to her, even without the aid of the latest Victor Mr. Templeton ordered just for her. Addition, subtraction, multiplication and division—numbers fascinated her, any which way she could figure them.

"Miss Renault. Come in here, please."

Mr. Templeton called her from his office at the rear of the small bank and sent her thoughts scattering. She rose quickly from her desk to obey.

Glass enclosed the crisp, efficient room where he conducted the most important financial transactions. Here, he could see each customer as they walked in and the tellers who assisted them. Here, too, was where the vault had been placed and, under Mr. Templeton's watchful eye, no one could enter the steel-enclosed chamber without his notice.

"My wife and son will be arriving soon," he said. Silver streaked the hair at his temples, though he was only a decade or so older than Lark's twenty-two years. His well-tailored suit showed not a speck of lint or unnecessary wrinkle. He was always fastidious about his appearance, from his meticulously trimmed fingernails to the shine on his leather shoes. "Show them in when they get here, won't you?"

"Certainly, Mr. Templeton."

"We'll be going to Omaha for the weekend, so I'll be leaving the bank early this afternoon. I'd like you to close up for me in my absence."

Pride swelled through her at this new responsibility. "I can do that, Mr. Templeton. Of course."

He smiled, gave her a brisk nod of dismissal and immersed himself in his work again. Upon leaving his office to return to her desk, she nearly collided with Mrs. Pankonin, the head cashier.

"So you'll be locking the doors today," she sniffed in a

voice their employer couldn't hear. She held a stack of bank notes in each hand and was on her way into the vault to store them.

"Yes, I will." Lark refused to let the older woman's antagonism deflate her pride. Perhaps if she wasn't so crotchety all the time, Mr. Templeton would be more inclined to depend on her more. As it was, most days he tended to avoid her. "Excuse me, won't you?"

Lark sashayed past her. From Mrs. Pankonin's perspective, she guessed, it wasn't fair that Mr. Templeton depended on Lark so much, not when Mrs. Pankonin had been employed longer than any of them, including Mr. Templeton himself. The woman knew the workings of the bank, inside and out. She was certainly capable of any task given to her.

Lark closed her mind to the woman's jealousy. She loved her job too much to let the pinch-nosed, whiny-voiced widow bother her unduly.

She had just finished figuring the interest due upon a draft and recording a customer's payment when Amelia Templeton arrived with her six-year-old son, Phillip. A cloud of expensive perfume alerted Lark to her presence, and before she could direct the pair into the president's office, Phillip pulled his hand from his mother's and darted toward Lark.

"I sit here, Mama," he said and crawled onto the chair closest to Lark's desk.

"But, Phillip," Amelia said with a doting smile. "Don't you want to see Papa? He has peppermint candy in his drawer for you."

"Don't want peppermint." The little boy shook his head emphatically. "I sit here with Lark."

"You must address her properly." Amelia's tone was

much too gentle to convince the child to obey. She glanced apologetically at Lark. "I'm sorry. What is your name?"

"Renault," Lark said, trying not to feel inferior that a six-year-old knew who she was but the bank president's wife didn't. "Miss Lark *Renault.*"

"Oh, that's right. I'd forgotten." She turned back to her son. "Did you hear, darling? You must address her as Miss Ree-no."

"No, no," Lark corrected quickly. "It's French. *Ray-nau.*"

Amelia blinked. Clearly, the woman didn't understand the differences in pronunciation, nor did she care about them either way. "Do you mind watching him while I see my husband?"

"Not at all." Lark forced a smile. What else could she say? Amelia was the bank president's wife. Lark had no choice but to be gracious and add child-caring to her duties for the time being.

Petticoats rustling, Amelia swept into the president's office. Lark busied herself double-checking her figures on the draft she'd just completed and found them accurate as usual. With no customers to assist at the moment, she turned to her young charge and found him staring at her in blatant curiosity.

She'd learned from Mrs. Pankonin that Phillip Templeton had been sickly since the day he was born. Lark was certainly no expert on children, but even she could tell he was small-boned and frail for his age. She doubted he played much outside at all—his skin was too pale, too smooth, too *clean.* He wore a neat little suit—a replica of his father's—and she couldn't help wondering if he'd ever dressed in dungarees, gotten dirt under his fingernails or scraped up his knees. Tiny, gold-rimmed spectacles sat on the bridge of his nose; his hair was slicked down and parted in a perfect line down one side of his head.

He clutched a drawing pad to his chest and continued to stare at her through the lenses. He stared so intently Lark had to resist the urge to scold him for his rudeness.

She forced a smile. "So, Phillip. I understand you're going to Omaha for the weekend."

The boy nodded somberly, his little legs swinging.

A moment passed. "Well, what will you do when you get there?"

Slender shoulders lifted in a shrug. "Don't know."

"Perhaps you'll go to a fine restaurant. Or attend a performance at the opera house."

Again, he shrugged. Obviously, neither option excited him much.

She grappled for something else to talk about. Up to now, she'd had pitifully little experience making conversation with small children. She indicated the pad of paper he held like it was his best friend. "Do you like to draw?"

For the first time, his bespectacled eyes lit up. He nodded vigorously.

"What's your favorite thing to sketch?" she asked.

"Outlaws."

Lark couldn't help a small gasp. "Outlaws!"

"Robbers is my favorite."

"Oh, Phillip. You shouldn't— It's hardly appropriate for a little boy to—"

"See?" He opened the sketch pad and thrust it at her.

She gaped at the penciled shapes on the paper, and though he was only six, the markings he'd drawn were appallingly precise.

Her heart began to pound.

"Here's a train," Phillip said. His small finger demanded that she look. "The outlaws are going to rob it. They got guns."

Oh, God, Lark thought in dismay, her gaze riveted to the trio of thieves riding on horses with their weapons smoking. One of them looked like a woman, her hair trailing from beneath her hat....

"And the train has a safe with lots of money in it, but I didn't drawed it 'cuz it's inside the train and you can't see it."

She pressed her fingers to her mouth, watched in horrified fascination as he flipped another page on his sketch pad.

"But I drawed a safe in this picture. See? The money's all gone. The outlaws shot the trainman, and he's dead."

Her eyes widened at the definite shape of a man, lying on the floor, the safe wide open. And empty.

"How can you know about such things?" she demanded, snapping his sketch pad closed. She was tempted to throw the thing in her waste receptacle, but thought better of it. Phillip was Mr. Templeton's son, after all.

"'Cuz Papa has a stereoscope."

"He has pictures of outlaws, too?"

He nodded. "He lets me look at them sometimes."

"He does, does he?" She clucked her tongue in disapproval. The newfangled viewer brought images on slides to life. The images were mostly created by actors posing as outlaws for a photographer, but sometimes the outlaws themselves posed, just for fun. Was it any wonder a little boy believed them real?

The child held the drawings against his chest again. "Mama doesn't like me looking at pictures of outlaws. She thinks I'll get scared from 'em."

Lark's mouth tightened. "They're bad people, Phillip."

"I'm not scared of outlaws, Lark. Are you?"

She gritted her teeth from the child's incessant chattering. "Some, I suppose."

"One of Papa's slides has a lady outlaw in it. You ever hear of a lady outlaw?" He grinned, clearly amused.

Lark glared at him. She didn't think the matter funny at all.

"Know what? Papa's scared that outlaws is going to rob his bank some day."

She rose abruptly. Enough was enough. She refused to listen to any more crazy talk about outlaws and bank robbers, and though Amelia expected her to watch over her son, Lark left him sitting in his chair while she headed to the vault to find something else to do. Mrs. Pankonin could keep an eye on him instead.

A small hand tugged at her skirts. Lark's step faltered, but she didn't stop. Phillip hung on, his shiny-shoed feet scampering to keep up with her.

"Where you going, Lark? Can I come with you?"

"I have work to do." She halted, pried his fingers loose from her skirt, and resumed walking, right into Mr. Templeton's office. It wasn't long before the boy was hanging onto her again.

"You going ___ the vault bef___ ignored his p___ siasm. It was an ___ boy into his mother's lap ___ take care of ___

Once inside the small room, Phillip stared owlishly around him. "O-oh. Look at all the money, Lark. There must be a million dollars in here."

His hushed voice gave her pause. The first time she had stepped into this room, she, too, was taken aback at the amount of currency and gold coins the vault held. Theirs was only a small-town bank; one in a large city would hold several hundred thousand dollars more. Still, to a little boy, the money would look like a fortune.

"No, Phillip. Not a million. Not even close," she said thoughtfully, and upon realizing he no longer clung to her skirts, she busied herself counting a stack of dollar bills.

"Can I help, Lark? Can I?"

"No, you may not."

"I can count good. One, two, three—"

"I'm sure you can count just fine." Exasperated, she stopped counting, her place lost. Now she'd have to start over again. "You can sit next to me and watch if you promise not to say another word."

Again, his eyes lit up. "I'll be real quiet."

Not at all convinced, she found a wooden stool, placed it right beside her and whisked Phillip into the seat. The child hardly weighed a thing, he was so frail, and some of her annoyance with him dissipated.

True to his word, he sat silently while she counted. He kept his drawings clutched to his chest, his fascinated gaze always upon her and the money she counted. She couldn't help glancing over at him now and again, just to make sure he was still sitting there.

He was being so good, something melted inside her. Impulsively, she reached out and patted the top of his head. She couldn't recall feeling affectionate toward a child before in her entire life.

"I'll bet you're going to be a banker when you grow up, just like your father, aren't you?" she said, banding a stack of bills and recording the amount in the proper column of her ledger.

He shook his head. "Nope. I'm going to be an outlaw."

The pencil lead veered past the ledger lines. She darted a quick glance into Mr. Templeton's office. He was engrossed in conversation with his wife, and neither overhead their son's declaration. Lark snatched a rubber eraser.

"That's the silliest thing I've ever heard of," she hissed. "What does your father have to say about it?"

"I didn't tell him."

"And if I were you, I wouldn't. Ever. He'd have palpitations from it."

Mr. Templeton was an upright and respected member of the community. All the tellers and cashiers at the Ida Grove Bank admired him. Lark knew he had high hopes his only son would receive a fine education and follow in his footsteps one day. What father wouldn't?

"Can it be our secret, Lark? I never told nobody I want to be an outlaw 'cept you."

Her eyes narrowed. Why he trusted her with his secret, she had no idea, but one thing was certain. She had no intention of telling a single soul.

"Well, look at you, darling! Are you helping Miss Reeno count her money like a big boy?" Amelia cooed from the doorway.

"Ray-nau," Lark corrected quickly, whirling toward her. "Remember? It's French."

"Naw. I'm not old enough," Phillip said, wriggling off his chair. Fearful he'd fall, Lark hastily helped him down. "She just let me watch."

His mother took his hand and smiled. "Someday, you'll be president of Papa's bank, and then you can count all the money you want." She turned to Lark. "Thank you for watching him. He's taken quite a liking to you, it seems."

"Hmm." Lark didn't know what to make of it.

"Tell the nice lady goodbye, Phillip. We're leaving for Omaha now."

"'Bye, Lark." His bespectacled gaze clung to her as his mother led him from the vault, as if he much preferred to spend the afternoon with her than with his parents in a carriage heading to Nebraska. Precise as always, Mr. Templeton gave Lark a list of instructions on how to close up the bank at the end of the day. Lark knew what to do, even without the list, but she nodded in all seriousness. Mr. Templeton's trust in her was not to be taken lightly.

Finally, his coat donned and his desk tidied for the weekend, he was ready to leave with his family. Amelia slipped her arm into his, and he patted her hand in obvious affection. Together, the three of them left the Ida Grove Bank.

Lark sighed out loud. He was obviously in love with his wife. Did Amelia know how lucky she was to have a husband like Mr. Templeton? Handsome, talented, with a keen mind for business and financial matters, he had *perfect* written all over him.

Sometimes, when she lay alone and pensive in her bed at night, Lark pretended Mr. Templeton wasn't married. She liked to think if he wasn't, he'd be infatuated with her instead. He would depend on her more than any of his other employees, not because of her skill with numbers, but because he *liked* her. Trusted her. And he found her attractive and feminine.

Feminine, most of all.

He visited a barber regularly and always looked like such a gentleman in his expensive suits. She loved to detect the faint smell of starch in his shirts when he happened to stand a little closer to her than he normally did, which wasn't often. He was much too proper to do anything which could set the tongues of his employees to wagging. Mr. Templeton detested scandal.

Another customer strode in the bank doors and shattered her reverie. What a fool she was, standing here, staring after her employer like a lovesick fool. He was long gone. More important, he was happily married.

She had to stop thinking about him. She was smitten only because he was so kind to her when she first arrived in Ida Grove. She'd been desperate, hungry, almost penniless. He gave her her first real job. A job she treasured. A job that kept her respectable.

Lark hastened back to her duties and immersed herself in them without another thought of what could never be. The afternoon passed swiftly, and by the time the clock read the fifth hour of the afternoon, she'd completed the list of instructions Mr. Templeton had given her. Twice. The monies in the vault balanced exactly to the ledgers. She'd checked and rechecked all the locks on the doors. All lights had been extinguished. Adding machines were silent.

Before leaving the bank, she swept a final, inspecting glance around the darkened room, then locked the doors behind her. She wouldn't be back until Monday morning. Two days stretched ahead of her with very little to do. While the rest of the Ida Grove Bank employees looked forward to weekends, Lark dreaded them. She'd work seven days a week if she could.

It'd be different if she had a family, she supposed, but she didn't. Not anymore. Lark had only herself to take care of and entertain. At first, that had suited her, but lately…

"Howdy, Miss Lark. All done for the day?"

She smiled at Ollie Rand, owner and editor of Ida Grove's only newspaper office, located on the corner op-

posite the bank. He always had a smoke about this time,
before he closed up for the day. Lark met him, just like this,
every night on her way home from work.

"All done, yes."

"Mr. Templeton left early, I see."

There was little that escaped Ollie's curiosity. His no-
siness would be annoying if he wasn't so likable.

"He took his family to Omaha for the weekend," she
said.

Ollie nodded at the news and kept puffing on his cigar.
Lark knew the tidbit would find its way into a column of
his weekly newspaper, the *Ida County Pioneer*, just in case
anyone might be interested. And most everyone was.
That's the way it was in a small town, Lark learned six
months ago. Thanks to Ollie, everyone knew about everyone else's business, private or otherwise. Made for fasci-
nating ruminating some days.

"Got any plans for the weekend?" he asked amiably.

"No." Her answer was always the same. She wondered
why he bothered to ask. "I might bake a few pies if Mrs.
Kelley needs the help."

"You'd make a fine wife, Miss Lark. You got to try a
little harder to find yourself a husband."

As usual, Lark simply smiled and kept walking. She had
chosen Ida Grove to live in because the town was quaint
and small. Peaceful and safe. Finding a husband here had
never figured into her plans.

"We don't have many men here needing a wife, but
strangers ride in nigh every day," Ollie called after her in a
jovial tone. "I'll keep my eye out for one needing marrying."

Lark couldn't help turning back to him with a laugh and
a wave. He answered her with a broad wink, tossed aside
his cigar and went back into his office.

By the time she arrived at Kelley's Boardinghouse only a few blocks away, however, a melancholy mood descended upon her. She could find no reason for it. Perhaps it'd been triggered by her silly thoughts about being infatuated with Mr. Templeton. Or perhaps it was Ollie's innocent comments about finding her a husband.

Regardless, the weekend loomed long and lonely. The night promised no better, and as she climbed the stairs, then unlocked the door to her room, she resolved to draw a hot bath and soak in it for a good long while. She could read a book after that. Maybe even order up a glass of wine or two.

A cool evening breeze fluttered the hems of the blue-flowered curtains hanging over the window. The room was unusually dark. Had she forgotten to part them?

She tossed her small handbag on the bed, added her hat after it. It wasn't like her to forget. Her geraniums thrived in this window. The sun poured in and drenched the blossoms every day while she was at work.

She raised up on tiptoe and pulled the window coverings open. The breeze danced against her skin. Enjoying the feel of the clean air, she lingered to savor it.

If there was one thing that detracted from the perfection of her job, it was being inside four walls all day. Once, a lifetime ago, she'd had no job, no home. The outdoors was all she knew….

A sound came from behind her, a sound so soft she might have imagined it. Had she? She kept perfectly still. Her muscles coiled. The fine hairs lifted on the back of her neck, her senses tuned—oh, God. She'd always trusted her senses. They had saved her life more times than she cared to count.

Lark would sell her soul to have a pair of Colts in her

hands. Instead, her fingers moved slowly, very slowly, to one of the geraniums on the windowsill, but before she could lift it, before she could crash the pot against the intruder's skull, he yanked her hard against him. His burly arm choked the air from her lungs. The other held a knife to her throat.

The stench of sweat and stale whiskey bit into her, throwing her backward in time.

Catfish Jack cackled in her ear. "Well, well, well. Damned if it ain't Wild Red."

Chapter Two

⟪⟫

The sound of his voice sent waves of horror crashing through Lark. Her life—the quiet, simple life she'd worked so hard to build—was in danger of collapsing forever.

Oh, God.

"How did you find me?" she demanded hoarsely. Only one person knew of her plans to settle in Ida Grove after her release from the Missouri State Penitentiary.

"You got talkative kin, Red. She was real helpful, yep, she was."

Laura. Laura Reno. Frank's youngest sister. The only one of them not to take up a life of crime. Lark had confided in her, never dreaming someone as ruthless as Catfish would come looking for her.

"Why are you here?" The blade kept her motionless when her instincts cried out to kick and claw her way free.

"Just renewin' our acquaintance, that's all. Been a long time, Red. I got to missin' you."

The lie set her teeth on edge. He wanted something. He needed it bad, too, for all the trouble he went through to find her.

"Let me go. We'll talk," she said.

Her mind worked every angle for his motive. She hadn't seen him since that terrible day at the Turf Club when the Pinkertons busted into their hideout. The Pinks and one lousy bounty hunter with blood on his hands.

Her blood.

When the smoke from the lawmen's guns cleared, only Catfish managed to escape arrest. From that day on, Lark suspected he'd been on the run.

"Not so fast, Red, honey. Not so fast." The blade pressed against her neck. Lark closed her eyes and dared not breathe. "You got to make me a promise first, y'hear?"

"A promise?" What did he want from her? She had nothing to give. "Holy hellfire, you forgot, Catfish. Wild Red don't make a promise she can't keep. But I'm not promisin' nothing until I know what it is."

She let herself fall into the old way of talking—guarded, evasive, crude. Outlaw to outlaw. As if the past five years had never happened.

"You'd best promise me. Or you die right here."

He was calling her bluff. He wouldn't kill her. Not yet, anyway. He couldn't get the information he needed from her if she was dead.

Heart pounding, she waited. Right now, he held the whole deck. She didn't have a single card to play.

"Don't scream. That's what you got to promise. And don't do nothin' stupid to make me run this blade right through you."

"What do you want?" she grated.

He cackled again. Shivers skidded over her spine.

"I want the money, Red, honey," he purred in her ear.

"Money?"

She blinked in confusion. The savings she'd amassed

in her account at the bank had been slow to build these past six months. She wasn't wealthy, not hardly, and even if she gave him every dime she owned, the total sum wasn't enough to make him search her out like this.

"Don't play dumb with me," he warned. Again, the blade pressed into her skin. "Tell me where it is."

"I don't have any money, Catfish," she said. She hated the desperation in her tone, but there was no help for it. "I swear I don't."

Suddenly, a new horror ripped through her. Had he somehow learned of her place of employment? Did he know Mr. Templeton was on his way to Omaha and had entrusted her with the keys to his bank?

Did Catfish intend to *rob* it?

Not if she could help it. Lark refused to be an accomplice, even an unwilling one. She'd never do that to Mr. Templeton. She would die first.

Catfish sucked in a breath of rage and spun her away from him. She grappled for balance and fell backward against the windowsill. A potted geranium toppled to the floor and shattered.

She hastily righted herself and kept him in her range of vision, especially the ominous knife clutched in his hand.

"I'm talkin' about the Muscatine heist," he snarled, teeth bared. "The loot you hid when you was ridin' with the Reno gang."

Her heart dropped to her toes.

The Muscatine heist. The thousands of dollars in gold coins, bank notes and stacks of greenbacks they'd taken from the county treasury there. She had helped John and Frank strip the vault clean. They'd taken it all.

Oh, God. Oh, God. Oh, God.

In the years since, she'd buried the crime in the recesses

of her mind, just like she'd buried the loot. Buried everything so deep no one knew that part of her past existed anymore. It was easier that way, except when the guilt came back to haunt her.

Guilt and a gut-wrenching fear of the consequences.

Her breath quickened as that fear grabbed her by the throat and squeezed, choking every gasp of air out of her lungs.

"I heard you talkin' about it that day at the Turf Club," Catfish said. "Remember? I was drivin' your rig. I heard every word."

The memory hurtled back. She'd been cocky then, talking to Frank without a care for the two men riding with them. She'd been so sure of herself.

So stupid.

She couldn't let Catfish see her fear, all that she had to lose. Her life. Her job. Her very reason for living.

Her fists clenched. "Those days are over for me, Catfish. I don't want to have anything to do with that money."

"Tell me where it is. Then you won't have to do a damn thing."

She shook her head. "The money's not yours to take. It's not mine to give, either, so I'm not going to tell you. I'm not going to tell anyone. Not ever."

He bettered his grip on the knife, took a step closer. "I always figured you for smart, Red. Guess I was wrong."

Lark let him talk. Keeping that money out of his greedy hands was the right thing to do. She'd made too many mistakes in her life to make another one now.

He halted only a foot or two away. His peculiar, mismatched eyes raked over her, from the hair she kept pinned close to her head, to her prim navy blue dress, right down to her new leather shoes.

"You've changed." He made the words sound like an

insult. "Made yourself into a right fancy woman, all hoity-toity. Like you're better than me."

"I served my time for the crimes I committed. I've started over. I'm never going to be an outlaw again," she said fiercely.

His raspy chuckle sounded like a snake slithering through the weeds. "Once an outlaw, always an outlaw, Red. You got Reno blood in your veins. Remember?" He shifted, and Lark detected the faintest loosening of his grip on the knife handle. "You hear that Frank got lynched?"

She steeled herself against a sharp bite of grief. "Yes. In New Albany, with William and Simeon. Laura told me." Three Reno brothers, pulled from their jail cells and killed in a night of vigilante justice. Lark had cried for days when she got the news. "Charlie Anderson swung from the noose with them."

"Yeah. All four of 'em at once."

Lark suspected Catfish had been as affected as she had. Every outlaw, no matter how cold or devious, held a secret fear of one day being a guest at his own necktie party.

Catfish, however, seemed to shrug off the ugly past with ease, considering. His hand tightened over the knife handle again.

"John still doing hard time in the Missouri State Prison?" he asked.

His interest in the whereabouts of the last remaining member of the Reno gang made Lark even more wary. "Yes. Twenty years left."

"Twenty years." A cold smile curved his lips. "Guess he won't be needin' that heist money for a good long while then, will he?"

A fraction of a second too late, she saw Catfish's intent, and before she could escape him, he shoved her against the wall with a fierce snarl, the blade once again at her neck. Pain exploded in her head, her back, her hips.

"Tell me where you hid the loot, Red, else I'll carve up your pretty face so you'll never forget you didn't help ol' Catfish find it."

She clamped her jaws shut, forced slow, even breaths through her teeth, kept her eyes and senses fixed on what he might do next.

"We'll split it." Frustration threaded through his voice. Lark clung to the knowledge he had to keep her alive to reveal the money's location. "Fifty-fifty."

"Go to hell," she grated.

He shook his head. "Not hell, Red. South America. That's where we'll go." His rank breath billowed into her face. "You wanted to do it that day, back in Canada. Remember? Hide out in South America. We'll go as soon as we can buy the tickets to get us there."

He was guilty of who knew how many crimes. And he expected her to help him elude them? Be no better than he was?

He could rot in jail first.

"Red, I'm warnin' you," Catfish said.

Her fingers closed around a potted geranium.

"It's been a long time," she said carefully.

He gave a quick, negating shake of his head. "Not a chance you'd forget that kind of money."

She tightened her grip on the pot. "It was dark. We were in a hurry. I-I'm not sure—"

"Think harder, damn it."

"How can I think when you've got that blade pressed

up next to me?" she demanded hoarsely. "You think I don't know how it could slip? Accidental or on purpose?"

He swore viciously and pulled the knife back a scant inch. She lifted the pot slowly, slowly...

"It might come back once I got in the general area." Now that he gave her some breathing room, she could goad him. Tell him what he wanted to hear.

Hope flared in those strange eyes. "Sure it would, Red. You'd remember just fine."

"Yes," she whispered. "I'd remember...."

She swung the pot hard against his temple, and he staggered back with a roar of pain. The knife slashed across her shoulder, but she felt no pain, only a searing need to escape him before he killed her.

And, oh, God, she wasn't ready to die yet.

He recovered with alarming speed and came at her with the ferocity of a wounded grizzly, but she met him with Mrs. Kelley's polished three-legged table. Wood splintered and snapped in two. Lark's bones rattled from the force of the blow.

Catfish went down, and his weapon skittered across the floor. Blood spurted from a gash across his cheek. Dazed and furious, he sprawled on the rug, then gave a quick shake of his head, as if to chase the stars away.

He glared up at her, venom spewing from his eyes. Lark gripped what remained of a table leg, one in each hand, her feet spread and pulse pounding.

"I been watching you for a while now," he said, his voice an ugly rasp. "You didn't know that, did you?"

Whatever she thought he'd say, it wasn't this. Lark's muscles coiled, one by one, the dread building with every beat of her heart.

"Your dandy bank president ain't going to like hearin'

his favorite bank teller used to ride with the famous Reno gang. No, sirree, Red, honey. He ain't going to trust you workin' for him anymore."

A sound of dismay escaped her. Mr. Templeton. Her beloved job…

"You'd make fascinatin' readin' in the newspaper, too. Lark *Renault,* alias Wild Red," he sneered. "Folks from miles around will know all about you."

And Ollie would print the story, she knew, her horror building in leaps and bounds. It was what he did. Print stories about people every week.

She'd be front page news.

Suddenly, with more speed than she thought him capable, Catfish reared up with a snarl and lunged for her again. She cried out and reacted with gut instinct, tossed aside the table legs and dove for the ceramic water pitcher on the dresser top. She hurled the thing at him, found her mark with more luck than skill. The pitcher shattered against his skull, and Catfish dropped like a lead weight, bringing her down with him.

He lay motionless on top of her. Her breaths came in frantic whimpers, and when she realized he couldn't hurt her, at least not now, this minute, she pushed against him with all her strength. The smell of his body, the ugliness of his greed and revenge, nauseated her.

He rolled, cadaverlike, off her, and she bolted to her feet. Panic wrenched a choking sob from her throat.

When he came to, Catfish would talk. He'd tell anyone who'd listen all about her. Everything. Her crimes. The Muscatine heist—the one robbery for which she'd never been charged. The citizens of Ida Grove, her newfound friends, and, oh, God, *Mr. Templeton,* would be shocked and scandalized.

She'd be a disgrace in town. Shunned. An outcast.

What would she do? Where could she go?

How could she survive?

Lark couldn't think, couldn't plan. The panic consumed her—a raw, debilitating despair of losing everything.

Everything.

Muffled voices sounded outside her door. Someone called her name, Mrs. Kelley maybe, or one of her boarders, concerned about the sounds coming from inside the room.

They'd be in here any second now. They'd see her standing over the ruthless outlaw, her sleeping room in shambles, her reputation on the brink of being destroyed.

How could she face them? How could she make them understand?

They wouldn't. They wouldn't. They wouldn't.

Lark pressed a fist to her mouth, and blinking hard, she made her decision.

The doorknob turned. By then, she'd slipped through the window and onto the second-story veranda.

Mrs. Kelley screamed, but Lark was already gone.

Somehow, she found herself in Ida Grove's only church. She sat in the farthest pew, alone, in the darkest corner. Her shoulder ached from the knife's blade, but she felt dead inside.

How she got there, she wasn't sure. Some inborn instinct guided her feet to seek the sanctuary of a holy place, a haven not even Catfish Jack would penetrate. Here, she was protected, if only for a little while.

She stared at the rows of tiny flickering candles on the altar. They burned steadily, silently, a tribute to the faith of whoever lit them. The candles, too, were sheltered from the outside world, just like she was. Here, they could burn freely. Undisturbed. Proud.

If only she could be so fortunate.

She was a tribute to no one. Instead, she was guilty of a great sin. Catfish intended to hunt her down and kill her if she didn't tell him where the stolen money was. Most likely, he'd kill her if she did, too, and take all that loot for himself.

Despair billowed inside her. He would've regained consciousness by now and given Mrs. Kelley the scare of her life. Lark prayed he didn't hurt her or any of the boarders who'd rushed to Lark's defense.

One thing she knew with miserable certainty. Catfish was looking for her at this very moment. Even wounded, he'd flee the boardinghouse to chase after her. It was only a matter of time before he found her again.

A sob pushed into her throat, and Lark covered her face with her hands. Never had she felt so helpless, so cowardly, so *afraid.*

Cool fingers touched her shoulder. She emitted a gasp and leapt from the pew bench. Her gaze clawed the darkened church behind her for a pair of peculiar, mismatched eyes.

Instead, she saw a starched white collar—and Father Baxter's worried expression.

"I'm sorry. I'd hoped not to frighten you, my dear." He whispered in deference to their sacred surroundings, but his tone was stricken with genuine apology.

Relief flooded through her, left her shaken, almost giddy. She pressed a hand to her breast; pain burned in her shoulder from the movement, but she hardly noticed. Father Baxter was pastor of the Ida Grove church, and she'd not known a man more kind than he.

"Is everything all right?" he asked.

"Fine, fine." She hesitated. She'd told her share of lies in her lifetime, but saying one to a man of the cloth, in a church no less, was wrong. She fought the ridiculous urge to cry. "No, it's not."

"I didn't think so." In the shadows, his teeth showed in a gentle smile. "Mind if I join you?"

Again, she hesitated. She'd come here for solace. For inspiration and time to think. Her time was running out, and she still had no plan to save herself from Catfish.

"Of course."

How could she refuse him? It was his church, his lot in life to console the afflicted. And God knew she was afflicted, all right.

His black frock coat rustled as he settled himself next to her in the pew. For a moment, neither spoke.

"You're deeply troubled," he said quietly. "Let me assure you, if you have a need to talk, everything you say to me will be kept in the strictest confidence. I have vows I must keep in that regard."

Lark stared at the candles, those silent, flickering candles. She couldn't tell Father Baxter her terrible secret. She couldn't tell anyone.

"I suspect the reason you're here is because of the attack against you at Mrs. Kelley's Boardinghouse."

At that, her glance flew to him. "Is she all right? Has anyone been hurt?"

"Mrs. Kelley is unharmed. Rattled to her soul, of course, but unharmed and quite worried about you. I was just there, you see."

Lark swallowed and thought of the chaos she'd left behind. "You were?"

"She always calls for me at the slightest sign of trouble, no matter where she is. A deeply religious woman, Mrs. Kelley. She feared your intruder was going to die. She wanted me to pray for him before he did."

Lark held her breath. "And?"

The good priest grimaced. "He was gone before I got there. Physically, I mean. They left him alone just long enough to get word to me, and by the time they returned, he'd escaped through the window."

Yes. Catfish would be that shrewd. That quick. It was how he'd evaded the law for so many years. Being shrewd and quick.

"He means to hurt you. That's why you ran away?"

She drew in a breath, let it out again. "He'll kill me if he gets the chance."

"God have mercy."

She felt the shock roll through him, heard it in his stunned words. "He wants something from me. I can't give it to him. Not ever."

"I see."

But he didn't, Lark lamented. How could he? How could anyone?

"Your attacker must be caught before he hurts you—or worse. You must enlist the sheriff's help, Lark."

"No," she said sharply. "No one must know. You promised, Father. No one. Especially the law."

He studied her for a long moment, so long Lark was sure he could see right into her dishonest soul.

"I have a solution to your problem, then, my dear Lark."

She eyed him doubtfully.

Father Baxter nodded in reverent satisfaction. "His name is Ross Santana."

Chapter Three

⚜

"And Mrs. Kelley said she saw him yesterday, right in front of the boardinghouse, walking real slowlike. She didn't pay him much mind because he's got a right to walk wherever he wants, just like everyone else." Chat Santana drew in a breath. "Of course, she never dreamed he'd sneak into her place the next day and attack one of her boarders. Poor thing." Chat stopped stirring her biscuit dough. "Her boarder, I mean. Not Mrs. Kelley."

Ross grunted and let his kid sister talk. At sixteen years of age, tall, slender and dark-haired, she loved to gossip, like the rest of the Ida Grove townspeople.

But he wasn't interested in the happenings in town. Never was. He made a habit to distance himself from the old hens who had nothing better to do than cluck about everyone else in the community roost.

He was determined to finish the design of his latest furniture project, a revolving bookcase, before he went to bed tonight. The fewer questions he asked, the sooner Chat would get her story told, and the sooner she'd get dinner on the table.

"There was a terrible commotion in her room. Sarah and I were in the library. We couldn't imagine what was happening."

Dishes clattered on the table behind him. She was in a hurry. She'd gotten home late from spending the day with Sarah Kelley, her best friend. Ross suspected dinner would be scorched more than usual because of Chat's tardiness.

"By the time folks rushed upstairs to see what was happening, she was gone. Escaped right through the window! Can you believe it? Why would she do such a thing?"

"Damned if I know." He jotted down a series of measurements and began adding them together.

"Then, her attacker escaped, too, when everyone's back was turned. Now, both of them are gone. *Pphht!* Like that!" Chat snapped her fingers. "Isn't it just the strangest thing? Why would she run? Why wouldn't she get some help for herself instead?"

"Can't say." He repositioned his ruler, drew a perfectly straight line, then measured it.

"Ross." Chat sounded exasperated. "Aren't you even curious who it *was?*"

"Figured you'd get around to telling me eventually."

The oven door slammed shut. "That pretty bank teller Mr. Templeton hired, that's who. You know, the one with the French name?"

"Never met her."

Ross had never set foot in the Ida Grove Bank, either. Nor did he intend to, not after what happened to Pa back in Muscatine. Ross had damn near sworn off banks because of it.

"She was the nicest person. Pretty with that rich, red hair. And smart with numbers. Why ever would anyone want to attack her?"

Ross grunted again.

"You know what I think?" Chat plopped into the chair next to his desk.

He narrowed his eye and contemplated the sketch in front of him, his mind more caught up envisioning the bookcase with beveled glass than his sister's opinions. Chat huffed a breath, reached over and plucked his pencil right out of his hand. He scowled and reached for it, but she held it behind her back.

"I think you should help her," she said.

He stilled. "Me?"

"Yes, you. Ross Santana. The best bounty hunter in this part of the country. She *needs* you!"

"The hell she does." Impatience rolled through him that Chat would even come up with the idea. She knew better.

"What kind of man would attack a defenseless woman? A *bad* one, that's what kind. And your specialty is hunting down bad men."

"Not anymore." He rooted in his desk drawer. Where was another pencil? "Those days are long over, so don't bring it up again."

He finally found one, but the lead was broken. He swore, then scrounged among the drawer contents for his sharpener.

"You lost an eye," she said. "So what? You can still shoot. You can still track. And you've got more guts than anyone else I know."

Ross gave up trying to find the sharpener. He tossed aside the worthless pencil and sat back in his chair. He glared at his sister with the one good eye he had left. The other, rendered useless when he took a hit from a shotgun blast, was covered by a black leather patch.

"Guts aren't worth a damn when a man has to defend

himself and can only see half of what the man shooting at him can." His words were a cruel reminder of all he had lost, the price he paid to enforce justice. At first, death had been preferable to partial blindness. The dizzy spells, the headaches, had been debilitating when he'd never been sick a day in his life. Worst, though, had been losing trust in himself. Who would protect him if he couldn't protect himself?

His abilities to hunt down some of the country's most wanted criminals were destroyed with a single pull of a shotgun trigger, and Ross had been devastated by the loss.

"Yes, but—"

"No buts." He made a gesture toward the kitchen. "Check those biscuits before they burn, will you? And you'd best finish getting the table set, too. It's getting late."

"Ross Santana, if you weren't my brother…"

She threw his confiscated pencil onto his paperwork and returned to the stove in a huff.

His determination to finish the bookcase design fizzled into frustration. He rose from his chair, strode outside into the night. He lived only a few miles outside of Ida Grove, and the town's lights shone like tiny white stars on the horizon. He leaned a hip against the porch rail and lit himself a cigarette.

He drew in deep, and his thoughts drifted to the woman attacked in her sleeping room. He tamped down the urge to think about her, about why a man would hunt her down with such calculated precision. He tamped down the urge to worry about her, too. About where she'd run to. Or why.

One thing was sure. She knew something—or had something—or else the lowlife who was after her wouldn't have gone through so much trouble to get it. And whatever it was must've been important for her to run like she did.

She was in deep trouble.

But those troubles were her own, he told himself firmly. He'd have no part in them, no matter what Chat wanted him to do.

So why was he thinking about her?

A buggy rumbled down the road, and his thoughts evaporated. Wasn't often he got company this time of night. Might be Chat had friends coming to call.

He lit the lantern hanging on a nail outside the door. The buggy pulled up, braked, and Father Baxter stepped down. Ross hid his surprise.

"Evenin', Ross."

"Evening."

His glance slid to the driver's seat, to the passenger sitting there. A woman, draped in a hooded black cape, as if she wanted to blend into the night.

"Would you have a few minutes to spare for us?" the priest asked.

Hell. Ross had a pretty good guess who the woman was. And why the priest had brought her here.

She needs you....

His resistance teetered from Chat's words. Ross wrestled it firmly back into place.

"You've wasted your time riding out here, Father." He inhaled again on the cigarette, forced himself to keep from looking at her. "I heard what happened in town. I know what you want. You've got the wrong man for the job."

"I'm convinced you're exactly what we need, considering the trouble she's in."

...the best bounty hunter in this part of the country.

His resistance teetered again.

"Hung up my guns a while ago," he said. "I'm out of the business. You know that."

"This time it's different. There's a woman involved."

A woman. His mouth quirked. Last time he took on a case that involved one, he almost got himself killed over her.

"A *woman*, Ross."

He dragged his gaze back to the driver's seat. She looked small inside that black cape. Vulnerable.

What if she was innocent? What if her attacker had chosen her at random? That she fled through her second-story window out of sheer fear for her life?

"Talk to her, at least," the priest pleaded. "Hear her story. Would you do that?"

Could be she deserved none of the trouble she was in, despite the speculation of Ida Grove's gossipmongers, and what was left of his resistance crumpled right through his fingers.

"All right. If she wants to talk, I'll listen." He took one last drag off his cigarette and flicked the stub into the darkness beyond the lantern light. "Come in, then."

Father Baxter inclined his head gratefully. "Much obliged, much obliged."

He helped the woman from the rig. They climbed the stairs in silence, but at the door, the priest halted.

"I won't be coming in," he said. "Not much else I can do anyway. You're the only one who can help her." He took the woman's hand and gave her a reassuring pat. "Things will turn out just fine, you'll see. You'll be safe with him."

From within the shadows of her hood, she looked doubtful. The priest nudged her firmly into the house, clambered back into the buggy and was gone.

Ross frowned. When was he coming back? And what was Ross supposed to do with her until he did?

Well, hell. His frown deepening, Ross pulled the door shut, then on an afterthought, locked it.

She stood before him. The tension in her was palpable, as if being here was the last place she wanted to be. Most likely, his reluctance to talk to her didn't help matters any. He hadn't been polite about it. Ross suspected if he didn't watch her close, she'd bolt first chance she got.

He held out his arm. "I'll take your coat."

She shook her head, and the hood slipped a little. "It's not mine, actually. Father lent it to me, so if you don't mind, I'll just keep it on."

"Ross, is someone here? I thought I heard voices." Chat stopped in midstride on her way out from the kitchen, a plate of darkened biscuits in her hand. The woman turned; her hood slipped down further, and Chat gasped. "Oh! It's her. Mrs. Kelley's boarder. The one I was telling you about."

The woman made a soft sound of dismay. "You know what happened? Already?"

"Yes." To Chat's credit, the word held a wealth of sympathy. She extended her free hand. "I've seen you at the bank. My name is Chat. This is my brother, Ross Santana."

"Yes." She turned back to him. "I know."

She didn't offer her own name, and he didn't ask. He strode toward Chat, took the plate of biscuits and set them on the table.

"Your room," he said.

Her eyes widened. "But Ross! Dinner's ready, and—"

"You heard me."

She slid a disappointed glance toward the woman, and her mouth curved downward in a pout. But she didn't argue. "All right."

After the door shut behind her, the woman lifted her chin. Weary pride shone in her expression.

"I'm intruding on your evening," she said. "I shouldn't have come."

Ross held her gaze. There was something about her he couldn't place. A stirring of familiarity.

"Evidently the good priest thought otherwise," he said. "Sit down." He indicated the couch, but she didn't move.

"This was a mistake," she said stiffly.

"I'll decide that."

"We have nothing to discuss. I shouldn't have bothered you. I'm sorry." She pivoted and headed toward the door.

What did she think she'd do? Walk back to town? Alone?

Not a chance, given her circumstances. And not until he figured out who she was, what happened to her to-night—and if he'd ever seen her before. He reached out, grasped her elbow. She cried out, and he immediately let go.

The attack against her was worse than what folks knew, evidently. No wonder she refused to relinquish the black cape.

"You're hurt. Let me see," he commanded.

"I'm not hurt. I'm fine. Thank you for your concern, but I'm leaving. Really, I must." She swung back to the door, faster than before, but Ross was wiser this round. He clasped her other arm in one hand, removed the cape with the other.

The left shoulder of her dress had been slashed open, and blood caked the fabric to her skin. He'd been knifed a time or two himself. He knew firsthand the wound hurt like a bitch.

"Who did this to you?" he growled.

"No one you know," she snapped, pulling against his grasp. "He's none of your business, besides."

"You've got that wrong, woman. You showed up on my doorstep bleeding and on the run. Whoever's after you could find you here. That affects me and mine, so I'm making it my business."

She sucked in a stricken breath. Obviously, she hadn't figured Chat into the repercussions.

"Sit down," he said, the command quieter, but no less firm.

This time, she obeyed. She looked more worried than ever. "I won't be staying long."

"I'll decide that, too." He hunkered in front of her, carefully pried the fabric from her skin. The blade had left a gash several inches long, but she didn't need stitches. "A flesh wound. You'll live."

At her silence, he glanced up. She stared at him intently, a slight frown knitting her brows. Maybe she'd never seen a one-eyed man before. Maybe the patch he was forced to wear repulsed her, or fascinated her in a macabre sort of way, like it did with most folks in Ida Grove.

He hated it when people stared at him. Hated it with a passion.

Did she pity him?

Ross stood suddenly. He needed space away from her. He didn't want her pity, and he had to break that odd pull she held over him.

It was easier to contemplate her when he wasn't so close, and he contemplated her with outright boldness. He could see her pride, her strength. She'd endured his probing of her shoulder with surprising tenacity, considering the burn she'd be feeling. He knew Chat wouldn't have been as stoic.

But the woman was pale, a sign she'd been hurting for awhile. Exhausted, too. Neither took away from the attractiveness she wore casually, as if vanity was never part of her thinking. Long lashes graced eyes that were a rich shade of brown, tinted with a hint of red, like the finest quality of mahogany wood. Eyes like that didn't often have hair with the same rich color, auburn, almost a deep red, and with wavy strands just a little wild…

"Who are you?" he asked in a low voice.

"My name is Lark," she said, sitting stiffly on the couch. "Lark Renault."

Ray-nau. French, like Chat claimed. Spoken in a tone that was low and husky. Easy on a man's ears.

But he'd never heard it before. He'd remember a name like hers.

"You work at the bank in town?" he said.

"Yes."

"The man who attacked you tonight. Is he a customer? Someone who might be dissatisfied with the bank's handling of his financial affairs?"

"No, no. Mr. Templeton insists that the bank's customers are treated fairly and with the utmost respect."

It was easy to see she held her job in high esteem. Ross knew she'd treat the people she dealt with the same way.

"A lover, then," he said. "Someone you've spurned lately?"

She rolled her eyes, made a sound of disagreement. "Not hardly."

She was a beautiful woman. Why wasn't she married? Or betrothed? Why didn't she have a half-dozen men panting at her skirts?

His mouth tightened. It wasn't like him to speculate about a woman and the men she might have attracted to her. Why was he doing it now? With her?

"I can stand here and interrogate you all night long, Lark," he said, his tone brusque. "Unless you tell me who's after you, and why, you're going to end up dead. And what a waste of time that would be for both of us."

Her throat moved in a hard swallow. His gaze followed the motion, and he was reminded yet again how strong she was. How stubborn. And determined as hell to keep him from helping her.

Seemed Father Baxter had made a mistake bringing her all the way out here. Fine. The least Ross could do was treat her wound, feed her some dinner, and take her back to town. Her decisions were her own. So were the ramifications that came with them.

But his scrutiny lingered. That pull again. That deep-down gut instinct which told him he'd crossed paths with her once before.

When?

"There's really nothing you can do," she said quietly. "I appreciate you trying. And you're right. This has all been a waste of our time. Father Baxter meant well, didn't he?"

Ross grunted. "Stay put. You need cleaning up, and I have some medicine that will help your pain."

He expected her protest, but she said nothing more. Just sat there, staring at him, looking small and vulnerable in that damn cape.

He strode into his bedroom and closed the door. He kept assorted pharmaceuticals on a shelf above his washbasin. But it was the bureau he headed for, and the bottom drawer he kept under lock and key.

Once he opened it, he found the flat, rectangular box he was looking for. He removed the lid, tossed it aside, his urgency growing as he rifled through the papers he kept within. Reports he'd penned. Payments he'd received. Documents from his past life as a bounty hunter.

Wanted posters.

He yanked out one in particular.

And there she was.

Lark Renault. Alias Wild Red. Once part of the notorious Reno gang. The artist's drawing was at least seven years old, crude at best, but it was her. Thick, wavy hair, spilling from beneath a wide-brimmed hat. Eyes, dark and direct. She looked young in the drawing. Thinner, too.

But it was her.

She'd been there that day at the Turf Club. Ross was hell-bent on arresting her, but things turned ugly. Out of control. He never intended to shoot her down.

Catfish Jack took care of matters with his shotgun primed and ready. Ross never saw him coming.

He shut off the memories, dragged himself back to the present. Now, at last, he could finish the case he never solved, and the one person who could help him do it was sitting on his couch at this very moment.

The Wanted poster slipped from his fingers. He rose, strode to the door and yanked it wide open.

But Lark Renault had disappeared.

Chapter Four

He knew who she was.

Lark's breath quickened in frantic desperation as she bolted into the shadows beyond his house. He didn't show it, didn't say it, but her senses had screamed with the certainty.

And she knew who he was. The bounty hunter who had gunned her down all those years ago. The lawman who would just as soon see her dead as take up space in a jail cell. She never heard his name until tonight, but the memory of him, of what he'd done, had haunted her for weeks, months, after her arrest. Until tonight, she'd almost forgotten Ross Santana existed.

Oh, God.

He knew who she was, all right. Why else had he gone into his room and shut the door? Her instincts had kicked in the minute he left, warning her that there was something in there he didn't want her to see, or he was going to do something he didn't want her to see him do. And once he left her alone, she had no choice but to run.

She halted at the first structure she came to, a small

building beyond the yard. Any second, Santana would open his front door, see her out here, and until she could get her bearings, formulate a plan of escape, she needed a minute to hide and compose herself.

To think.

Thankfully, the door to the structure wasn't locked. She slipped inside, making sure the door was latched tight behind her. She stood in darkness so deep, so black, she couldn't define where she was, and for a moment, she didn't move. The stark silence and pungent scent of fresh-cut wood told her there were no livestock near to betray her presence.

She sagged against the door. She tilted her head back and sucked in a long, miserable breath. She, Lark Renault, respectable bank teller and Mr. Templeton's prize employee, was forced to hide out in a woodshed like a common criminal.

Which she was, of course. Once.

Now, Catfish Jack was after her. Ross Santana, too, and the longer she hid in here feeling sorry for herself, the sooner one of them would find her.

She had to keep moving. But how? Steal one of Santana's horses to make her escape? And where would she go? How would she defend herself?

How would she survive?

She'd find a way.

First, she needed money. Clothes and food. Which meant a trip back to her sleeping room at Mrs. Kelley's. After that, the Ida Grove Bank to withdraw her savings. Mr. Templeton wouldn't approve of her sneaking into the vault so late at night, and who could blame him? But she had to, and—

Voices outside shattered her frenzied thoughts. She

leapt away from the door, pulling her black cape tighter around her as she sought something, anything, to hide behind.

But, oh, God, she couldn't see, it was so dark. Unexpectedly, her knee knocked against a solid heap and sent the whole pile clattering to the floor with a terrible racket. She cried out at the contact, her balance lost, her arms reaching out to break her fall. She landed hard, and pain from her lacerated shoulder bit into her nerve endings.

Holy hellfire, Santana would know where she was now. He'd be here any minute—any second—but still she scrambled to hide, scurrying on her hands and knees like some kind of disgusting, nocturnal insect.

The lowest of all creatures.

Tears of frustration, of fear and utter dismay, welled up. Her cape tangled around her legs, hindering her escape, stealing away precious time. She clawed at the yards of fabric, and just as she freed herself, the door burst wide open.

Lark twisted. Lantern light jumped into the room. Chat Santana stood in the doorway.

"Miss Renault?" she said in a careful tone, worry in her expression. "You'll be all right. I'm not going to hurt you."

Maybe she wouldn't, Lark thought. But Santana would. He'd throw her in jail so fast her teeth would sing. He'd hold her responsible for all the trouble at the Turf Club, when in truth, *he* was the cause of it. That wagon full of Pinks, too. Worse, he'd want to know all about the Muscatine heist.

"Just leave me be," Lark said, appalled at the quiver in her voice. A tiny part of her realized how pitiful she must look, sprawled on the floor, sawdust covering her cape. She scrambled to her feet. Her mind worked to find a way past Chat and the doorway she stood in.

Chat shook her head slowly. "I want to help you."

Lark wanted to believe her. She wanted to be convinced that Chat was nothing like her brother.

But Lark couldn't be that gullible. Chat was a Santana, and she'd be as justice-minded as he was.

"Let me go, then," Lark said. She took a step toward the door. She was older, stronger, could push her way past the girl if she had to.

"I can't do that. It's not safe for you to leave here. Let us *help* you, Miss Renault."

Lark's resolve wavered. Chat spoke her name perfectly, a tribute to her intelligence. She sounded genuine and nice. Kind. Lark wanted to believe her so badly it hurt.

"Us?" Lark couldn't help the derision in her tone. "Your brother has no reason to help me. Why would he?"

"I know this is hard for you, but you have to trust him. He's very good. He's just who you need right now."

Lark took another step toward her. Toward the door. She'd lost too much time already. "No, I don't need him. I don't need anyone. I just need for you to step aside and forget you ever saw me."

"Don't play us for fools, Wild Red," Santana growled from somewhere behind her. "You're not going anywhere."

Lark spun in alarm. She hadn't known there was a back door to the place, or that Santana had gotten inside, slick as a snake. But there he was, tall, shrouded in shadow, with a Colt .45 in his hand.

Her instincts had proved right. He knew who she was. Or had been.

"Don't call me that," she snapped. "I'm not her anymore."

He smirked. "Once an outlaw, always an outlaw."

Catfish had taunted her with those same words only a

few hours ago. Before Lark could declare she'd never go against the law again, Chat made a sound of protest.

"Ross, please," she said. "Put your gun away. Give her a chance."

He ignored her. He strode toward Lark with the smooth, powerful stealth of a man comfortable on the hunt.

Which he was, of course.

Ready to close in for the kill.

Lark trembled. She stood with Chat at one door, Santana at the other. Sandwiched between them, with no hope of escape.

"Let's go in the house." Santana stopped a few feet away. He kept the revolver aimed at her chest, but his voice had lost some of its edge.

The last time she had a weapon pointed at her, blood had spilled. Her blood. Santana had pulled the trigger, and if she resisted him now, her fate would be even worse.

He'd shoot her dead.

She had to cooperate with him. For now. But she'd not make things easy, and she intended to escape him first chance she got.

"Now." Santana grasped her elbow to nudge her forward.

Lark jerked free. Her shoulder hurt when she did. "Don't touch me."

His jaw clenched, though he made no move to take her arm again. "Chat will walk with you into the house. I'll be right behind."

"Fine." Lark swung away. She noticed the fresh-cut lumber scattered over the floor, the pile she'd stumbled over earlier and yet another mess she'd made tonight.

"Leave 'em," Santana said, as if he knew what she was thinking.

She skirted the pile and drew closer to Chat. Lark estimated her to be the same age she was when she fled to Canada, already guilty of a long string of crimes. Where Lark had been hardened by the lawless side of life, Chat had been protected from it. Santana would've seen to that.

Lark sensed the questions the girl longed to ask, but didn't. Too, she expected to see pity in her eyes, but there was none. Only gentleness and concern, and a burst of emotion pushed into Lark's throat.

"You must be exhausted after all that's happened." Chat held the door open. "Things will get better from here on out. You'll see."

Lark swallowed hard and eyed her dubiously. After all, Lark had a Colt pointed at her back, a bounty hunter determined to make her pay for her crime, and a ruthless outlaw on her tail who would forever destroy the new life she'd worked so hard to build. How could things be any worse?

When they were in the house, Santana locked the door a second time, then went about the place pulling curtains snug over their windows. Chat led Lark into the kitchen.

"You need something in your stomach, and dinner's ready. Won't take but a minute before we eat, then you and Ross can talk," she said. "You can wash up in here. I'll take your cape for you."

She extended a hand for the garment, but Lark drew back. She didn't think she could eat at Santana's table as if there was nothing between them, as if this night was just a pleasant social occasion. Didn't Chat understand all Lark had at stake?

"She's been knifed," Santana said, joining them. He set the Colt on the table, out of Lark's reach, but close to his own. "The wound will need tending before she can have dinner."

"Knifed! Oh, my God. I had no idea. I'll get your medicines," Chat said, rushing toward his room farthest from the kitchen.

Santana's glance drifted over the death grip Lark held on the cape. "Take it off, Red."

She glared up at him. "If you think I'm going to make it easy for you to arrest me, you're a fool."

"You've got some explaining to do. If I decide you need arresting after that, then I will."

"There's nothing I care to tell you. Ever."

Chat reappeared, brown bottles and bandages in both hands, and Santana's mouth tightened. Clearly, her arrival diffused his terse response.

Lark choked down her own argument. Her battle with the bounty hunter wasn't something his sister needed to witness, not when she had showed Lark more kindness than Santana ever could.

He reached out and tugged at Father Baxter's black cape. Lark let him take it. The lacerations needed looked at, she conceded. He tossed the wrap onto the couch, and specks of sawdust drifted to the thick floral carpet.

"Sit down. Here." He pulled out a chair.

Lark glanced at it, then up at Santana. In the next few minutes he'd be standing over her. Touching her. Once, she'd hated him with every fiber of her being. Now, she had little choice but to let him take care of her.

She eased down into the seat and clasped her hands tight in her lap. Santana removed a small knife from his hip pocket and unfolded the blade. Chat set the pharmaceuticals down with a clatter and stared at the blood staining Lark's shoulder.

"Does it hurt much?" Chat asked in a sympathetic whisper.

Now that Lark was thinking of it, the wound hurt plenty. Santana's blade ripped through the fabric of her dress. He used the tip to lift a stubborn piece of fabric caked to her skin.

"Not really," she lied.

"Well, it looks like it hurts *a lot*. Can I get you anything?"

A good stiff drink. Lark caught herself before she said the words. "Coffee, please. But only if you have it."

"I do. Ross drinks it all day long. We always have a pot on the stove. I'll be right back."

Chat hurried off, and Lark angled her head to get her first peek at what Catfish had done. Santana bent over her shoulder, studying the wound. Her forehead brushed against his, but he didn't seem to notice.

"You've lost a good amount of blood." His voice was low, subdued, as he poked the skin with a gentle finger. "But it's stopped now. You need a good cleaning before I wrap you up."

Lark's stomach lurched at the crimson that had streamed down her arm and onto the swell of her breast. Maybe it was worse than she'd thought. "Holy hellfire."

He glanced up at her and frowned. "You going to be sick?"

With Santana to watch? There'd be nothing more humiliating. "No."

"Put your head between your knees if you feel it coming on." He rose and slid the knife back into his hip pocket. Taking the Colt with him, he headed to the kitchen.

Lark glared at his back. Evidently, he'd give her no more sympathy than that. Well, fine. She didn't want his sympathy anyway. The bastard.

"Here you are, Miss Renault. Coffee, black and hot."

Chat set a cup on the table, sloshing some of the brew onto the table top in her haste. "Unless you prefer cream? Sugar?"

"No, no. Black is perfect. Thank you."

Lark looked for something to wipe up the spill. Santana returned with a bowl of water and a bottle of Old Taylor whiskey. He poured a portion into her coffee.

Lark eyed the mixture. She should've been annoyed that he took the liberty, but the truth was she hadn't had anything stronger than the occasional glass of wine since the day of her arrest back in Canada.

"It'll calm your nerves," Santana said, lathering the wet towel with a bar of castile soap. "Drink up."

It unnerved her how he knew what she was thinking. And needing. She lifted the cup to her lips and sipped. The whiskey-laced brew slid down her throat, warming her clear to her toes. It tasted so good, she sipped again.

The coffee gave her something to concentrate on while he cleaned her shoulder. She didn't want to be too aware of him and what he was doing. Or how close he was. She wanted to pretend he wasn't there.

Which was impossible, of course. Santana had muscled his way back into her life. Worse, she had the uneasy feeling he intended to stay awhile.

"He cut you clean," he said, rinsing the towel yet again. The water turned a darker shade of red. "You'll heal, but you'll have a scar."

This new one would pale compared to the one *he'd* given her. The thing was a constant reminder of how he'd tried to kill her five years ago.

The thought sent a prickle of rebellion through her. Santana appeared to sense her shift in mood and regarded her. Steadily. As if he dared her to confront him about her imperfection when he bore one, much worse, of his own.

Losing an eye wouldn't have been easy, she knew. Some of her defiance fizzled. She couldn't hold his hard gaze, and she dropped hers back to her shoulder.

The blood was gone. She hadn't noticed until now how her dress had sagged. She felt half-naked with him. Looked it, too. Her chemise was too thin, too low-cut to afford her any measure of modesty, and she yanked up what part of the bodice she could.

"You've ruined my dress," she said, refusing to look at him for fear he'd see the stupid blush in her cheeks.

"You can change into something of Chat's later." He smeared an ointment of some sort over the wound, then reached for a roll of bandages. "Until then, I'll get you one of my shirts to wear."

"We'll draw a bath for you, too." Chat laid a large platter of warmed-over roast beef and vegetables in the center of the table. "Hurry, won't you, Ross? Dinner's getting cold."

He wound the fabric strips over Lark's shoulder and under her arm, tying the ends snugly in place. At last, he stood.

"There's laudanum in the ointment that will numb the pain. If you're still hurting, though, I can give you a powder." He held up one of the bottles for her perusal.

The ointment he'd used had already begun working. Or was it the whiskey and coffee? Lark didn't know for sure, but what discomfort remained she could tolerate. God knew she'd been hurt worse than this before.

"That won't be necessary." She forced herself to meet his gaze square. There were words that needed to be said, though they galled her to say them. "Thank you."

He grunted, an indication he knew her pride had been tested, and gathered up the bottles. "Start filling our plates, Chat. I'll be right back."

"Finally," Chat muttered after he left.

All over again, Lark dreaded the prospect of sharing a meal with the man who had thrust her into long years of jail time. "Really, I shouldn't stay. I'm feeling much better now."

Chat's head came up in alarm. "He won't let you leave."

Lark bit her lip. No, he wouldn't. He'd made that threat quite clear, and it'd be pure futility to even try. She'd just have to get through the next few hours, bide her time, find an opportunity to escape.

"Let me help then. Is there something I can do?" Lark asked. She wasn't accustomed to being waited on. Even at Mrs. Kelley's, she'd pitched right in at mealtime and done her share.

"You just stay sitting, Miss Renault," Chat said. "Won't take but a minute to dish this out. I hope you're hungry."

Santana returned, a clean white shirt in his hand. He tossed it into Lark's lap. "Put this on if you want."

Chat indicated the bodice Lark was forced to hold up and frowned at her brother. "You were pretty rough on her dress, Ross. She has nothing else with her, you know."

"Couldn't be helped."

"And what is she to wear until we take her back to town again?"

Lark nearly yelped. She had no intention of being escorted by either of the Santanas back to Ida Grove. The young girl meant well, but she clearly hadn't an inkling of Lark's predicament.

"The dress can be washed and mended," Lark said quickly, though she suspected the end result wouldn't be suitable for public wearing. She donned Santana's shirt as she spoke. Under the circumstances, she couldn't be choosy about who it belonged to. "Truly, it wasn't his fault. The dress was torn before I ever arrived."

"We'll set about laundering it first thing in the morning, then," Chat said.

The shirt was a good solution, Lark discovered. Her modesty was intact. The garment was too big, of course, but rolling the cuffs sufficed. She'd have to take it with her when she escaped, but she'd make arrangements to have it cleaned and returned after she was gone.

"Men. They just don't understand, do they, Miss Renault?"

With all the plates filled, Chat settled into her chair and laid a napkin over her lap, and though her tone was scolding, the glance she tossed her brother's way was amused and held a wealth of love.

But Santana wasn't looking. He stared hard at Lark, a bird dog homing in on his kill. Could he see into the workings of her mind? Did he know she planned to escape him first chance she got?

"Take your dinner into your room, Chat," he said.

Chat gasped. "What? Why?"

"Miss Renault—" he taunted Lark with the name "—and I have matters to discuss."

Chat's glance bounced between them. "But I want to know what happened, too!"

"Do as I said."

Lark's heart began a slow pound. This was it. The confrontation that had been simmering between them for five long years. Santana knew she had one secret left. Did he think she'd give it to him without a fight?

Chat crossed her arms over her chest. "I'm not going to

my room this time. I'm sixteen, Ross. Almost full-grown. I don't need you protecting me all the time."

His dark head swiveled toward her. "The hell you don't."

"Someone is after Miss Renault. Father Baxter brought her out here so you could help her. That means she's in danger." Chat leaned forward. "Does that put me in danger, too?"

Santana's jaw clenched. Chat had zeroed in on her brother's weak spot. She hit pay dirt and knew it.

"Then I have a right to know what's going on, don't I? Same as you," she said.

Chat made a strong argument, but still Santana hesitated. In the coming moments, Lark knew, he intended to cut her wide open, make her bleed out the truths from her past. It was understandable he'd want to shield Chat from the ugliness of all that happened between them at the Turf Club.

Lark suspected, though, he was protecting her, too, for as long as he could. A gallant attempt to preserve her new identity and the respectable life she'd built in Ida Grove, the only one Chat had ever known.

Maybe Santana had a streak of honor in him. In spite of everything, he deserved to understand the threat Catfish Jack presented. Chat did, too. And Lark would do them both an injustice by not telling them.

She drew in a breath. "I'll talk."

Santana's attention jumped back to her. "Damn right you will."

"But I want Chat to stay."

He seemed to ponder that, kill some time while he reached for the bottle of Old Taylor and poured himself a stiff one. Finally, he met his sister's hopeful glance. He met Lark's, too. And swore softly under his breath.

After throwing back a quick swallow of whiskey, he lifted his glass in a mock salute.

"Well, then. Talk away, Red. We're listening."

Chapter Five

❧❧❧

"**Y**ou're not really Lark Renault, are you?" Chat asked quietly.

"Yes. I am."

"But Ross called you Wild Red."

Lark chose her words carefully. Besides Santana, Chat would be the only other person in Ida Grove, in all of Iowa for that matter, who would know of her past life.

Except Catfish Jack, and he didn't count.

"My father was born in France, and his family name was Renault," Lark said. "When he was a young man, he came to America and brought his brother with him."

"Wilkinson Reno," Santana said.

Lark glanced at him in surprise. "Yes. How did you know?"

"I always investigate the men I'm hunting for. Besides, Renault and Reno sound alike." Santana speared a chunk of beef with his fork. "And given your association with them, it makes sense."

After she was released from prison, Lark depended on the anonymity her legal name would give her. Santana was quick with details. It'd been in her favor he hadn't made the connection between the two names until now.

"So your father and uncle chose to go by 'Reno'?" Chat asked.

"Yes. Reno was easier to say. Easier to spell, too." Lark finished off the last of the whiskeyed coffee. "After my parents died, Uncle Wil took me in. I was raised right along with his daughter and sons."

"And took up their life of crime, too," Santana said, his tone rough.

Lark hesitated.

"Yes," she said finally.

There. She'd admitted it. Now Chat knew the truth.

"*Those* Renos?" Chat's eyes widened. "You rode with the Reno *gang?*"

The guilt stung, but Lark lifted her chin high. Nothing she could do to change all she'd done. "I'm afraid so."

Chat gaped at her in disbelief. "You can't possibly be an outlaw."

"I'm not. Not anymore," Lark said. "Prison convinced me to change my ways. I'm an honest citizen now."

"Are you?" Santana taunted in a low voice.

Her gaze slammed into his. Damn him for not believing her.

"Well, sure she is," Chat said before Lark could answer. "Everyone in Ida Grove knows it, too. She works in a *bank,* Ross!" She turned to Lark. "But you still haven't explained why he calls you 'Red.'"

Lark shifted a little in her chair, giving Santana her back in a deliberate snub. "Outlaws are often given nicknames. Mine was Wild Red." She flicked the curls that crowded around her nape. "Because of my hair."

Clearly fascinated, Chat nodded in understanding.

"Where is your former gang now? Don't they want you to ride with them anymore?"

"They're dead," Ross said and shoveled in a forkful of vegetables.

Lark's lips tightened at his callousness. "They were lynched by a mob of vigilantes. Except John. He's in the Missouri Penitentiary serving out his sentence."

Chat hadn't touched her dinner, which wasn't nearly as interesting as the sordid tale Lark had to tell. "Folks aren't going to believe this, Miss Renault. They're going to be positively shocked!"

Santana stood abruptly.

"Not a word to anyone about her," he thundered, stunning Lark with his protectiveness.

Chat's fingers flew to her mouth in instant remorse. "No, no. Of course not, Ross. I'm sorry. I didn't think—"

"Damn right you didn't." Santana braced both hands on the table and leaned toward her. "What's said between these walls stays here. And I mean it." Though the timbre of his voice had lowered, the fierce intensity of his words left no doubt he meant every one.

"I know, Ross. I know."

"You think those gossiping hens in town wouldn't have a heyday with this? You think news about her wouldn't spread like wildfire? That she wouldn't be tried and convicted all over again in their narrow little minds?"

Eyes shimmering, Chat's head bobbed again and again. "You're right. You're right."

"We don't know who's after her yet. Or why. Or where he's at. If we're to keep her alive, you can't say a word to anyone. Not Sarah. Not Mrs. Kelley. Not *anyone*, Chat."

"I won't. I promise. You can trust me, Ross. I *promise*."

Lark didn't move. It appalled her to be the reason for

their disagreement, that she'd disrupted their lives and their thinking. And, oh, poor Chat. In her youth and innocence, what would she know of outlaws and protecting one?

Worse, it seemed they'd forgotten she wasn't an outlaw anymore. She was honest, respectable Lark Renault. Mr. Templeton's favorite bank employee.

Chat turned to Lark, her dark eyes pleading. "Please know that you can trust me, too." Her voice quivered with the tears she fought to hold in check. "I won't tell anyone of your past. And I'm so sorry if I led you to believe otherwise."

Lark battled miserable tears of her own. "No, no. I'm the one who's sorry for putting you in this situation. I should never have come here. This has all been a terrible mistake."

What could Father Baxter have been thinking? She rose from her chair. She couldn't cry. She had to be strong, but she had to get away, too. She had to find some hole to crawl into and hide forever.

Long fingers clasped her wrist before she could bolt. She whirled back toward Santana and tugged against his grip, but he held her fast.

"You're not running off again," he growled.

"I don't want to be here." Sometime in the last five years, Lark had turned soft. She never cried, but she was precariously on the verge of it now. "I just want to leave and forget this horrible day ever happened."

He drew her closer. Suddenly, he was taller, broader, more dangerous than she ever remembered.

"Like it or not, you're safest here," he said. "No one else around who can give you protection like I can. Except maybe Sheriff Sternberg, and the best he can do is his jail."

Lark swallowed. She knew the man, had handled his accounts at the Ida Grove Bank. His lack of tolerance for lawbreakers was well known throughout the county. Because of him, Ida Grove remained peaceful and safe.

He was the last man Lark could turn to.

"You've run out of options," Santana said, ruthless in driving home his point. "You can stay here, convince me whoever's after you needs to be caught and punished for attacking you. Or you can run and fend for yourself until he finds you again."

His words circled in Lark's head like a flock of angry crows. Catfish would kill her when he caught up with her. Even if she told him where the Muscatine loot was, he'd kill her so he could keep all that money for himself. The knife wound on her shoulder was proof he'd have no mercy to get what he wanted.

"What'll it be, Red?" Santana asked, his voice low.

Humiliation seared through her that she needed him, just like he said she did.

"Her name is Lark, Ross," Chat said, calmer now.

He merely grunted. Lark stood unmoving, pathetically indecisive about being dependent on a vengeance-seeking bounty hunter who would only turn her in when he learned the whole truth.

"Sit down," he said finally, making the decision for her.

Miserable, she complied. She took a breath and let it out again.

He propped a booted foot on his chair seat, rested his elbow on his knee. She tensed at the change which came over him. An attitude. A grim power that made her even more uneasy.

"Who attacked you in your sleeping room tonight?" he demanded.

Lark had no choice but to meet that power head-on. "His name is Catfish Jack."

Santana straightened and stared at her. "He's here? In Ida Grove?"

"You know him, then."

She wasn't surprised. They were all there that day at the Turf Club. Santana, Catfish, herself. Frank, Charlie, the others. And a horde of those damn Pinkerton agents.

There'd been so much chaos. So much yelling, shooting, *blood.* Lark couldn't keep track of what happened to whom. After she got shot, she didn't care much either way.

"Yeah. I know him." He looked grim, and Lark imagined his brain sifting through the ugliness, same as hers was. "Why did he come after you? After all these years, why now?"

"He wants something I don't have."

Santana waited.

"When I told him I didn't have it, he didn't believe me."

Still, Santana waited.

"So he got mad and attacked me."

Santana's mouth went hard. "He didn't believe you. Which means he's convinced you have what you say you don't. Which also means he'll hunt you down until he can force you to give him whatever it is he wants." Santana paused. "Knifing you is only the beginning."

Santana had a cold way of looking at things. But an accurate one. Her misery doubled.

"Yes," she whispered.

She braced herself for the question he'd ask next. What it was Catfish wanted. Or did Santana already know about the money she'd hidden?

"You fight him back?" he asked.

His unexpected question brought her head up. What did he think? That she'd just *let* Catfish attack her? "Of course!"

"How bad?"

"I hit him on the skull with a potted geranium. And Mrs. Kelley's table. And a water pitcher."

Chat, wide-eyed, emitted a sound of shock.

Santana nodded in satisfaction. "He's hurting then."

Lark glanced away. She found no gratification in violence, even against a cutthroat like Catfish. "Yes. I, well, I knocked him out, but—" her uninjured shoulder lifted "—Father Baxter assured me he came to again."

"Most likely, he's in no shape to ride. He'll have to lay low a day. Maybe two." Santana hooked a thumb in his hip pocket, stared a pensive moment at the curtain-covered window, as if he could see through the fabric and into the Ida Grove countryside. His bounty hunter mind would be working. Calculating Catfish's next move. He'd be thinking like the outlaw would, staying one step ahead of him.

"He's out there," Santana said, almost to himself. "Somewhere close."

"Yes," she said.

He turned back to her. "But he doesn't know you're here. That buys us some time. You're safe, so try to relax." He pointed to her plate with its dinner long since gone cold. "Eat up."

Lark forgot to breathe. That was it? No questions about Catfish's motive in hunting her down? No demand to know about the money she'd stolen?

Holy hellfire, the relief. Her secret was still intact, buried deep inside her where no one could find it. The one stroke of good luck she'd had the whole wretched night.

Santana strode away from the table, again taking his

Colt with him. His meal, Lark noticed, was finished. "Chat promised you a bath. I'll draw some water while you eat."

His sister stood. "Ross, wait."

He turned toward her.

She looked worried. "Are you still mad at me?"

The hardness faded from his expression, and he opened his arms. Chat flew into them, throwing her own around his neck. His embrace lifted her high from the floor.

"I know you'll help me protect her," he said quietly, setting her down but keeping her in his arms, talking as if Lark wasn't right there with them. "You just needed reminding how important it is to be discreet with the folks in town. It could mean her life."

"You can trust me, Ross. I *vow* it."

"You're a Santana. I do trust you." He kissed her forehead, released her, and gave her a gentle nudge toward the table. "Finish your dinner. It's getting late, and the kitchen's a mess."

He left the house, then, without a single glance back at Lark. Chat sat and dug into her meal. She caught Lark watching her and smiled, all her worry gone.

Lark lifted her fork. The bounty hunter's show of affection left her bemused. She couldn't shake the image of his embrace. Or the way he'd kissed Chat with brotherly ease.

But mostly, Lark couldn't help wondering what it'd feel like to have someone like him love her, too.

Ross sat at his desk, the design for his new revolving bookcase laid out in front of him once again. He'd hoped to calculate the final measurements before turning in tonight, but his figuring was off, and he couldn't find the mistake.

She was the problem. He couldn't concentrate. The

numbers kept blurring on the paper. Even more frustrating, the strain on his eye had brought on a low-grade headache.

Wild Red wasn't 'fessing up to everything she knew. And maybe Ross couldn't blame her, under the circumstances. Hell of a jolt to have her old crime come back, turn her new life upside down. She'd worked hard to put her sins behind her and start over in Ida Grove. Understandable she'd want to keep her mouth shut to keep from losing all she had.

But the law was the law. If she broke it, she'd have to pay the price.

His gut told him her silence had something to do with the Muscatine heist. All those years ago, suspicion had run high among lawmen and local citizenry alike that the Reno gang took the money, but without a single witness, no one knew for sure.

Ross intended to find out.

How Catfish Jack fit into the picture, Ross could only speculate. As far as he knew, the desperado had never ridden with the Renos. Yet Catfish had gone through a helluva lot of trouble to track Wild Red down. Why? What did he want?

Ross intended to find that out, too.

The revenge would be sweet when he did. He had scores to settle, and only Wild Red could help him do it.

She was plenty skittish, though. He'd have to be careful. Take his time. Earn her trust before he could get her to talk.

Even more important, he had to keep her alive. He owed her that much. She'd been hurt too much already. Thinking back, Ross guessed he'd hurt her more than anybody.

For the dozenth time, his gaze strayed to the open door

of Chat's bedroom. Once dinner was over and cleared away, Red took the bath Ross prepared for her, and Chat helped wash her hair since Red's lacerated shoulder kept her from doing it herself. Now she sat cross-legged on the bed in a borrowed nightgown while his sister brushed the wet mass, running the bristles through the waist-length strands again and again.

Inexplicably, his blood warmed just thinking of all that hair. How it'd feel wet. How it'd feel dry...

He tore his glance away with a muttered oath. He determinedly jotted down a series of fractions on a piece of scrap paper. Before his brain could convert the numbers into inches and feet, his ear strained to catch the bits of conversation drifting out from the bedroom.

He couldn't decipher what they chatted about. Female things probably, since they seemed to get along well enough. But then, Red didn't have to do much except sit and listen. Chat was prone to do most of the talking.

From what he could tell, the responses Red made were polite and reserved. Maybe she tended to be closemouthed, even on the best of days.

He narrowed his eye over the series of numbers he'd written and tried to remember what part of the bookcase they were for. He heard Chat set the hairbrush on the bedside table and stride toward him.

"Ross, we're ready to go to bed now. I'll give Miss Renault my room tonight," she said. "Do you want to sleep on the couch or shall I?"

He gave up on the measurements. "Give her my room. I'll take the couch."

Red made a sound of alarm. She unfolded her legs and slid off the mattress, then padded toward him on bare feet. Chat's nightgown ran a little short on her. A bit snug around the chest, too. His gaze clung to the provocative wobble of female bosom under the white cotton.

"I will not sleep in your bed tonight," she said in a husky voice.

His brow arched. Did she think she had a choice? That he wouldn't anticipate any covert moves she might try to make in the middle of the night?

"Oh, it's no bother, really," Chat said, clearly oblivious to the undercurrent of rebellion brewing between them. "Whenever we have overnight guests, which isn't often actually, but when we do, they always stay in Ross's room. His bed is bigger and more comfortable than mine. He made it himself, you know. Come here. I'll show you."

Chat headed toward his bedroom, but Red stayed behind. She glared at him, her slender feet spread in a defiant stance, but Ross sensed her vulnerability.

Her worry.

About what? That he was lying? Or had no intention of sleeping on the couch but would share the bed with her against her will?

He held her glare with one of his own. He was guilty of a long string of mistakes in his life—shooting her in an arrest gone wrong among them—but he'd never put raping a woman on the list.

"Miss Renault? Are you coming?" Chat waited in the doorway of his room.

"I'm not going to hurt you." Ross's low voice rumbled with the vow only Red could hear. "Damn you for thinking I would."

She appeared taken aback by that, but the rebellion in her lingered. "You're a bounty hunter, Santana. I've never trusted one. Why should you be any different?"

She swung away from him, depriving him of a terse response, leaving him with no choice but to watch her go and the sway of her hips when she did.

"Isn't his furniture beautiful?" After Red joined her, Chat strolled past his tall bureau to the nightstand with its kerosene lamp on top. She turned the flame higher, and the glow splashed into the room. "He designed and built all the pieces himself. The quality can't be matched, and his workmanship is flawless. He's brilliant, don't you think? I'm so proud of him."

Ross gritted his teeth against his sister's gushing. He figured what talent he had spoke for itself. Chat didn't need to do it for him.

Yet as he busied himself rolling up the revolving bookcase designs and tidying his desk for the night, he strained to hear Red's response.

"And why is it your bed is so much smaller than his? And not nearly as new?" she murmured.

"Oh, well, when we moved out here several years ago, Ross offered to build me a bedroom set of my own, but I decided to wait until I was married. I want the set for my dowry. To share with my new husband."

"I see."

"When Sarah spends the night, she stays in my room," Chat babbled on. "And that's why I offered it to you, but truly, Ross's room is so much nicer. And don't worry about him sleeping on the couch. He's slept in places far worse." Chat laughed.

Red slid a haughty glance his way. "I'm sure he has."

"Well, it's settled then, Miss Renault. Is there anything else I can get you?"

Red reached out, laid a gentle hand on Chat's arm. "No, but thank you for everything. You've been most kind. And please, call me Lark. I insist."

Chat smiled. "All right. Good night, Lark." She turned and headed for her bedroom. "Good night, Ross."

"Good night."

Chat disappeared inside her room and closed the door.

Ross's gaze locked with Red's. He rose from his chair, strode toward her, taking his time.

She stood without moving, watched him come.

He halted. Her head tilted back.

"If you touch me, I'll kill you," she whispered.

A corner of his mouth lifted. "Killing's not your style, Red. Only stealing."

She sucked in a breath, and he knew his taunt cut deep. "Go to hell, won't you?"

"I've been there, darlin', thanks to you and your kind. And I don't care to go there again."

"My kind." She whirled away. One fine-boned hand gripped the top edge of the bed's carved footboard, hard enough to turn her knuckles white. She probably wished it was his neck instead.

But when she faced him again, her features were cool. Controlled. He had to admire her for the dignity she found, then wore like a diamond-studded crown.

"My name is Lark," she said quietly. "Your insistence to call me anything else is not only rude but infuriating."

He scowled. Did she have an inkling how many times he'd thought of her over the years? She'd become indelibly imprinted in his mind. He doubted he'd ever think of her as anyone but Wild Red, reputed outlaw and thief.

He strode toward the bureau, opened the top drawer, removed his toothbrush and powder. But, hell. He might as well use her legal name, since it meant so much to her if he did. He needed her to capture Catfish Jack. No sense in getting her hackles up every time they had a conversation.

He tossed a clean towel over his shoulder and faced her. Her hand, he noted, still gripped the footboard.

"You can't stand there all night. You need to rest to keep your wits about you tomorrow," he said. "No telling what might happen. We both need to be ready for it."

"I'm not sure I can do this." She glanced away, her teeth finding her lower lip again.

His eye narrowed. "Sleep in my bed?"

"A *bounty hunter's* bed."

Impatience rolled through him that she despised him so much. He yanked back the coverlet. "Get in."

She met his gaze square. Now that her hair had begun to dry, wisps of auburn curls were collecting at her temple and cheeks. "Fine. Like you, Santana, I've slept in places far worse, I suppose."

The barb had the effect of both annoying him and amusing him. She sat on the mattress and drew her knees up, then busied herself fluffing the pillow behind her, more to avoid looking at him than to see to her own comfort.

Ross stepped closer, grabbed a shapely ankle with one hand, the chain and leg iron he'd attached to the bedrail with the other. In the breadth of a heartbeat, he clamped the shackle around her ankle.

The iron held fast.

He ignored her yelp of outrage, gathered his toothbrush and powder, and left the room, closing the door behind him.

Chapter Six

Lark gaped at her leg in horror. Santana had tethered her to the bed like a disobedient dog.

Furious, she lifted her ankle and pulled, but the chain wouldn't give. She bent forward, grasped the links with both hands and yanked. They didn't budge. She leaned over the side of the mattress, found the end attached to the bed's iron frame and tugged there, too, all to no avail.

The brute.

She flung herself back against the pillows and fumed up at the ceiling. She could call out for Chat, but what good would that do? Santana wouldn't give in. Besides, Lark didn't want his sister to see her manacled to the bed. Was there anything more humiliating?

She glared daggers at the closed door and thought of him on the other side. He'd caught her completely unaware with the leg iron, had probably rigged the thing when she was bathing in Chat's room. Was he snickering right now? Gloating? And just when she was beginning to think staying here might not be so bad after all....

It was only Chat's kindness that made Lark delay her

plan to escape. So did the trouble Santana went to by readying her bathwater. Making sure she was fed and treating her wound, too. Lark admitted she'd been pretty scared at first. Both of them had gone to great lengths to put her at ease.

Except for the sleeping-in-Santana's-bed part.

Santana didn't trust her any farther than he could throw her, and, well, as reluctant as Lark was to admit it, maybe she couldn't blame him. He hadn't built his reputation as a shrewd bounty hunter by being stupid in his dealings with the lawless.

Not that she was lawless. Not these days, at least.

So he made sure she wasn't going anywhere any time soon, which would ensure both of them a good night's sleep. She'd be safe from Catfish Jack, too. Even though she hated Santana for his underhanded way of keeping her where he wanted her, she could understand his reasoning for it.

The fury within her faded, and she didn't bother to revive it.

She slid her gaze about the perimeter of his room with wary curiosity instead. He liked his surroundings simple, clean and uncluttered. A man's taste, she supposed. One who wasn't prone to pretentiousness. He merely surrounded himself with the things that meant the most to him.

Like a picture of Chat on his dresser when she was several years younger, still wearing braids and ribbons. Next to it, a photographer's shot of an older couple, staring boldly into the camera lens. His parents, perhaps. On the wall, there was a framed photo of an Arabian horse, dark coat gleaming from the sun. One of his prized mounts?

And the furniture pieces. Solid and strong, like the man

who built them. The lantern's glow shimmered across the smooth, polished surfaces of the deep mahogany bureau and dresser, shadowed over their carvings and curved rolls, and glinted off the handsome matching mirror.

The furniture signified permanence. That Santana had set down roots, something she'd never done until she moved to Ida Grove, and maybe not even then. Everything in this room was a part of him, either something he created or loved and most likely both, and how fortunate he was to have it all.

Some strange sort of longing stirred within her. Lark had never owned a piece of furniture in her life. Nothing in her sleeping room in town qualified as hers, except a few potted geraniums. She was only renting the furnishings from Mrs. Kelley. Why had that never bothered her before?

Catfish Jack threatened to take away even that small semblance of stability in her life. If Santana ever found out the truth about the Muscatine heist, he *definitely* would.

Lark shut the troubling thoughts down. There was nothing she could do to change the horrific events of the afternoon. What mattered more was how she would deal with them in the morning. To do that, she had to sleep. As Santana said, she'd need her wits about her to deal with everything that had happened.

The chain contained a gang ring in the middle, giving the leg iron length so Lark could move about in reasonable comfort. She reached over to turn down the lamp, and the room plunged into darkness. Mindful of her sore shoulder, she settled into the pillow, pulling the covers to her chin. Her eyes closed. If she didn't think about them, she wouldn't be aware of the manacle on her ankle or that she was lying in a bounty hunter's bed.

From within the linens, Santana's masculine scent rose up to surround her.

Her eyes opened again.

A disturbingly male blend of fresh-cut wood and tobacco. Not a bounty hunter's scent, but a *man's*.

Lark didn't want to think of him as being one. She didn't
want to think of him lying in this bed with his skin bare
against the sheets and his long, lean body relaxed in sleep.

The breadth of the mattress would hold a woman as
well, and an image of him tangling his arms and legs with
hers lingered in her mind.

She swallowed, not wanting to think of him in that way,
either.

She shifted to her side and forced a new round of
thoughts into her brain. Important thoughts, like her job at
the bank and how she treasured it more than anything. Mr.
Templeton with his wife and little Phillip, enjoying their
trip in Omaha. And, oh, Mrs. Kelley.

The dear woman would be fretting over Lark's safety
and whereabouts. Never in a million years would she think
Lark was here, in Ross Santana's bed, desperately in need
of his help and protection to save herself from a cutthroat
like Catfish Jack.

Lying in the darkness, alone in an unfamiliar bed, the
homesickness rolled through Lark in churning waves. She
missed her sleeping room, Mrs. Kelley's cooking, the comfortable, boring routine she had become accustomed to day
in and day out.

Would she ever have it back again?

Lark's eyelids fluttered open. She'd managed to fall
asleep at some point, for the night had slipped away, and
with it, worries and apprehensions. A shy morning sun
peeped through the closed muslin curtains, keeping Santana's room pleasantly shadowed and serene.

She had no qualms about where she was. Or why. The time would come soon enough when she'd have to deal with harsh reality again, but until it did, she was content to simply lie in Santana's bed, snuggled beneath the covers, deliciously warm, comfortable and safe.

The house was quiet, but Lark detected the faint scent of brewing coffee. If Chat was up already, preparing to cook breakfast, she was careful not to wake anyone. The girl was a gem, and Lark had liked her from the start. If only—

The muted squeak of the door creeping open on its hinges scattered the thoughts. Lark rolled over and lifted a hand to push away the mass of curls that fell against her cheek.

Santana stood in the doorway. He wore Levi's and nothing else except for a towel around his neck. Clearly, he'd just bathed somewhere; droplets of water still dotted his chest. His hair was casually finger-combed back, a stubble of beard darkened his cheeks, and with that black leather patch over his eye...

Heat unfurled in her belly. He looked primitive. Powerful. Purely male.

"Did I wake you?" he asked in a low voice.

"No." The hushed tone of her voice matched his— husky, strangely intimate.

"I forgot my razor last night. You mind if I come in and get it?"

She couldn't stop a small smile. It was his room, after all. And she was shackled to the bed frame.

"Feel free," she murmured.

"Thanks." He strode toward the washstand, a fine accent to the other pieces in the suite. He hesitated, then turned back toward her. "As long as you're already awake, I could just shave right here."

"You could."

"Is that a yes?"

"It is." His need for her agreement amused her. What would he do if she said no?

"I won't be long." He lit the kerosene lamp, took down his straight razor from the shelf above the basin.

"Take your time. I'm not going anywhere, thanks to you."

She yawned and shifted to her side to see him better. What else did she have to do but watch him? Her lacerated shoulder made only a mild protest, a good sign the wound had begun to heal.

"I made coffee. You want a cup?" he asked.

A leather strop hung from a nail next to the shelf. He dragged the blade across the cowhide, back and forth, again and again, giving the razor a smooth, sharp edge.

"Maybe later." She was much too comfortable to think about doing anything but lie there.

"For what it's worth, I didn't have a choice chaining you up last night." The muscles in his back bunched and bulged from each stroke and left Lark fascinated by their play. "You would've run first minute the lights were out."

Lark dragged her gaze from him. She didn't want to be fascinated. "Maybe."

"No maybe about it. You would have."

She didn't bother to deny it, but found herself watching him again. He took his shaving mug from the shelf, dipped its brush in water, stirred the bristles into the soap in the bottom.

Their eyes met in the mirror. He had a strikingly dark gaze, rich as molasses, and he held her captivated.

Santana had the power to make a woman forget things she shouldn't.

"Did you sleep well?" he asked, his tone husky again.

"Hmm. Surprisingly so."

"In a bounty hunter's bed." He grunted, lathered his cheeks with the frothy soap. "Imagine that."

She scowled at his sarcasm. Or was he teasing her? "I'd punch you if I could get to you, Santana."

Amazingly, he chuckled at that. "Good thing you're shackled then."

"Are you going to leave me like this all day?"

He placed the straight razor at the base of one sideburn, ran the blade down his cheek in a smooth swipe. "Depends."

"On what?"

"On whether you plan to run or stay."

She snorted. "Do you think I'd tell you if I intended to run?"

"I've learned to read the signs." He rinsed the blade, the set of his jaw telling her he was dead serious. "You wouldn't have to tell me a damn thing."

His words gave her pause. Had she underestimated him?

"And what are my signs telling you, Santana?" she asked softly.

"You're torn about it." Again, the blade journeyed down his cheek, until all the soap was gone. "You're straddling two worlds. The one you lived in as an outlaw, and the one you're living in now as a respectable citizen." He jutted his chin, then ran the razor over its curve. "That means I can't trust you."

She raised up on an elbow. In spite of everything, his declaration stung her hard-won sensibilities. "Regardless of what you think, I am completely trustworthy, Santana. Mr. Templeton trusts me in his bank day in and day out.

Don't you *dare* think I didn't earn that from him by being honest in every way."

Santana tossed her a hard glance. "Circumstances the way they are, your point is moot, Red." He cleared his throat. "I mean, Lark."

His use of her name failed to assuage her, and she fell back against the pillow in frustration. Why did he have to be so brutally frank?

"All right." Damn him. "You have my word."

"About what?"

"About escaping from you."

The razor hovered in midair. "Say it."

She rolled her eyes. The man truly didn't trust her, and why did that bother her? "I promise I will not try to escape you. Leastways, today. Unless you give me reason to."

"Or unless I fail in my protection of you." He regarded her steadily. "Agreed?"

She hesitated only a little. The addendum assured her he took his intent to protect her seriously. God knew she needed it. "Agreed."

The razor slid over the other side of his face with the same expert strokes of the first. He was silent so long she began to get worried.

"Do you believe me?" Lark asked.

"Yes."

"Do you have a plan?"

"About what?"

"About me. Now that I'm here, what am I supposed to do?"

"Nothing. And neither will I. But I'm going to send Chat to town."

"Chat?" Vague alarm filtered through Lark. She didn't

want the girl involved. What if she got hurt? "But what can she do?"

Santana cleaned the straight razor and returned it to the shelf. "She knows a lot of people who love to gossip same as she does. If Catfish has been seen around these parts, she'll hear about it."

Lark eyed him dubiously. "You're the bounty hunter. Not her."

Remnants of shaving soap remained on his face. He wiped them away with the towel, then tossed the linen aside. "I don't go into town much. Hardly ever. If I ride in, start asking questions, folks are going to wonder." He turned toward her, hands on hips. "Chat, on the other hand, goes to town most every day. No one will find it unusual that she's there."

Still, Lark worried. "I hope you're right."

"I am."

He stood next to the bed, tall, bare-chested and...*male*. His rich molasses gaze lingered over her hair, wild and tangled on the pillow, as it always was when she woke up in the mornings, lingered so long that a tiny tremor of fear rippled through her.

What was he thinking? What did he intend to do?

When Chat left, Lark would be alone with him. Just the two of them, with no one else around.

I'm not going to hurt you.

Damn you for thinking I would.

She took heart from the words he'd spoken the night before, as if he was offended that she thought otherwise.

"If I'm to stay here, I want to make myself useful," she said quietly, looking up at him.

"You've got enough to do just staying alive right now."

"I've intruded on your lives. I've kept you from your

room and bed. Now, Chat will have to go into town to scrape up information, all on my account."

He fished a small key from the pocket of his Levi's and found her ankle beneath the covers. "You hear us complaining?"

"I'll not stay here and do nothing."

He slid the key into the leg iron, and the shackle fell free. Santana frowned at the faint ring the iron left on her skin. He sat beside her and rubbed it gently with his thumb.

"What do you want to do?" he asked.

Her mind sifted through her talents, few that they were. Numbers were her strong suit, but would good would that do her here?

"I don't know." She shrugged. "I can cook, I guess."

"Yeah?" His thumb stopped rubbing.

"I was assigned to kitchen duties in prison. I cooked every day for five years."

"Chat damn near burns everything she makes."

Lark remembered their dinner last night, the too-dry beef and too-dark biscuits. The meal had been rather taste-less, but then, Lark hadn't been of a mind to enjoy much of anything, no matter how well it had—or hadn't—been prepared.

"Mrs. Kelley is an excellent cook. She's taught me how to fix numerous dishes, so I'd be happy to…"

Santana rested his hand on her foot and distracted her with his boldness. Long, lean fingers curled around her ankle, loose and casual, as if he didn't even realize they were there. But the warmth of his skin, the clean scent of his shaving soap, his close proximity on the bed sent awareness zinging through her like buckshot.

She pulled her foot from his grasp and sat up, drawing her knees to her chest. Her toes curled into the mattress.

She eased out a breath. "I'd be happy to perhaps show Chat a few—a few things."

Brow furrowed, Santana straightened. "Never been much good in the kitchen myself. Mother passed on when Chat was barely six, so she's not had a female around to teach her what she needs to know. The proper way, at least."

No sisters, then. And no father? Lark refrained from asking. What business was it of hers who made up the Santana family?

"You've done a fine job with her," Lark said softly. "She's a lovely girl."

"That she is." He stood. "She does what she can the best she knows how."

Which didn't include much success in the kitchen, evidently. Lark eyed him with sympathy. She'd lost her own mother what seemed like forever ago. How different would her life be if Mama had lived?

"I'll cook breakfast then," she said.

He inclined his dark head. "If it'll make you feel better."

"It will."

"Chat's still sleeping." He strode toward his dresser, removed a clean shirt from the drawer. "I've got chores to do. I'll see you a little later."

She watched him go. Keenly aware of the privilege he'd given her, that of moving about his home with a semblance of freedom, but mostly of trust, she slipped from the mattress.

It moved her, that trust.

She'd be a fool to abuse it. He'd given her no reason to, besides. And so she took great care in making his bed, smoothing the sheets first, then pulling the quilt up and seeing that the sides hung even and straight. She plumped the pillows, laid them next to one another and stepped back.

Ross Santana, she had to admit, had a wonderfully handsome bed.

Her gaze dallied over the quilt with its bold-colored squares in varying shades of blue, rows and rows of them, each perfectly stitched by deft, experienced fingers. His mother's? Grandmother's?

Lark could only imagine the wealth of time and love that had gone into the creation. She had no such keepsake, and she swallowed down a little welling of sadness from the loss.

She shook it off. She had more important matters to think about than not owning a family quilt.

Her dress was still in Chat's room, she recalled with a grimace. She'd taken it off in there before her bath, then cleaned the blood from the fabric in the leftover bathwater. Lark didn't want to risk waking Chat to retrieve it. Besides, the bodice needed mending, and she had no idea where to find needle and thread.

That left her with Santana's shirt again, to use as a robe. Lark contemplated the garment, hanging on a hook near his bureau, where Chat had left it last night. Odd that it no longer bothered Lark to wear the thing.

She slid her arms into the sleeves and adjusted the shoulders to fit better over hers. Her fingers worked the buttons, and she breathed in the scent of starch.

Mr. Templeton always smelled of starch, too. Always wore crisp white shirts, like this one. Preferred his surroundings neat and tidy, just as Santana did.

But, Holy hellfire, there couldn't be two men who were more different.

Had it been only yesterday that Mr. Templeton had honored her with the responsibility of closing up the Ida Grove Bank in his absence? That she'd thought of him, spoken with him, had envied his wife his love and affection for her and their son, Phillip?

A lifetime ago.

Once he learned the truth about her, she would never be his favorite employee again.

Chapter Seven

Ross led the last of Chat's milk cows out of the paddock to graze in the pasture beyond the barn. He'd already strained their milk and carried the pails to the cellar where they would chill and set for the cream she'd skim tonight. He'd skimmed the cream from last night's milking, too, and left the jug on the back step.

Might be Lark could use some for their breakfast.

The cows were Chat's responsibility, but Ross did her share of chores this morning, just so she could sleep in some. She wouldn't be expecting him to do her work for her, but he figured he'd owe her the favor. Sending her into town to do a bit of discreet investigating would be more than worth a few minutes of milking time.

He strode from the barn to the house, but paused on the front porch. Thoughts hung heavy on his mind, and he had a need to sort them through. He leaned his hip against the rail to have a smoke and realized he'd done the same thing the evening before, when Father Baxter had ridden out with Lark.

Funny how the morning had a way of putting a different perspective on things.

He struck a match, cupped a hand around the flame, and lit a rolled cigarette. He'd wanted nothing to do with her then. But sometime during the night, he'd come to think of her less as an outlaw and more as a woman.

Right there, that would get him into trouble.

Seeing her in his bed, that wild mane spread out on his pillow, sleep-tossed and thick with those auburn curls, had stirred his blood with a slow fire. He shook out the match and drew in deep on the tobacco.

A slow, lusty fire.

She'd mess up his head if he wasn't careful. He had to stay focused. Detached. In control. After all these years, she was his one chance to capture Catfish Jack. He might not get another. And if he recovered the money from the Muscatine heist in the process, well, that was just sweet sugar icing on the cake.

He exhaled, squinted against a haze of blue-gray smoke. If nothing else, her need for his help awakened in him a hunger for the justice he'd years ago buried deep inside him, so deep he didn't think about it much anymore, deep enough he pretty much believed that hunger was dead.

It was still there.

Justice.

The thrill of the hunt, too.

It was what had earned him his reputation as a damn good bounty hunter. Gut instinct. Raw nerve. The ability to think like a hunted man would think.

But as he studied the burning end of his cigarette, nauseating fear rolled in his belly.

Could he do it again? A one-eyed, has-been bounty hunter, protect himself? Lark? Chat? Was he man enough to protect them all?

Sweet Jesus, he didn't know.

He dragged his stare to the yard, to his workshop and the woods beyond, and, as always, endured the sickening sensation of having the images only half of what they'd once been.

The blast from Catfish's shotgun had destroyed all vision on his right side. He wouldn't see anyone coming at him from that angle, would miss the most subtle of movements, most likely the most obvious, too, until it was too late.

Catfish Jack would take advantage of that.

Ross sighed heavily and dropped the cigarette stub to the porch floor, then mashed it to ashes with the toe of his boot.

The sight of the stub jolted him. The thing reminded him of what he'd become. A wasted, ground-out imitation of his former self.

He stared once more into the woods past his shop and met the half vision head-on. Lark had thrown him into a do-it-or-die-trying kind of situation, and damned if he was going to run from it. He had a thing or two to prove to himself. To Chat. And, yeah, Lark, too.

At the knowledge, his acceptance of it, an unexpected vein of anticipation hummed through him. He turned, pushed open the front door and froze at the myriad of aromas that greeted him.

Breakfast.

His mouth watered. When had the house smelled this good? Sausage frying. Coffee simmering. And something that smelled vaguely of cinnamon.

Lark's cooking?

He headed toward the kitchen, but halted before going in. She stood at the stove, barefoot and wearing his shirt again, right over her nightgown. Her hair hung in a queue down her back, with a ribbon tied at her nape to hold the auburn ringlets in place. Standing over hot burners bloomed a delicate flush in her cheeks, and damn if that fiery lust didn't start flickering inside him again.

She glanced over her shoulder. "Oh, I didn't hear you come in. I won't be much longer."

"Take your time." He eyed the sausage in the skillet, the bowl of light batter next to it.

"I found the waffle iron in the pantry." She held her hand over the long-handled utensil Ross hadn't seen in a good long while, sitting on the burner over a brisk fire, gauging the metal's heat with her palm. "I hope it's all right I'm using it."

He'd given the irons to Chat a couple of Christmases ago. "We've only had waffles but once or twice that I recall."

She stilled, looking worried. "You don't like waffles?"

"I happen to favor them. So does Chat. But the last time she used the irons, she had such a mess going, she hasn't used them since."

"They can be difficult to clean," Lark conceded carefully.

"Might be she just wasn't using them right."

"Perhaps."

Lark looked apprehensive. Ross wondered if his comment made her question her choice of menu for breakfast.

"They'll be a nice change from eggs and bacon every morning," he said.

She relaxed a little at that. "Mrs. Kelley serves them on Sunday morning to her boarders. They're quite popular with us."

"Make plenty then. We'll eat 'em up." He remembered the jug he'd left on the back step. "There's cream if you can use it."

She made short work of buttering the irons, then ladling batter on top. A soft smile curved her lips. "I love fresh cream in my coffee. Thank you."

She sounded so pleased he felt ridiculously pleased himself that he had thought to mention it. He set the jug on the table, and not finding her cup, took one from the sideboard, filled it with black brew and added the cream.

She stood with her back to him as she removed browned sausage from the skillet, setting each one on paper to drain. He extended the coffee toward her, and her glance flew up at him in astonishment.

"My, my." She put the fork down, took the cup from him, the tips of her fingers barely brushing his when she did. "I didn't know bounty hunters could be this thoughtful."

"Only when we're fed waffles, so don't get used to it," he muttered roughly.

The tinkle of her laughter surprised him. Surrounded him. Her femininity, too, and the delectable aromas of breakfast cooking, and damn, how could she be guilty of the crimes she'd committed?

He had to work hard at remembering the kind of person she was, or at least used to be, and the one crime she needed to be held accountable for. For the life of him, he couldn't think of a thing to say, or do, and so he stood there, looking at her, feeling like a hapless little spider caught in the delicate web of confusion she'd managed to spin around him.

Chat burst into the room, saving him.

"Oh, I'm sorry! I completely overslept. Why didn't you wake me, Ross?" She froze, her eyes widening. "Miss Renault, I mean, Lark, what are you *doing?*"

"Fixing breakfast." Lark turned from him to resume

her work at the skillet, one hand still holding her cup. "Are you hungry? There's plenty."

"But you're our guest. You shouldn't be cooking. Ross, why are you letting her?"

"She wanted to. Besides, she's good at it, it seems." He stepped away, went in search of his own coffee in hopes of clearing his head of the effect she had on him.

"I should say so. Everything smells delicious," Chat said.

Lark finished with the sausage, set the plate aside, and moved the skillet to the back burner to cool. "Thank you."

Chat's incredulous gaze settled on the hot irons. "Are you making *waffles?*"

"I am. And this one is ready, I think." Putting her coffee down, she lifted the top handle. A round, golden waffle appeared.

"Oh," Chat breathed. "How did you get it to turn out so perfect?"

"I've helped Mrs. Kelley many times, and we made them now and again in—" Her uncertain glance darted to Ross, then slid ruefully back to Chat. "Well, since we all know where I once was, I'll admit I helped make them when I was in prison."

"If they look this good, who cares where you learned how?" Chat asked, arching a brow at Ross in silent challenge for him to deny it.

He didn't. Prison had its place, namely to reform those who needed it. And reform included teaching lawbreakers new skills for them to use on the outside. In Lark's case, forcing her to work in the penitentiary's kitchen had paid off.

She lifted the waffle from the iron with a fork and eased it on a plate. She dusted the top with powdered sugar, sprinkled cinnamon on top, added several browned sausages, and handed the whole thing over to Chat.

"Give this to your brother, won't you? I'll make another. Unless you'd like to try making one yourself?"

"I would." She set the plate on the table with a hurried clatter, leaving Ross to retrieve his own fork and napkin. He didn't mind. Chat needed tutoring in more than just waffle-making, and Lark was well-suited for the job.

He'd owe her for that, he supposed, taking a bite of the warm cake and liking the taste of it on his tongue. Chat had a great deal of admiration for her. If this breakfast was an indication of all Lark had to offer, Ross hoped Chat would learn from everything she had to say.

"But your batter is so different than mine was," Chat said, dipping the ladle in, then raising it and letting batter spill back into the bowl. "Mine was much too thick, as I recall."

"The trick is to set it aside in a warm place until it gets very light, then add a little flour and butter," Lark said. "Make sure the iron is greased well, too, and hot enough to sizzle."

Chat made a sound of understanding.

"When you pour the batter onto the iron, don't fill it too full. Otherwise, batter will leak out the sides," Lark went on. "The waffle expands as it's baking."

"It'll burn, too," Chat said. "I know that for a fact." She rolled her eyes. "What a mess."

"Now you won't do it again." Lark closed the iron. "And that's it. Simple, really. In a minute or two, this one will be ready."

By the time enough golden waffles had been made for them all, Ross was on his third plate. After his belly had its fill, he leaned back in his chair and contemplated the two women at the table with him, both barefoot and still in their nightgowns, their hair uncombed, but their conversation animated and relaxed. In time, he knew, they'd be fast friends, if they weren't already.

That troubled him.

He had to keep their feet on the ground. He couldn't let them forget what had happened yesterday, what might happen tomorrow. They could be allies today, now, this minute, but in the next, they could be enemies.

It all came down to survival. Lark's survival. She'd do what she had to do to save her neck from the noose, whether she knew it or not. And if that forced her to turn against them, Ross and Chat both, well, Ross would understand it.

Chat wouldn't.

And that troubled him, too.

"I want you to go into town today, Chat," he said grimly.

Whatever they'd been talking about ended. Chat and Lark swiveled, their full attention upon him.

"Sure," Chat said. "Any special reason?"

"Information."

Somber, she nodded. "About Catfish Jack."

His gaze slid to Lark, lingered over the wild curls which coiled against her temple. What were the old hens in Ida Grove saying about her? Had they shredded her reputation to ribbons by now?

"Among other things," he said. "Catfish was wounded when he attacked Lark in her sleeping room. Might be he needed medical attention."

Chat nodded. "I'll see if Doc Seeber knows something. I'll be discreet, of course."

"*Very* discreet," Ross said.

"This isn't a good idea, Santana." Lark sat stiff in her chair, looking miserable.

"We can't stay out here with our heads in the sand," he said, the words rougher than he intended. "Any piece of news Chat can find out for us will help keep you safe."

"But the risks!"

"I won't draw attention to myself," Chat said quickly. "I promise."

"You don't understand how underhanded Catfish can be," Lark said. "Neither of you."

"The hell I don't," Ross growled.

"I'll be careful. Truly, I will." Chat jumped up, carried her dishes to the sideboard. "It's getting late. I'd best dress and get going." She dashed off to disappear inside her room.

Lark rose, gathered her own dishes. "If anything happens to her, I'll never forgive myself." She leveled Ross with a reproving glare. "Nor will I forgive you for sending her."

Her words stung, but Ross took their bite.

Because if he failed in protecting either one of them, he'd never forgive himself.

Chat draped a flour sack over her basket of eggs and slid the wicker beneath the buckboard's seat. "I'll be back well before supper, so don't start cooking again before I arrive."

Lark managed a small smile and thought of the long hours that lay ahead. "It would give me something to do, you know."

"Who says you have to do anything? Just be lazy today."

Lark detested "lazy." "I'll be fine. Don't worry about me."

Chat cocked her head. Looking young and carefree in a fawn-colored skirt and ivory pearl-buttoned blouse, one would be hard pressed to guess the true purpose for her trip to town.

"You could get to know Ross better," she said.

Lark's gaze was steady. "I do believe I know him well enough as it is."

"He needs a woman like you in his life."

"Hmm." She squinted into the sky. "I don't think so."

"It's true. He's been different since you came here." Chat shrugged, thoughtful. "I don't know. More alive, maybe."

"I imagine I've given him something different to think about, that's all."

"Better you than his boring furniture all the time."

Lark could feel Chat watching her, but she refused to meet the girl's gaze. What if Chat saw the truth in her eyes?

"He's a little gruff at times, but he's one of the most gallant men I've ever met," Chat went on. "Truly."

Chat idolized him, and that affected her thinking. But Lark had seen a side of him that Chat hadn't—the violent, justice-minded side—and she held no doubt Santana wouldn't have a gallant bone in him if he ever unlocked her secret and had to drag her off to jail because of it.

"I'm sure any woman around could give him far better company than I could," she said.

And why were they having this conversation anyway?

"He won't let them."

Intrigued in spite of herself, Lark glanced at her. "Why not?"

"Oh, he could have any female he wanted, believe me. But he's pretty much sworn off all of them. His eye, you know. His lack of one."

Santana approached from the far side of the house, and Chat shifted her stance to keep her voice from reaching him. Lark suspected he'd never approve of his sister talking about him like this, and to Lark, especially.

"He's a proud man, Lark. He doesn't want anyone's pity, and for some reason, *female* pity is the worst for him." She reached for her hat, which was sitting on the wagon seat, her movement casual and relaxed, as if they merely spoke of the weather. "You're different, though. You treat him like a normal man, like the eye patch doesn't exist."

Her brow arched. "Normal?"

Santana had the power to destroy the honest citizen she'd become. How could that be normal? Couldn't Chat see Lark's fear in that? Had she hidden it so well?

Santana knew, though. And was only biding his time until the truth came out.

He drew closer, and their conversation had to end. Chat smiled brightly up at him.

"Everything loaded up?" he asked.

"Yes. My eggs and six crocks of butter to sell at the dairy." She patted her skirt pocket. "And money for a few supplies at the grocery store." She smiled. "As usual."

"Make sure it stays that way." He dropped a few extra coins into her palm. "Here. When you meet up with Sarah, treat yourselves to a doughnut at Nell's Bakery. Find out if Sarah's heard or seen anything around her mother's boardinghouse that might indicate Catfish Jack's whereabouts."

"She'll tell me if she has."

Santana frowned. "Be careful. We don't know if he's working alone or if he has a gang hanging around town listening for word of *Lark's* whereabouts."

"I know most everyone in town, Ross. So I'll recognize a stranger when I see one. If there's news, I'll hurry back with it."

He bent and kissed her forehead. "Be careful."

"You've told me that a hundred times already." She rolled her eyes in exasperation and tied her stylish brown velvet hat under her chin, covering the brunette hair she'd earlier crimped and braided into a coil around her head.

Her attractiveness made Lark keenly aware her only dress still needed mending and that she stood in the yard with her toes buried in the grass, that she was still wearing Chat's nightgown and Santana's white shirt as a robe.

He placed his hands at Chat's waist, hefted her into the wagon seat. "Be back by midafternoon. No later."

"I will."

"Earlier, if there's trouble."

"There won't be."

She took the reins and smiled conspiratorially down at Lark.

"Remember what we talked about," she said, giving Lark a wink that Santana couldn't see.

"It's better that you remember what your brother has told *you*," Lark replied quickly and with far more seriousness.

"I'll remember." She slapped the reins, and her horse took off with a clatter of wagon wheels. "See you both this afternoon."

Lark watched her go. Santana did, too, both of them standing in the yard, at each other's side. Like parents, worried about a child's safety.

"What did she tell you?" Santana asked when a cloud of dust was all that remained of her and the wagon.

"She told me I wasn't to cook in her absence." Lark tilted her head back and looked him square in the eye. She thought of the true way of the conversation, that of Chat's matchmaking, and what would he think of *that?*

His masculinity crept into her awareness again. Lark

had never looked at him like this, boldly and without trep-
idation. She wasn't particularly curious about the black
patch he would always wear. Certainly not repulsed by it,
either. She'd lived the life where men who survived by
their guns were maimed by them, too. Her own body carried the scar left behind by a lone bullet.

Santana's bullet.

Instead, the dark depths of that single orb he had remaining kept her standing in front of him. Motionless,
hardly breathing, as if he wove a peculiar riveting spell
around her. The eye was a beautiful deep brown, and oh,
how it must have devastated him to lose its mate.

She looked away. She couldn't think of Ross Santana's
pain, an ugly consequence of the days he'd once lived, like
she had. Days which were filled with vengeance and violence.

She chose a safer route, thoughts that wouldn't snap the
tenuous truce that had unexpectedly formed between them.

A truce she didn't want to destroy.

She tucked a loose curl behind her ear and studied the
empty road, prolonging the moment when she'd have to
go into the house, envying Chat her freedom.

"Chat sells butter in town?" she asked.

"Yes. Eggs, too. She raises several dozen chickens."
He glanced over his shoulder with a wry frown. "Can't you
hear them?"

Her ear tuned to the squawking fowl somewhere behind
them, and she smiled. Evidently, he had little patience for the
creatures. "She has a small business going for herself then."

"It's only been since this past spring that I've let her try
her hand at it."

"She must be succeeding. I've seen her at the bank now
and again. Making deposits to her account."

He nodded, his approval evident. "I want her to be independent. If anything should happen to me, she has to be able to take care of herself financially."

He was all she had, Lark knew. Again, she wondered about their parents, their absence in his and Chat's lives. The transition from bounty hunter to guardian of his younger sister would've been a difficult one.

"You've been successful, too," she mused.

"With Chat?" His dark gaze regarded her. "Or building furniture?"

"Both."

He shrugged. "Either one gets supper on the table, I guess."

His modest logic amused her. "That's not what I meant."

"Yeah, well, a man has to do what he can when his life takes a turn for the worse."

Her amusement faded at the harsh reminder of what had happened to him back in Canada. Her part in it, most of all, however unintentional.

"But then, it all depends on a man's perspective, doesn't it?" she asked in a frosty tone.

"It sure as hell does." He stepped away with a scowl, their truce gone, the old bitterness in its place. "I'll be out in the shop. When you get dressed, join me there."

Her hackles rose with his imperious tone. "So you can keep guard over me?"

A cold smile formed. "Exactly."

Chapter Eight

Lark was taking her own sweet time coming out.

He had it coming, Santana supposed. Having to wait. He'd been short with her, and she'd gotten miffed with him over it.

She hadn't deserved it, either.

He'd been an ass.

Just when things were getting polite between them. Breakfast had been a…pleasure. She'd given him a glimpse of what a normal family life could be like. Of what having a *woman* in the house could be like.

And Lark Renault was all woman.

He blew out a self-deprecating breath, picked up another board and set it neatly on top of one just like it. Until now, he hadn't had the opportunity to straighten up the lumber she'd scattered last night after she ran into the pile, trying to hide from him. It'd been dark as pitch. A wonder she didn't break a bone when she fell.

Then again, this same lumber kept her from escaping him. The racket she raised alerted him to her presence and—

Escape.

Ross muttered an oath. He should've thought of the possibility sooner, and he bolted to the door. If she wasn't in the house, if she'd taken one of the horses, if she'd *left* him, by God, he'd—

A few steps beyond the shop, he saw her. Coming out the front door. She wasn't wearing Chat's nightgown anymore, and she'd done something to her hair, and damn if his heart wasn't pumping hard enough to burst right out of his chest.

He eased backward, took a minute to regain his control. She couldn't see him from this proximity. Not that she was looking. She pulled the door closed and paused with her hands clasped behind her back, her head angled toward the road that led to Ida Grove.

What was she thinking?

Whatever it was, she didn't appear troubled by it. She finally lifted her skirts and descended the steps. In no hurry. Again, she paused, this time in front of Chat's flowers, bordering one side of the porch. The bed was colorful with black-eyed susans and vibrant primrose, and Lark bent to finger the delicate petals, admiring each one. She eventually straightened and crossed the lawn, but in the drive, she stopped a second time. She perused the barn, the chicken house, the Iowa countryside. At last, she turned toward his workshop.

Ross slid back into the doorway. Throughout her dawdling, her expression registered curiosity, nothing more, and the relief that swept through him was a tangible thing.

He couldn't have her figure out what he'd thought about her. That his trust in her had slipped. She had kept her promise about not trying to escape, even complied with his command to meet him out here in his shop.

But on her own terms. When she was good and ready.

Ross conceded that her rebellion was understandable. Might be he'd act the same way if he was in her place.

He stacked the last of the boards and acted as if she hadn't been on his mind most of the morning. By the time she appeared at the doorway, he had the design for the revolving bookcase spread out in front of him. He stared hard at the lines he'd drawn, the numbers he'd written, distracted as hell by her presence but not acknowledging it.

For long moments, neither said anything, each waiting for the other to speak first. In the end, it was Lark who made the first move with a casual stride toward him.

"I neglected to bring the leg irons," she said coolly. "Should I have?"

She halted in front of his workbench. He straightened, meeting her gaze. "You tell me."

She rolled her eyes, like Chat did now and again. Why did women do that when they were annoyed?

"Believe me, Santana. If I wanted to escape you, I'd find a way."

The sun shone in behind her, wrapped her in a soft light. She'd mended her dress, he noticed. The neat, tiny stitches made the tear on her shoulder almost unnoticeable. The blood was gone, too, and the fabric pressed crisp. She'd piled her hair on top of her head, but a few curls managed to break away and coiled at her temple.

It freed a man to see her neck, with all that hair held back.

She had a nice neck, shaped real graceful and feminine. Nice skin, too. Creamy and smooth. She looked prim, though, in her buttoned-to-the-throat dress. Respectably proper, and this was how folks saw her every day in Ida Grove.

Prim. Proper. Respectable. Without an inkling of her past life.

Most likely, he knew more about her than anyone. And not just her life as an outlaw. He'd seen her with her hair down and scattered across a pillow. He'd heard her voice early in the morning, husky from sleep. Only thing missing was how she'd feel in his arms—

He shut the thoughts down. He had to scramble to remember what it was she'd just said.

"Seems to me we had an agreement, Santana. I'll hide out for a while with you, at least until we see if Chat has news about Catfish."

"So?"

"So your part in the deal was to trust me."

He hadn't, of course. He should have. And now he'd offended her.

"Yet you still feel I need to be *guarded*," she said stiffly. "I heartily resent that."

"Considering the situation—" he growled in an attempt to defend himself.

"The situation, Santana, is that you insist on feeling sorry for yourself because you lost an eye."

He stood there, unmoving. The accusation came out of nowhere. "That's enough, Lark."

"And you hold me responsible for it."

"It wasn't your gun that shot me."

"No. But it may as well have."

"You're wrong."

Wasn't she?

"Think what you want about me," she said, her voice revealing the barest of quivers. "But you weren't the only one who's suffered because of that awful day. The difference between us, though, is that you've moved on. I, on the other hand, am still dealing with the consequences."

"You think I'm not 'dealing with consequences'?" he

demanded. "Every day I see this patch in the mirror I'm dealing with them."

She gave him a hard look. He guessed it was all she could do to keep from giving him a good shake.

"But you don't need to be 'guarded,' do you?" she asked.

Ross blew out a frustrated breath. Well, hell. Now that he could see her side of it, he realized he really had hurt her feelings and maybe she had a right to be mad about it.

It'd been so long since he'd had a prolonged conversation with a full-grown woman, he'd lost his knack for it. Now he had the uneasy need to apologize.

He hooked a thumb in the hip pocket of his Levi's. Shifted from one foot to the other. The silence stretched out between them.

"Look," he said finally. "I shouldn't have said—I shouldn't have thought—I'm sorry, all right?"

She rolled her eyes again. Made a tiny *oh, sure, you're sorry* sound with her tongue.

Not only was she driving him crazy, that need in him to make amends didn't go away. When it came to choosing sides—getting along with Lark or arguing with her— he found himself wanting the getting along part most.

He searched his mind for something intelligent to say. Or something humble, considering the predicament he was in. Either way, her wounded silence was proof she wasn't going to make it easy for him.

She refused to look at him. Just stood there in front of him with her fingers twined tight together, slender and female and still properly miffed.

If Ross didn't know better, he'd never guess Lark was who she was. Or had been. The transformation from a reckless young outlaw to a grown-up, beautiful woman with principles was intriguing.

To say the least.

"You look nice today," he ventured.

Her gaze flew to him.

"What's that supposed to mean?" she asked, her eyes narrowed in suspicion.

"Just what I said." He made a vague gesture. "Your dress and the way you did your hair. Nice."

"As opposed to what I *used* to wear? Pants and a pair of Colts hanging on my hips?"

"Yes. I mean, no. Hell, Lark. Just take the compliment for what it's worth. You look nice, that's all."

Her reluctance to accept the praise puzzled him. Hadn't she been flattered by a man before?

She regarded him, as if trying to decide his motive. Finally, she nodded, accepting his attempt at conciliation. "Forgive me for jumping to conclusions, then. Thank you for—for your kind words."

His mind worked over the possibility no man in Ida Grove claimed the privilege of courting her. If that was true, why not?

"You're welcome," he said.

He'd have to ask Chat about it. Might be she knew something about Lark's personal life and the men she favored.

Not that he should even care.

But he did.

"This is what I wear to the bank," Lark said, smoothing her skirt self-consciously. "Nothing fancy." A delicate pucker formed at her brows. "I don't recall seeing you there. Chat a time or two, yes, but not you. I—I would have remembered."

"I don't frequent them," he said.

"Banks?"

"Swore off 'em years ago."

"Oh. I see."

She didn't, of course. How could she? She'd learn the ugly truth soon enough. When he found the money stolen from the Muscatine treasury.

The thought sobered him, and he rooted through the papers on his bench. He had work to do. Standing here talking to Lark—thinking about her—wouldn't get it done.

"So this is your workshop?" Her gaze swiveled around the place, a small-scale factory of sorts he'd built himself.

"Yep." He found the sheet he was looking for, frowned at the numbers he'd jotted down last night.

"It's big."

"Has to be. Furniture takes up space."

"What do you make? Besides bedroom sets?"

"You name it, I can build it."

"Really?"

She sounded impressed. Ross glanced up. She'd meandered to the far side of the shop to see the projects he had scattered in organized confusion throughout the open area, all in various stages of construction.

"Really." Her awe gave him pause. It wasn't often someone unfamiliar with carpentry came into the shop.

"How?"

"How what? Do I build things?"

"Yes. You must start somewhere." She strolled closer, her gait graceful. Relaxed.

"I start with a design."

"Do you draw your own?"

He nodded. "Mostly. Sometimes the customer buys one. From a company out East, maybe, that sells the design only. Then he'll hire me to build the piece for him."

"But sometimes the customer needs you to draw the design, too."

"That's right." Again, he perused the numbers, but her presence shot his concentration.

"I suspect your customers are not just from around Ida Grove."

"Some are. Some are from Omaha. A few from Chicago and St. Louis."

"I see." Again, she stood before him, in front of his workbench. "You have quite a business going for yourself, don't you, Santana?"

The huskiness in her voice stroked him. "Keeps me busy, if nothing else."

Her mouth curved. "From a bounty hunter—" her arm swept outward "—to this. How did you learn it all?"

"My father." Ross ignored a nibble of grief. "He was a master in the trade. Taught me when I was a kid."

"But you really wanted to chase outlaws."

"Yes." Much to William Santana's disappointment.

"It's amazing all you've accomplished."

He grunted. "As if I had a choice."

"Because of your eye?"

Her frank perception unnerved him. No one, with the sole exception of Chat, spoke as openly about his loss as Lark did. And lest he be accused of feeling sorry for himself again, he kept his mouth shut. She didn't need his response.

But his mind crept inward to the past, to the despair that had descended upon him when his surgeon gave him the news. Despair which had turned him into a recluse and inspired a fierce devotion to furniture-making.

Because furniture didn't stare. Furniture didn't think of him as a has-been bounty hunter. Furniture didn't ask nosy questions. Or mock him.

Or pity him, most of all.

"Seems to me there's a world of good that's come out of losing that eye, Santana," she said quietly. "A lucrative business being at the top of the list."

"Don't make it sound easier than it's been, Lark."

"Lucrative," she insisted. "And you don't even have an account with Mr. Templeton. Why?"

He stiffened. "I have my reasons."

"You could be investing the profits. Mr. Templeton is very good—"

"I choose not to. And what business is it of yours what I do with my money?"

She drew herself up a little taller. "You're right, of course. It's none of my business. None at all."

Ross heard the hurt in her tone, and he plowed a hand through his hair in frustration. She had his best interests at heart, nothing more, and why did she manage to bring out the worst in him?

"If you think I'm plotting a way to steal your money or—or something, then you're—"

"Hell, Lark. I'm not. Why would I think that?"

"Because you're always so blasted cross with me. You're suspicious, too, and I am *not* the person I used to be, and until you're able to accept that—"

"I'm sorry."

The words came out easier this time. He was getting good at it, apologizing to a woman twice in one morning, yet the need to take her into his arms, to use his body instead of words, ran strong within him.

If not for the workbench that stood between them, he would have.

"Well." She drew in a breath, let it out again. "We're having a difficult time of it, aren't we?"

He vowed to go easier on her. They had the rest of the morning and most of the afternoon together, just the two of them, and if they were to get through it, he'd have to think before he opened his mouth and be more…likable.

"I can show you what I'm working on. If you'd like to know, that is," he said stiffly.

She blinked at him in surprise. "All right. Of course."

"A revolving bookcase." He came around the workbench to stand beside her, bringing the design and its measurements with him. He laid it all in front of her. "The project is in its earliest stages, but the sketch will give you an idea of what it'll look like when it's finished."

"Oh, how beautiful," she breathed.

Her admiration stroked his ego, his pride. Compelled him to keep talking.

"The case will be three shelves high and have beveled glass here and here." He bent a little toward her, caught her clean scent, like prairie grass in the spring. "As soon as I'm finished figuring the measurements, I can get started."

"The design looks complete to me," she said, her fascinated gaze taking in every detail. "What do you have left to finish?"

"The second tier is figured wrong." He reached for his calculations. "I need to find the mistake before I go any further."

"May I see?" She leaned over the paper, a slight frown of concentration tugging at her brow. In what seemed only a few moments, she smiled in triumph. "There." Her finger tapped the page. "You carried a one instead of a two when adding your fractions. That's where your mistake is."

He saw his error and shook his head. "You know how long I've been trying to find that?"

She angled her head toward him, her mass of curls narrowly missing his chin. "I've always found numbers easy to cipher."

It'd been a long time since he'd stood so close to a woman, and Ross had no desire to pull away from this one.

"Lucky for me you do," he murmured.

Their gazes locked, and damned if time didn't stand still. He could lose himself in those eyes of hers, that intriguing blend of brown and mahogany. He could lose himself in her scent, too. Just breathe the freshness of her all day long. He could take her mouth to his and taste its softness....

But of course, he couldn't do *any* of those things.

He stepped back, snatched up his design and wondered how in the hell he was going to keep his hands off of her for the rest of the day.

Chapter Nine

Catfish Jack huddled in the shadows of the Hungry Horse Saloon and pulled a sack of Bull Durham from his shirt pocket. He needed both hands to get the tobacco on the paper, and even then, some of it drifted into the dirt. He licked the seam and pinched the ends closed, found a match and scraped the tip across his thigh. The flame leapt at the end of the cigarette, and Catfish drew in deep.

Yesterday, he could've rolled his smoke one-handed while sitting on a spooked horse in a high wind. Today, his head hurt, his hands shook and his eyes saw two of everything he looked at.

All because of Wild Red.

After she knocked him out cold back there in her sleeping room, he came to and found her gone. The red-haired witch had always been a fighter. Catfish had forgotten that, her being a fighter.

He wouldn't forget again.

She was hiding somewhere, same as he was. She had too much at stake to run just yet, what with the new life she'd built in this peashooter little town. She'd be scared, too. And real careful. But he'd find her, all right. Give her a taste of her own medicine for what she'd done to him.

After she told him where the money was.

Might be she didn't think ol' Catfish meant what he said, helping her find the Muscatine loot, splitting it fifty-fifty. Didn't matter what she thought, though. Or if he ever did what he'd said he'd do. He needed that money she'd taken. Needed it bad.

He had to get to South America. The law was after him in most every state this part of the country. If he got caught, they'd have him gargling on a rope fast as lightning.

Just thinking about it made his skin get up and crawl.

A ticket south was the only thing that would keep him alive, and if he couldn't find Wild Red, make her talk, maybe even lead him to the money, then he was good as dead.

"Hey, Catfish. You starin' at that boardinghouse again?"

Catfish started. He'd been so deep in his ruminating he didn't hear Jo-Jo Sumner come up behind him.

"Keep your fool mouth shut, boy. Too many folks around to hear you."

"Sorry."

Catfish took another drag on the cigarette and hid his annoyance. He had to tolerate the kid. His pa, Eb Sumner, owned the Hungry Horse Saloon. He'd been letting Catfish sleep in the supply room at the back since the day he rode into town to scout for Wild Red. Charged him a tall penny for the privilege, but kept quiet about it, at least. Catfish figured the deal was worth it, except he was almost out of money, and what would he do then? There was no other place he could stay as banged up as he was.

His hope lay in the kid. Jo-Jo was somewhere on the shy side of eighteen, born lazy, bored with life in Ida Grove and itching for some excitement. Meeting Catfish had given him some of that, Catfish guessed. Might be the kid could convince his old man to let Catfish hide out in the saloon for a little while longer after his money ran out. At least until he learned something about Wild Red's whereabouts.

Catfish focused his sights on the boy. Lanky, with crooked teeth and a drawling way of talking, he was eager to please and real curious about Catfish's outlook on life. His tricks of the trade, so to speak.

Some of Catfish's annoyance faded. The kid *liked* him for his law-breaking tendencies. 'Course, Jo-Jo had broken a few laws of his own. Petty stuff, mostly. Nothing of Catfish's caliber yet enough of an irritation to be a thorn in the side of the local sheriff.

The thought helped Catfish feel better. Superior, too, which made it easy to be a mite more friendly toward him.

"You really think she'd come back?" Jo-Jo asked, keeping to the shadows, same as he was.

Catfish stared at Kelley's Boardinghouse, across the street and one block over from the saloon. It'd been against his better judgment to tell Jo-Jo who Wild Red really was, but when Catfish had stumbled into the back room of the Hungry Horse with his skull cracked open and bleeding after his run-in with her, he didn't have a choice but to take the kid into his confidence. He'd kept back pertinent details, of course—he wasn't that stupid—but he'd revealed enough about her to keep Jo-Jo interested.

"It's where she lives," Catfish said. "And she's a woman, ain't she? She didn't have time to take anything with her last night. She'd want to come back and pack up some gear if she was intendin' to leave town."

"Hard to believe Miss Renault used to ride with the

Reno gang," Jo-Jo said. "Folks just ain't going to believe it when they find out."

Footsteps sounded on the boardwalk just beyond the saloon's shadows. Catfish slid his hat lower over his face, hiding the bandage wrapped around his head. An elderly couple walked by, arm-in-arm, oblivious to their presence. After the footsteps died down, Catfish smacked Jo-Jo against the shoulder.

"Keep quiet!" he snapped. "The whole town's looking for me. I ain't got a hankering to get caught just 'cuz you can't keep your voice down when we're hidin' out like this."

The kid was smart enough to look alarmed. "Sorry!"

"Don't you go openin' your mouth about Wild Red just yet, either," Catfish warned. "When the time's right, and not a minute sooner!"

"I won't!"

Catfish slid a disgusted breath through his teeth and lifted his hat brim to better see the boardinghouse again. A buckboard wagon pulled up in front, and a young girl got down from the driver's seat.

He'd seen her before. Real pretty, she was. From what he could tell, she was a friend of the daughter of the lady who owned the place. He'd seen them together most every day since he'd been in Ida Grove, watching for Wild Red.

Catfish prided himself on remembering details, and his gut told him the girl was one detail he should remember. She carried a basket in her hand, and from the way she was swinging the thing, it was empty. She climbed the stairs, opened the door to the boardinghouse just as free as you please, and disappeared inside.

Jo-Jo's thin lips curled in a lusty grin. "Sure would love to get under her skirts, wouldn't you?"

Catfish wasn't particularly discriminating when it came to the female gender, but he drew the line at one so young.

"Who is she?" Catfish asked after a thoughtful pull on his cigarette.

"Her name's Chat Santana. Lives with her brother outside of town."

Santana. A common enough name.

Catfish frowned. Or was it?

"What else you know about her?" he asked.

Jo-Jo shrugged. "Not much, 'cept she's got all the boys pantin' after her. She's best friends with Sarah whose ma owns the boardinghouse."

Santana. Chat Santana...

The name stuck with him, raised the hairs on the back of his neck some.

He shook off the uneasy feeling.

"So have you done it yet with her?" he asked.

Jo-Jo blinked in confusion. "Done what?"

He sighed. "Gotten under her skirts yet."

Jo-Jo shuffled. "Hell, no. Her brother would filet me alive if I did."

"Her brother." Catfish smirked. If *he* wanted a woman bad enough, no one would stop him from having her, didn't matter who he was.

"Ross Santana," Jo-Jo added in hasty defense against that smirk. "Word is he used to be a bounty hunter."

Catfish nearly choked on his own spit.

"You heard of him?" Jo-Jo asked.

Catfish needed some time to recover, get his heart to beating again. "Yeah, I've heard of him."

Most every outlaw this side of the Missouri had heard of Ross Santana. Catfish recognized him that day at the Turf Club. Acted fast when he did. A blast from his shotgun had thrown Santana to the floor. Sure the man was dead, Catfish took the opportunity to run, but in all the confusion— damn.

Santana was alive and kicking. Right here in Ida Grove.

He'd have a score to settle with ol' Catfish for shootin' him, for sure.

Catfish swallowed hard at the nasty wrinkle in his plan to find Wild Red.

"What do you know about Santana?" he demanded.

"Not much. He don't associate with folks. Only thing that brings him to town now and again is if he has an order to pick up from Bowman Lumber, that's all."

"But his kid sister comes in."

"Most every day. Sells butter and eggs at the dairy." Jo-Jo shifted his attention back to the street. "She's coming out again, and ain't that strange."

"What?" Catfish demanded.

"She's comin' from the back of the house, like she doesn't want no one to see her."

Catfish strained to focus. That was her all right, carrying the basket on her arm. But this time, there was something in it. Heavy, too, by the looks of it. She seemed in a real hurry to stuff the basket under the wagon's seat, but then she just stood beside the rig, waiting, acting real nonchalant. Her friend—Sarah—came out, they both got in the wagon and rode off.

Jo-Jo was right, though. Real strange Chat didn't come out the front door, like other folks. Only reason for that— she was hiding something in her basket.

"What do you make of it?" Jo-Jo asked.

"I'm thinkin'."

His mind gathered the details, sorted them through. Did Santana know Lark Renault's true identity? That Wild Red was living in Ida Grove, right under his nose? And what about the money she'd stolen from the Muscatine County Treasury? Did he know about that? Or had he given up on the case?

Catfish didn't think so. Any bounty hunter worth his salt would give both his balls to find the missing money.

Same as Catfish would.

Catfish figured he had a couple of options. He could bribe Wild Red into talking, threaten her with telling Santana who she was, who would throw her back in jail and ruin her new life. There was always that newspaper editor, Ollie, who would make her secret front-page news. And if Santana didn't cooperate, well, there'd be ways of getting his attention, too.

Like putting his pretty little sister in a compromising position.

Nope, Wild Red wouldn't have no choice but to tell ol' Catfish exactly where the money was.

Might be he had her figured wrong, that she was on the run, after all. Still, he'd cut her good on the shoulder and well, most likely she was still around these parts.

He could *feel* that she was.

Suddenly, a new thought burst through the others bouncing in his brain—maybe Wild Red didn't know Santana was who *he* was.

Maybe, since Chat was the Kelley girl's best friend, and since Wild Red had one of her ma's sleeping rooms, they was all in cahoots with another, helping Wild Red—Lark Renault—hide out.

Stranger things had happened, and if there was one man who could protect her, it was Ross Santana.

Would Wild Red risk trusting him?

Catfish intended to find out.

He just had to find her first.

It'd be like finding a flea in a barn full of straw. As much as he hated to admit it, given his present physical condition, he needed a little help to get the job done and lay low at the same time.

He dragged his gaze from the boardinghouse back to Jo-Jo. Thought again how much the kid idolized him.

He put on his best smile. "You've been a real good friend to me, boy. Have from the time I first rode into town."

Pleasure lighted Jo-Jo's features. "Thanks, Catfish."

"Been thinkin' I could use a partner. Someone I could trust, no matter what."

"Yeah?" Jo-Jo grinned. "Well, you can trust me, Catfish. You know you can."

"Times like these, we outlaws got to stick together. Give each other a hand when it's needed."

"You need somethin' done, Catfish? Just name it."

He saw the kid's eagerness, plain as red paint on his face. And nodded in satisfaction.

"Follow the Santana girl home," he ordered. "Mosey around her place a little. See if she's got company."

"And if she does?"

Catfish finished his smoke, flicked the stub into the dirt. "Then it's high time they get some unexpected callers."

"I'm not very good at finding information," Chat said with a small pout.

The late-afternoon sun dipped low on the horizon and smeared bold hues of crimson, orange and gold against the sky. Warmth from the day still lingered in the air, and at Chat's return from town, the porch seemed a good place to gather to hear what she had to say.

Lark handed her a glass of lemonade. "Dare we hope there was no information to be found?"

"But surely there was *something* I could've learned today," she said. "Folks are plenty worried about you, and there's talk about *that,* but of course they would be. When has a defenseless woman in Ida Grove ever been attacked in the privacy of her sleeping room, then forced to escape with her life before? Never. Absolutely never. Then to have the same defenseless woman just disappear—poof!—into thin air, well, the town is positively *buzzing* about it."

Ross settled on the porch floor, his back against the rail post, one knee drawn up. The old hens were having a heyday in their speculating, hashing and rehashing Lark's story until it was so misconstrued no one knew what was fact and what was fiction.

Of course, he had the advantage. He *knew* Lark was safe. No speculating about it.

But only for now. Only until Catfish tracked her down again.

Lark handed him his glass of lemonade, and he made sure his fingers closed over hers, keeping her in front of him. He read the worry in her eyes, worry she kept from Chat. Worry that said no word about Catfish didn't mean he wasn't around, sniffing her out.

Their gazes held, and he willed silent reassurance through his. She had to know he'd do all he could to keep her safe, didn't she? That he'd find a way to keep the ruthless outlaw away from her?

Her lashes lowered, and she pulled away. They both knew she couldn't hide out forever. He couldn't watch over her twenty-four hours a day, either. And when he thought of all that could go wrong when she wasn't with him, of what Catfish was capable of, well, it pretty much turned his blood cold.

He swung his attention back to Chat. "Tell us who you talked to. Start from the beginning."

Lark took the last glass of lemonade. Chat made room for her on the swing he'd built, and in the way of most women, they set it to a gentle rocking motion.

"Well, before I ever headed to the dairy, I decided to pay Doc Seeber a visit," Chat said. "He closes at noon on Saturday mornings, so I had to hurry before he did. He was just finishing up with Myra Perkins. Her baby is always colicky, you know. Doc thinks it might have something to do with what she's feeding the poor thing. She weaned him much too soon."

Ross had to keep Chat's gossip on track, or else she'd launch into a detailed history of all Doc Seeber's patients' ills.

"What about Catfish?" he asked.

"Well, just as Myra went out the door, Sheriff Sternberg came in."

Lark held her breath. "And?"

"He wanted to know if Doc had a patient come in last night or this morning with head injuries needing medical attention. I must admit, I was glad it was the sheriff asking. Doc was prone to tell him much more than he might ever tell me, and he wouldn't be as curious about it, so I just waited and listened. But Doc didn't have anything to report."

Lark sighed. "Catfish wouldn't be that obvious."

"But it was worth checking out," Ross said.

"Of course it was," Chat agreed. "The sheriff said he had wired neighboring counties to be on the lookout for a man of Catfish's description and injuries, but that's all he could do without more evidence to go on. After Sheriff Sternberg left, so did I. I didn't have anything to glean at that point, but just so Doc wouldn't think it odd that I stopped by, I left him a dozen eggs for a treat."

"A whole dozen?" Lark said in dismay. "That's profit you lost."

"That's okay," Chat said quickly. "I'll just sell an extra dozen next week."

"What about the grocery store, Chat?" Ross urged, getting her back on topic again.

"Nothing there, either. I dawdled for as long as I dared. Folks were talking about Lark, all right, but no one had seen or heard anything. I bought my supplies and left."

"And Sarah?"

"I went to the boardinghouse last, but like everyone else—nothing."

"How is Mrs. Kelley?" Lark asked.

"She wasn't home. Sarah said she was at the church, saying a novena for you with Father Baxter."

Touched, Lark pressed her fingers to her lips. "A novena. For me."

"For your safety," Ross grunted and hoped the age-old ritual helped. Catfish Jack was the devil himself.

"Mr. Kelley is prepared to defend his family and each of the boarders," Chat said. "Why, he had his rifle out, all polished and ready if Catfish comes back."

"Which he won't," Ross said roughly. "Not without Lark there."

"No," Lark concurred. "He'd have no reason."

"Oh, I nearly forgot." Chat leaned over and slid her egg basket across the floor toward Lark's side of the swing. She lifted the flour sack on top. "I brought something for you."

Lark gasped in surprise. "My clothes!"

Chat smiled. "I convinced Sarah to let me see your sleeping room."

"How did you do that without making it seem suspicious?" Ross demanded.

"I simply told her I wanted to see how Catfish escaped. We weren't allowed in there then, you know. When everything happened. We had to stay in the library until Sarah's parents felt it was safe for us to come out." Chat cocked her head at Lark. "They have it all tidy and clean now. Mrs. Kelley insists upon keeping it available for you. I had no problem taking your belongings."

"Thank you," Lark said. "But surely Sarah didn't know you did?"

"No, and I don't feel guilty for it, either. Not a bit. They're yours, after all, and the Kelleys will never know they're missing," she said, emphatic. "I left by way of the back stairwell, came around front and hid the basket in the wagon. Sarah never had an inkling."

"I hope not." Lark gave Ross a worried look.

"You're sure no one saw you?" he asked Chat.

"Positive."

"And no one followed you home?"

"I would've known if they did."

He nodded. And wondered if she would.

"So, if not for this—" Chat nudged the basket with the toe of her shoe "—the afternoon was a waste. I accomplished nothing."

"Wrong," Ross said. "Because you learned there's no information in town, we have to assume Catfish is wounded too bad to get around. Which means he can't ride yet. Which means he's still around these parts. And we have to be ready for that."

"You don't suppose he crawled into a hole somewhere and died, do you? After Lark hit him on the head?"

Lark made a sound of alarm. "Chat!"

"We couldn't be so lucky," Ross said drily.

"Listen to me, both of you," Lark said, gesturing at them fiercely with her lemonade glass. "For all the grief Catfish Jack has caused, I do *not* want him dead because of me."

Chat blinked. "Why not? He tried to kill *you*."

"He attacked her to scare her, Chat," Ross said. "He doesn't want her dead. Yet. But he will, in the end."

"Yes. But not if I can help it." Lark stood, and the swing jerked from the abrupt movement. "This conversation has taken a depressing turn. I'm hungry. How about you two?"

Chat exchanged a glance with Ross. Clearly, she wanted to keep talking, but a single shake of his head ordered her silence.

She gave Lark a bright smile and stood, too. "I'm starved. And I'm hoping you'll cook because I can't wait to see what kind of magic you can stir up. I'll help, of course."

Ross hoped to catch Lark's attention before she went inside, but she seemed determined to keep from looking at him. He wanted to do something to comfort her and cursed his inability to do so.

She left him alone on the porch. Alone with his thoughts, too. Thoughts about how companionable their day had been. Once the awkwardness of being together was gone, their conversation turned relaxed, easy, as if they were just two ordinary people, alone in his workshop for the afternoon.

They weren't, of course. Ordinary. Their differences would destroy the fragile relationship that had budded between them. No longer man and woman, but enemies, each on the opposite side of the law.

How much time did they have? Days? Hours?

The uncertainty churned in his stomach. Suddenly rest-less, Ross set aside his lemonade, left the porch and strode across the yard. Chores were far from his mind, but Chat's horse needed unhitching from the buckboard. The rig still sat in the drive, and he led her piebald toward the corral, where he kept his own mount, a fine-blooded sorrel he'd ridden since his bounty hunter days, and an aging stallion that once belonged to his father.

Freed from the harness, the piebald trotted through the gate, and Ross locked it. He hooked a boot heel on the bot-tom rail of the fence and considered the three horses in-side.

He could take Lark somewhere, he mused. Ride some place where Catfish would never find her. Ross could help her start over in a different state, clear across the country, where she'd be safe. Free from worry.

She'd done it once before. And while Catfish had found her in Ida Grove, it didn't mean he'd be able to find her again.

But then again, it could.

An agitated whinny erupted from the sorrel's throat and captured Ross's attention. The horse tended to be skittish on the best of days, but Ross had learned to his advantage the sorrel's instincts could be trusted. A ruckus rose up among Chat's chickens, too, and his senses leapt into place.

Something made them nervous, something beyond Ross's range of vision. Uneasy, he straightened from the corral fence, ran a slow, discerning glance around him. Might be a skunk in the brush. A fox, maybe.

Or someone hiding in the shadows.

A weasel skittered from the direction of the henhouse and disappeared into the thicket beyond the corral. It wasn't long after that the sorrel quieted. Even Chat's an-noying fowl fell silent, and Ross's unease gradually lifted.

A final searching glance yielded no other movement, and he headed toward the house. On the porch, he scooped up the wicker basket holding Lark's belongings and went inside for dinner.

Chapter Ten

The next day, by the time the morning tumbled into afternoon, Lark had done every household chore she could think of.

She folded the damp dish towel into a neat rectangle and hung it over the stove handle to dry. Two golden loaves of bread and a pan of hot cinnamon rolls cooled on the table. Now that she'd washed all the dishes and put them away, she had nothing else to do the rest of the day.

Earlier, Chat had ridden into town for Sunday services. She'd been reluctant to go, preferring to stay home and keep Lark company instead, but Ross insisted, because going to church was what she always did. Folks would wonder where she was if she didn't. Besides, plans were in full swing for the Ida County Fair and its annual melodrama. Chat had one of the lead parts. She had a rehearsal to attend. She couldn't miss it.

A melodrama.

Lark envied Chat her busy social life. She envied the happiness Chat lived with every day, too, that of being part of a close-knit community who accepted her as one of their own. But most of all, Lark envied the snug, secure world Chat took for granted. The world Ross had created for her. The one he kept safe.

And when had she begun thinking of him like that?

Ross, not Santana.

A glum mood descended over her. Maybe she was getting too comfortable here, in his house, with his sister. With him. Like they were a family.

Which they weren't. Not at all.

Her time here made it too easy to forget "why" and made her think "what if."

Lark sighed and meandered onto the front porch. The morning's baking left the kitchen hot and stuffy, and she lifted her face to catch the light summer breeze against her flushed cheeks. If only the wind could chase away her melancholy thoughts, too.

She sat down on the top step, propped her chin in her hands. She couldn't stay with Ross and Chat forever. Tomorrow, Monday, the Ida Grove bank would open bright and early, ready to begin a new week. Mr. Templeton might be traveling back from Omaha at this very moment. He would expect her to be at her desk, punctual as always. So would Mrs. Pankonin and all the bank's customers.

Ross wouldn't. He'd say she couldn't go back, that it wasn't safe, and Catfish Jack would only find her and kill her.

Ross was right, and oh, God, what was she to do about it?

Her gaze slid in the direction of his workshop. He was inside, she knew. Working. Had been ever since Chat rode into town for church. He left Lark to her baking, had trusted her not to escape. And she hadn't.

But she must tell him she intended to leave. Tonight.

She was going back to her sleeping room and her job and her life. She had consequences to deal with. *Terrifying* consequences. She had no recourse but to meet them head-on.

She had to survive. Without him.

The workshop door opened, and he stepped out, his arms full of scrap lumber. Without a break in his stride, his gaze swung toward her. As if he'd been thinking of her then, at that moment. He carried the load with little effort, and though the pile must be heavy, his gaze lingered.

He made no acknowledgement of her presence there on the porch. He strode to the side of the workshop and added the wood to a pile of the same, scraps he'd cut into kindling later. Instead of returning inside, however, he headed toward the house.

Toward her.

Her stomach did a funny curl. He strolled toward her with the easy confidence of a man who knew what he was capable of and accepted it, who took what he wanted, when he wanted it, who possessed his own brand of honor, all in the name of justice.

And, oh, what would it be like to be loved by him?

He halted in front of her, sending her heart into a sloppy rhythm. He wore his gray cotton shirt open at the throat, the sleeves rolled to his elbows. A fine layer of sawdust covered the dark hairs on his forearms, and her hands clenched so she wouldn't reach out and brush it away.

"Let's go for a ride," he said in a low voice.

Her breath caught; her brain scrambled to figure his motive. Chat had taken the buckboard into town. And ride where, for heaven's sake?

She tried to feel suspicious, but failed. Two days ago, she would have succeeded. Yesterday, too. But she had learned Ross would never suggest the outing if he didn't feel it was safe for her to go.

"Why?" she asked, curious.

His arm swept outward, as if indicating the obvious. "Because it's a nice day, that's why."

Her glance lifted to the pure, azure sky. Indeed, it was, with the sun shining and the breeze just bold enough to chase away the heat. Even so, she refused to be convinced on such a flimsy reason. "You always work on Sunday afternoons. Chat told me so."

"Today, I'm not."

"Why?"

He appeared amused. "Because it's a nice day."

She narrowed an eye at him. "So you want to go riding. With me."

"I do."

Had he sensed her need to return to Ida Grove? Did he hope to divert her thinking? Or did he have an ulterior motive?

Her perch on the step allowed her to meet his gaze straight-on. He regarded her intently, as if to soak in the sight of her, imprint it on his memory like ink to paper. She wondered if her cheeks were still too flushed, her curls too wild and why should she even care what she looked like to Ross Santana?

Because she was a woman, and he was pure, vibrant male, and God help her, she *wanted* to go on a ride with him.

"I haven't ridden since I was sent to prison," she said softly, knowing she'd never make the admission to anyone but him.

"You'll still know how."

"Probably. Yes." From the time she'd been old enough

to sit a horse without falling off, she'd been comfortable in the saddle. Excitement stirred within her to climb into one again, after all these years.

"Lark." His voice—smoky, coaxing—wobbled her defenses. "Ride with me."

The man could be persistent when he needed to be. How could she refuse? Her mouth softened. "All right."

He gave her a quick nod. "Meet me out by the corral in half an hour. Pack something for us to eat first. We'll be gone most of the afternoon. And find one of Chat's hats to wear."

She rose. Not even his bossy manner could subdue the anticipation building inside her, and without questioning the wisdom of what she'd be doing, Lark hurried inside the house to do as he said.

She was out there, ten minutes early.

Ross took that as a good sign. He wasn't prone to impulsive decisions, especially when that decision concerned a woman, but hell, the words to invite Lark to ride with him were out before he could stop them.

She'd been on his mind all morning. She'd gotten restless hiding out with him and Chat. He could feel it. Catfish did a fine job of playing hide-and-seek. Until they got wind of his whereabouts, about all Ross could do to keep Lark's mind off her situation was to distract her a little.

He carried Chat's saddle from the tack room out to the corral and glimpsed Lark waiting for him by the fence. He couldn't remember the last time he'd wanted to spend some leisure time with a woman. Odd that it would be one like Lark....

Might be he was making a big mistake. Things were sure to turn ugly between them and what then? Last thing he wanted was to hurt her by sugarcoating the circumstances between them.

Circumstances neither could pretend didn't exist, but Lark seemed willing to sweep them under the rug for the time being. He'd do the same.

He set the saddle on the ground with the rest of the gear, caught the piebald on the far side of the corral, bridled him, then led him toward Lark.

"He's beautiful," she said from over the top rail.

"That he is. Chat picked him out for his coloring." Ross's glance skimmed the striking black-and-white hide before he draped a blanket over the back. "He's lady broke, too. Helped her get through the grief after our father died."

"I see."

"She's had him four years now." The saddle dropped onto the blanket. Pa had been gone only that long. Some days, it felt like forty. "I bought him for her as a colt the same year we moved out here."

"He's grown up with her, then."

"You could say that."

"And she won't mind if you let me ride him?"

"Not a bit." He buckled the cinch, checked to make sure it fit snug against the belly. He straightened. "Climb up. I'll adjust the stirrups for you."

The gate opened, and she slipped through. She wore one of the dresses Chat had brought back from the boardinghouse for her, a deep emerald-green color that looked real nice with her hair. A wide satin ribbon helped hold the wild curls in some manner of order, and when she put on Chat's wide-brimmed straw hat, Ross regretted seeing them disappear beneath the crown.

"Hmm." Lark peered up at the piebald as she tightened

the hat's cord under her chin. "Funny how big a horse seems when you haven't ridden one for so long."

"He's just the right size for you."

She nodded and tucked their lunch into the saddle bag. "Yes. I think so."

"Need some help climbing up?"

She regarded him with surprise. "I haven't needed any since I was a baby."

Ross noted she still hadn't made an attempt to mount. "Lots of women expect a man to help. They like it when he does, too. Nothing to be embarrassed about."

"I'm not embarrassed." She sounded defensive, a little annoyed. "I just don't expect anything from a man when I can do what he can myself." Finally, she reached up for the saddle horn and tucked a foot into the stirrup. "My Reno cousins made sure of that."

Ross scowled. "I'm nothing like them, though, am I?" He grasped her waist and lifted her higher. She swung a leg over the cantle, and Ross planted a firm hand beneath her rump to help her up. "And don't you forget it."

She plopped into the seat. He drew away to adjust the stirrup, but she reached down and grabbed his wrist.

"No. You're nothing like them," she said quietly. "Please don't think I ever thought otherwise." She hesitated. "Frank and John's courtesies toward women were limited to wooing them into the bedroom. Nothing more. They always treated me like I was one of the boys. I learned never to expect to be treated any better than that."

"And what a damned shame that is." Ross vowed to remind her of her femininity as often as he could in the time he had left with her.

"Yes." She straightened, letting him go, and the feel of her skin against his lingered. Her attention shifted to adjusting her skirts. "It feels strange to ride astride in a dress. Pants are much more comfortable."

"I imagine so." After making sure the stirrups hung at her comfort, he handed her the reins, then took hold of the chin strap. He tugged the piebald into a slow walk around the perimeter of the corral. "We'll get you some riding clothes if you feel a need for them."

"And what would you have me do? Shop in town, as bold as I please?"

"If you wanted them, I'd find a way."

"Thank you, but unfortunately, it's much too risky. What are we doing?"

"Giving you a feel for being on a horse again."

"I won't fall off."

"Just making sure you don't, that's all."

A moment passed. "You're being very sweet, you know."

They approached the sorrel, standing patiently at the water trough. His tail flicked at a persistent fly. Sweet? Ross suspected his motive was far more selfish than that.

"I'm responsible for you. Can't have you hurt on top of everything else going wrong in your life. How's your shoulder?"

"Doing well. Most of the time, I forget Catfish cut me."

"Good." They halted next to the water trough. Ross released the chin strap and set his hands on his hips. "Now canter around the corral a few times. If you're comfortable enough, we'll head out."

She smiled at his fussing. "Still afraid I'll fall off?"

"Just do it."

Her expression indicated she'd comply only to keep peace between them. She turned her mount and nudged him into an easy lope.

In moments, Ross's misgivings disappeared. She rode like she was born to it, as if five years away from the saddle had never passed. Her body flowed with the motion of the horse, a grace any rider would envy to achieve, and damned if she wasn't something to watch.

After a few trips around, she reined in next to him. Her eyes sparkled with a teasing light. "See? I haven't forgotten. You fussed over me for nothing."

She looked a little too smug, and he did his best to muster a scowl. "It was the fussing that got you started right."

She laughed at that, and the sound wound through clear to his soul. "Now you have to hurry, Ross."

"Why?" The sorrel was already saddled. He went for his rifle, propped against the side of the barn.

"Because I don't want to ride in a corral." Sensing her excitement, the piebald pranced. She held him in line with no trouble. "I want to ride far. And fast."

"Yeah?" Ross sheathed the Winchester into his scabbard and swung into the saddle, leather creaking from his weight. Her excitement was contagious, all right. "Ride too long, though, and you'll get sore."

"But then you'll find a way to make that right for me, too."

Her words and what they might imply pretty much kicked the breath right out of him. By the time he could think again, she'd trotted out the gate.

Pure and exhilarating, the adrenaline soared through Lark with an abandon she hadn't felt for a very long time. It was more than the thundering staccato of iron hooves against the earth, more than the feel of powerful horseflesh between her thighs or the wind in her face, more than the fun of the race with a man who, if she wasn't careful, could very well steal her foolish heart.

It was freedom.

Ross's horse rode nose to nose with hers in their spontaneous run to the Maple River—a race where neither cared who won or lost. The exhilaration inside her built and built until it escaped her in an exuberant whoop, and as they pulled up next to a stand of cottonwood trees growing at the river's edge, she couldn't stop the laughter from spilling out, either.

"You hold your own in the saddle, woman," Ross said. Admiration broadened his grin. "Damn, you're good."

Her hat had blown off her head and hung by its cord against her back. She pushed at a spray of curls fluttering at her cheek.

"I've ridden all my life, that's all, and oh, how I've missed it."

She bent and gave the piebald an affectionate pat on the neck. Her ability to stay on the back of a fast horse had saved her sorry hide more than once when she'd ridden with the Reno gang and needed to make a quick escape.

"It's human nature to take for granted what we have until we don't have it anymore. In your case, a horse." Ross dismounted and came around to her. "We'll let them rest a spell. They've earned a good long drink."

He held her mount while she got down, and when Ross would've stepped away, she placed a hand against his chest to keep him there. Behind her, the piebald snuffled and lowered his head to the grass. The sorrel moseyed to the water.

"Thank you for asking me," she said. "I can't remember when I've enjoyed riding more."

"You were due, is all."

"Yes."

Why hadn't she taken the time before?

Because for five long years, she'd shut that part of her life down. Riding a fast horse was something Wild Red once did every day.

Lark Renault didn't.

Regret spiraled through her from the freedom she'd wasted, and just thinking of those Catfish threatened to destroy…she felt positively ill.

"Hey." Ross nudged her chin higher with a finger. "You're getting real serious all of a sudden. What's the matter?"

She'd lost her knack for a poker face—hiding her female emotions around men who all but ignored them. Certainly, John and Frank never tolerated worry or fear, not in her or any member of their gang, and she'd eventually grown adept at burying her feelings, even those of knowing right from wrong.

Her years in prison had taught her to feel again, and her time in Ida Grove even more so.

Ross, of late, with a vengeance.

She pasted a bright smile on her lips. "Nothing's the matter."

"The hell there isn't."

She tried to step away, but he angled his body so she couldn't. She smelled the wind on him. His maleness. He left her flustered and without a steady breath in her lungs.

His thumb slid across her lips, as if to wipe away the false smile she struggled to keep in place. "You were happy not a half a minute ago. What are you thinking about?"

"Really, Ross. I'm fine."

"I like seeing you happy." From the rumble in his voice, she guessed the admission didn't come easy. "It's become important to me."

The emotion burned a little more inside her. "Why should it matter? I can't want a happy life right now. Nor can I want this—a fun ride with you on a Sunday afternoon."

"But you do."

She swallowed hard and fought a mortifying rise of tears. "Yes."

"Let me give it to you, then. While I still can."

She moved away toward the shade of the cottonwoods, quicker than he could stop her. Her emotions flowed free. "I can't *want* anything right now. From you, especially. Probably never. Don't you see?" He knew all she had at stake, that she would likely lose everything she had. He *knew* it. "Are you just feeling sorry for me?"

"What?" he asked, his voice rough. Stunned.

"Maybe we shouldn't be here." Her arm lifted, indicating the beauty, the freedom, of their surroundings—the serenity of the gently flowing Maple River, miles of rolling Iowa grassland, green and thick. "Maybe it just makes things worse."

"I want to be with you, Lark," he said. "If I didn't, you can be damn sure I wouldn't be thinking of you now like I am."

She shook her head, rejected all he implied. "I'm in deep trouble, Ross. My life right now is most precarious, and I'll probably end up in jail again, and oh, I don't want to think of you, either. Like I am."

The words left her in a rush. By the time she'd finished spilling her guts to him, he was right there, close in front of her. She didn't think to dart away before he slid his arm around her waist and pulled her to him. She didn't even mind the way his belt buckle pushed into her belly because he held her so tight.

Her knees went weak, her breathing all crazy. She didn't have a choice but to put her hands on his shoulders to steady herself in a world suddenly gone sideways. He had a hard mouth, and he looked rugged and dangerous with his black patch. The brim of his Stetson shadowed his face, but she read the fire of desire in his gaze.

He excited her like no man ever could before.

"God help me, I want to make everything right for you," he growled. "I swear I do."

There was that word again. *Want.* Before she could think on the futility of it, his head lowered, and his mouth covered hers with a hunger he only barely kept under control. It fed hers, that hunger, and her arms climbed higher to curl around his neck.

She wanted to believe him. She pressed closer, *needing* to believe him. He had the power to save her or destroy her. He knew it as well as she did, and maybe it was tearing him apart, too.

He angled his head and coaxed her lips apart with a bone-melting caress with his tongue. She opened, unable to deny him when she craved the very taste of him. Never had she been kissed by a man with this intensity, this unbridled passion, and why did it have to be Ross Santana?

His embrace tightened, as if he tried to enfold her into his very being. Her every thought, every logical reason, fled. She knew only the feel of his hard body, the solid breadth of male muscle against her, and how she wanted him to kiss her like this forever.

Breathing rough, he dragged his lips against her jaw, her neck, making her believe he wanted to keep on holding her forever, too.

"Tell me you have someone in town who's courting you, and I'll stop," he said in a husky rumble.

"There's no one." She wasn't yet ready to open her eyes. Her nerve endings tingled wherever he touched, and she savored each sensation. "Isn't it too late to be asking?"

"Been meaning to find out from Chat for a while. It's only now that I got serious about it."

She managed to smile and took his mouth to hers again. He absorbed her worries, sent her down a new road filled with longings that could never be.

His head lifted, just enough to draw her lower lip between his teeth, to nibble and suck at its softness. "Why are you alone, Lark? Why isn't every man in Ida Grove pounding on your door to claim you for their own?"

Her eyes slowly opened. His low-voiced demand yanked her back down to reality. She eased away, though his arm still banded her waist. "Because I've been afraid."

"Of what?"

He already knew the answer, she suspected. "Of finding love, only to lose it because—because of what I've done."

"Seems to me a man who loves a woman deep enough could forgive her for it."

Bemused, she uncurled her arms from around him, slid her hands down to his chest. His heart beat steady and sure, strong like the man he was.

"How odd that you would find it possible to forgive anyone who deserves the justice that means so much to you," she said.

The slight flaring of his nostrils proved her words struck a raw spot deep inside and left him at a loss for words of his own. His hand lifted and gently tucked a wild tendril behind her ear.

"Lark," he began, but stopped.

Perhaps he intended to say more. Or perhaps he

couldn't say anything. She only knew he intended to kiss her again. That she wanted him to. The anticipation built in her, and his arms tightened—

Thwap!

A jagged hole appeared in the trunk of the nearest cottonwood. Bits of bark flew. Lark cried out, Ross swore and they both dove to the ground for cover.

Chapter Eleven

"**H**ell!" Ross scrambled over to Lark and flung himself on top of her, his body a shield against another bullet. "Are you hit?"

"No." Her head came up, twisted toward the direction of the shot. "Did you see anything?"

"No." He hadn't seen a damn thing. But then, his attention had been on her. All of it. Which had nearly cost them their lives.

"It's Catfish. I know it is." Lark pushed against his shoulders. "We have to go after him, Ross."

He didn't move. He stared hard through the thin scattering of cottonwoods that gave them the barest of protection. This side of the river, there was only flat rangeland covered by grama grass and the occasional yucca, but beyond, a few bluffs, at the base of which stood a thicket, just like this one.

And that's where the shooter—Catfish—had been. Watching them. Waiting. They'd been wide-open targets, and from that distance, a bullet finding its mark would've been hard to do.

But Catfish had come close.

He'd wanted a shot at Lark real bad to risk revealing himself like he had. The shot was a warning to her—and Ross—that he was serious. Impatient, too, and time was running out.

He hadn't fired again, which only meant he was sitting back. Letting Ross and Lark make the next move.

She had her hands full with him, Ross thought grimly. Most likely, Catfish had recognized him, would wonder why she was with him. But it was Lark he wanted, not Ross, and he'd get real trigger-happy to keep from getting captured.

Ross eased off Lark, but kept his attention on those trees by the bluffs. She tried to sit up, her attention on them, too, but he pushed her back down again.

"Does Catfish like to work alone?" he demanded.

"I don't know. It's been so long—"

"Is it his style to?" he persisted.

"I think so. At least he didn't have a gang with him back at the Turf Club. And he didn't mention anyone when he attacked me in my room."

Ross nodded. "Good."

His gaze swung to the horses. Spooked by the gunshot, they'd bolted farther down the river. Unfortunately, the rifle was in the scabbard. Getting to it would make Ross an easy target all over again.

The adrenaline for revenge stirred inside him. Been a good long while since he'd felt it. Even longer since he had the opportunity to satisfy it.

But with the adrenaline came the old fear. His blind side. His weakness. Failure. His heart pounded. He could likely get them both killed.

Lark followed his gaze, seemed to know what he was thinking.

"I'm going with you," she said.

He turned toward her. "The hell you are."

Her brows shot up in protest. "I'm not staying here alone!"

"It's safer to stay put."

"It is not!"

"You're not armed. How're you going to defend yourself?"

"How am I to defend myself *here* if Catfish isn't alone?"

Ross couldn't keep arguing with her. Time was ticking. He'd just have to have her ride as fast as she could to his place while he took care of matters without her. Getting her back on the piebald, though, would be the hard part.

They had to risk it.

Half-blind, *he* had to risk it.

"All right. We're going to make a run for the horses. I'll cover you while you catch yours, then I want you to ride as fast as you can back home. I'll distract Catfish while you do."

She gave him a brisk nod, pulled Chat's hat onto her head and tightened the chin cord.

"Let's go," she said.

Ross marveled at how cool she was, how she distanced herself from the danger. He took her hand and tugged her to a standing position. Together they left the protection of the trees and sprinted toward their mounts.

"Run!" he yelled as they drew closer to the sorrel. He pushed her toward the piebald and leapt into his own saddle, grabbing the rifle at the same time. He whipped the butt to his shoulder and twisted, raking his gaze across the distant thicket, ready to defend her against a charging attacker.

He saw no one and chanced a look behind him. Lark

caught the piebald and jumped into the saddle with an impatient yank on her skirts, then kicked the horse into a run toward him.

"Get out of here, Lark!" he shouted. "Go!"

"No! I'm staying with you."

She rode past him into the cottonwoods, giving him no choice but to follow. He drew up next to her with a terse pull on the reins.

"I'm staying," she said again before he could repeat the command. "We both want Catfish caught. We'll work together to do it."

He spat a savage oath. The woman needed a good tongue-lashing on the importance of following orders. But he knew her side of it. Capturing the outlaw would mean a heap of worry off her mind. "Stay behind me, then. Don't do anything until I tell you to, you hear me?"

Her glance jerked toward the thicket. "He's not shooting at us. He's waiting us out, isn't he?"

"I suspect so. We'll circle around. Make him think we're running for home. Maybe we can catch him from behind."

"I'm ready when you are."

He was as ready as he'd ever be. No time to think otherwise, and they broke into a fast gallop past the stand of cottonwoods. Once over the low rise of a bluff, they rode a wide circle back toward the thicket and slowed their run before going in.

Still no gunfire. No horse and rider that they could see, either. Ross puzzled over the possibility Catfish might have slipped through their fingers after all, satisfied with his warning shot declaring he was on to them, but too skittish to stick around.

They dismounted and took cover in front of a large outcropping of rock which seemed to have been belched from the earth, the only jagged protrusion on the sprawling grass-covered range. Over time, the brush had crept up from a ravine and spread into the prairie. Fed by the Maple River, a tangled copse had formed.

"There are more trees here than I thought," Lark said. She'd taken a position on his right, he noted. His blind side. "Catfish could still be in there and we wouldn't know it."

Ross ran a slow assessing glance around the perimeter of the grove. "Yeah, more woodland than thicket. Could hide a rider real easy."

"You got a plan, Santana?" Lark asked softly.

His heart took on an uneasy rhythm all over again. He'd never been a coward, but he could taste the bitter temptation to be one now.

"I'm going in. See what I can find." He leveled her with a hard look. "Alone."

Suddenly, a bullet slammed into the rock and ricocheted off. Ross lunged toward Lark and shoved her to the ground.

"Hey, Santana!" a voice bellowed out. "I know you're out there!"

He strained to hear. All those trees muffled the words. Laying low made it hard to figure where they were coming from.

He didn't respond, not until he knew where Catfish was hiding. Ross inched up around the rock, dared a careful inspection of the woods again. Lark touched his arm, pointed to the left, and he shifted his glance.

A faint spot of yellow appeared through the leaves. Ross lifted the rifle, slow and easy.

"C'mon out, then. We'll talk," he yelled back.

"Let me see Wild Red first."

Alarm flitted across her face. Ross caught the look, gave her a single negating shake of his head. What did she think he'd do? Give her up?

His gaze slid along the trees, one side to the other.

"Not until we make a deal," he said, not finding the snippet of yellow.

He didn't like the sound of the silence. He stared hard for any sign of movement, listened for the slightest noise. Lark, too, close beside him, as tense as he.

Abruptly, she gasped. "There, Ross! On your right!"

He swiveled, heard the pounding of hooves before the horse and rider bolted out of the woods. Ross swung the Winchester around, finger on the trigger. The outlaw came fast, hunched low in the saddle. He barely cleared the brush before he started shooting.

Thwap! Thwap!

The business end of those bullets lodged in the dirt, too close to suit Ross, and he fired back with instinctive split-second speed. Catfish jerked, let out a high-pitched yelp and dropped from his horse.

Ross kept the rifle trained on him. The bastard didn't look in any shape to retaliate, but Ross wasn't taking any chances. He strode closer to have a better look. Lark followed, on his heels.

The outlaw laid face down in the grass. The revolver was gone, lost somewhere in the brush. Ross flipped him over with the toe of his boot. Blood soaked the front of the yellow cotton shirt, but it sure as blazes wasn't Catfish wearing it.

Lark sucked in a breath. "Oh, my God."

"Who is he?" Ross asked, as taken aback as she.

"Jo-Jo Sumner."

He tossed her a sharp glance. "Eb Sumner's boy?"

"Yes." She let out her breath, long and miserable.

Ross had slaked his thirst at the Hungry Horse only a few times over the years. He'd never seen the kid before.

No question, though, the kid knew him. Lark, too. Had a vendetta against them both, and Ross intended to find out why.

He lowered the rifle and crouched at the kid's side to yank open the shirt. One look at the scrawny chest told Ross the bullet wound did some serious damage. Jo-Jo moaned, which meant he wasn't dead yet, but he didn't have much time left.

"Jo-Jo." Ross gave him a slight shake.

Glazed eyes fluttered open. Recognition cleared them.

"Santana." His wheezy breath carried the heavy odor of stale beer. Ross figured he must've been drinking most of the day. "He warned me…you carried a mean gun…wasn't afraid to use it, neither."

"Who?" Ross pulled a clean bandanna from his pocket, pressed it to the wound. "You working for Catfish Jack?"

"Guess I won't…be no more."

"We'll get Doc Seeber for you," Lark said quickly. "I can ride to town. I'll hurry."

Ross's hand snaked out, grabbed her wrist before she could leave. "Won't do any good."

She paled, but managed a jerky nod, and stayed put.

"Why'd you come after us, Jo-Jo?" he asked. He noticed a brown beer bottle wedged in the waistband of the kid's pants; Ross pulled it out, saw that it was still half-filled with brew, and tossed it aside in disgust. "Catfish tell you to?"

"I was gonna get a cut of…the money."

"Yeah? What money?"

He had a pretty good idea, of course. The Muscatine heist. He just needed Jo-Jo to say it so he'd be sure.

"Ask Wild Red." The glaze came back in the kid's eyes. His lids fluttered down. "She knows…everythin'."

Lark pressed her fingers to her mouth. Real hard for her to hear the words, Ross knew. Her secret not being a secret anymore.

"You were going to get a cut of the money if you found her and brought her back to Catfish. Is that right?" Ross demanded.

Jo-Jo didn't move, didn't speak. His lungs rattled with every labored breath.

It wouldn't be long for him. Minutes, if that. Not much time to get the kid to spill his guts, but Ross had to keep trying.

"Might as well talk, Jo-Jo," he said, pulling no punches. "You've got nothing to lose, you know that? Catfish Jack won't help you. No one can." He slid his arm beneath the kid's head to help him breathe better, give him some comfort, too, if nothing else. "You tried to kill her, Jo-Jo. Is that what Catfish wanted you to do?"

The kid grimaced. "Didn't matter if I hurt her…just bring her to him so she…could tell him where she hid the money."

"You tried to kill me, too."

"…promised me a bigger cut if I did."

"Oh, Jo-Jo," Lark whispered.

As if he only now realized she was there, Jo-Jo blinked up at her. "We was goin' to South America, Wild Red." He managed a slack-jawed grin. Blood trickled from the side of his mouth when he did. "Goin' to have our own gang down there, me and Catfish was…"

Then, his eyes rolled back, his head sagged limp and Ross let him go.

Lark sat on the ground and hugged her knees to her chest. She stared at the Maple River flowing in the distance, numb, unable to bear another look at the lifeless young man lying in the grass behind her.

It was her fault Jo-Jo Sumner was dead. It didn't matter that Ross's finger pulled the trigger or that Catfish Jack had bribed him to hunt her down. It didn't even matter that Jo-Jo *wanted* her hurt. Or Ross dead. The fault came back to her in the end.

The immensity weighed heavy on her. She'd been all kinds of a fool to think burying the loot from the Muscatine County Treasury would make the consequences of stealing it go away. Now, Jo-Jo was dead before his time. She'd have to account for her part in it.

The grass rustled behind her. Without turning, she knew that Ross approached, paused, stood over her. Watching her. She didn't have to look at the hard set to his jaw, the grim line of his mouth, to know the condemnation he'd be feeling.

"Lark."

His low voice penetrated the despair that all but made her physically ill. She didn't move, couldn't speak. It was all she could do to keep breathing.

He squatted down behind her, and her skin prickled at his nearness. Odd she'd be so aware of him when the grief burned inside. The warmth of his body soaked into her back, though he'd yet to touch her.

"I'll find a way to help you," he said. "I'll do everything I can."

Her eyes misted that he wanted to help her at all. Considering the man he was, and all he stood for, she didn't deserve it. "It should be me lying back there dead."

"It almost was."

"He was only a boy, just barely—"

"He was a man, with a man's gun in his hand, Lark,"

Ross said roughly. "How many times did he need to shoot at you before you can understand that?"

She rebelled against his logic. The thinking of a bounty hunter. "I was his age when you shot me at the Turf Club. Remember?"

Ross's arm slid around her shoulders, pulled her back against him. His jaw pressed at her temple. "Sweet mother, yes."

His chest rumbled with the admission. Did the memories haunt him still? As they did her?

She shuddered. God, but she wanted him to hold her. To scoop her up into his embrace and surround her with his strength. She had so little left of her own.

Instead, she sat stiff in front of him and curled her fingers around his forearm, satisfying her need for his touch. "I know the glamour of riding with a gang, Ross. I found it exciting. And I felt invincible. All of us did. Jo-Jo felt the same way. I know it."

"Don't make excuses for him."

She twisted toward him. "I'm not."

"What he did was wrong."

She let go of Ross's arm. "He was young and impressionable, like I was at that age."

"Damn it, Lark!" Abruptly, Ross released her and straightened to his full height in one fluid, angry motion. "Catfish knows you're hiding out with me. It doesn't matter how he found out. He'll finish what he sent Jo-Jo to start."

She went cold inside. "I know."

"You can't hide anymore."

"I know that, too. You think I don't *know* that?"

Restless, frustrated, she stood, the fear and dismay roiling inside her all over again. She crossed her arms over her chest and shivered, though the summer sun shined high, bright, in the sky.

"We have to talk," Ross said.

She refused to look at him, knew what he wanted to hear. "I can't."

"You have to tell me what Catfish wants. It's the only way I can protect you."

"I can't." She hung on tight to her resolve. "I won't."

He had to understand that. Revealing the location of the buried loot would be the clear, the *final,* admission to her guilt, which meant she'd have to go back to jail, lose everything she had, and she couldn't do that.

Not ever again.

"Catfish wants the Muscatine County Treasury money, doesn't he?" Ross asked quietly.

Lark stilled.

"You helped the Renos steal it back in '67. December nineteenth, to be exact."

The dread in her built, higher and higher.

"Would you like to hear the amount, Lark? Because I can tell you, right down to the last dollar."

The shock rolled through her. He knew more details about the case than she did. But then, she'd stuffed the crime away inside her, crushed it so deep that, until Catfish stormed back into her life, she'd almost forgotten it was there.

In the time she'd been with him, Ross had never let on how much he knew about her crime. He strung her along, helping her, winning her trust. Oh, God, he'd even *kissed* her. He'd made her think of him in ways different than she'd thought of a man before.

And wasn't that just like a bounty hunter?

Rebellion stirred inside her. She tried to hate him for it.

But couldn't.

Would she have done the same if she were him?

"How can you be sure I rode with the gang that night?" she taunted.

"I'm not. No one is." He regarded her with a long, measuring look. "You and the rest of the gang were good at breaking the law. You blew the safe open in the middle of the night, and all that money was gone by dawn. Without a trace. No witnesses. Nothing." As if he suspected she'd bolt, he took a careful step toward her. "But my gut told me it was you. The Reno gang. The scenario, your style, it all fit."

Now, with Frank dead, John locked away in prison, there was only Lark left to deal with the consequences, Jo-Jo being dead only one of them.

Her rebellion, the futility of it, died.

"I don't want to see that money ever again." The panic came back, hot and biting. "I want to leave it right where it is."

"You can't. Catfish won't let you."

He stepped closer. She stood her ground, watched him come. "And you won't, either."

"No."

He stood directly in front of her. She had to tilt her head back to meet his dark, shadowed gaze.

Lark thought of the decision she'd made, to leave him and return to her job in the morning. She thought of Catfish, who knew where she was, who would stop at nothing to find the buried loot, even killing her if she didn't cooperate. She thought of Jo-Jo, too, his untimely demise, and how her fate could very likely be the same.

And then…Ross. His honor, his need for justice. Bounty hunter or not, he could do nothing else but see it done.

As if he knew the despairing trail of her thoughts, he opened his arms and took her hard against him. She soaked in his heat, his strength, his power, and wished to her very soul things could be different between them.

She closed her eyes, pressed her cheek into the solid bulk of his shoulder. "I'm afraid, Ross."

His hand fisted in her hair; his arms tightened further still. "Me, too."

Chapter Twelve

Using the light from a pair of lanterns behind him, Ross made a final check on the rope holding Jo-Jo Sumner's body to his horse. Satisfied each knot would hold for the trip into Ida Grove, he turned his attention to the two women on the porch.

Chat was quiet for once. She stared wide-eyed at his cargo, having never seen a dead man before, their father excepted. Might have been easier for her if Jo-Jo had been a stranger, but the kid had gone to school with her before dropping out a year or two back. Didn't matter that Jo-Jo didn't have many friends; Chat knew enough about him for her shock at what he'd done to run deep.

Lark concerned Ross most. She stood at the porch railing looking grieved and miserable. Blood stained her dress. She'd wrapped Jo-Jo in a blanket out there by the river, then helped Ross drape him across the back of his horse before tying him on. She hadn't taken the time to clean herself up afterward. Ross had decided she needed a good strong shot of whiskey before she did.

She drank the glass dry, and he figured the liquor mellowed her some. She still looked vulnerable, though, and his arms craved to hold her again, like he had this afternoon by the Maple. He wasn't sure it did much good, but she seemed to have wanted the comfort from him, and he'd been quick to oblige.

Hell of a predicament he found himself in. This attraction for her—he had trouble separating her from the outlaw she'd once been and the woman she was now. A damned fine woman, too, and she fired up his blood. Made him think of things he shouldn't.

The freedom to kiss her whenever he wanted for one, and that near the top of the list. Since she was on his mind just about constantly, that meant, hell, he could go on kissing her for a good long time. Holding her, too. Feeling those full breasts pressed against his chest...

Her slim body felt right against him. Like it was meant to be there.

He stifled a grim sigh, pulled himself out of the reverie and picked up the holster containing both his Colts. He'd already made sure each chamber was loaded. The lantern light glinted on the cold metal as he placed one in Chat's hand.

"Keep this with you until I get back," he said. "Don't let it out of your sight."

She nodded, though she held the weapon as if it was a piece of rancid meat. "Do you really think Catfish Jack will come?"

"We have to expect that he will," Ross said.

"He could be watching us right now." Lark accepted the weapon Ross handed her with an ease Chat lacked. The quiet huskiness of her voice reached out to him, but her attention centered on the yard beyond.

"Yes," he said and recalled last night, before dinner, how

the sorrel had suddenly gotten skittish in the corral. Ross was as certain as he could be it hadn't been from a weasel as he'd first thought.

Ross studied the yard, too. The darkness where the lantern light failed to reach. This afternoon, he'd decided to wait a few hours before bringing Jo-Jo back into Ida Grove. Figured it'd be better to go at nightfall than to ride in at broad daylight with a dead body in tow. No one knew yet Jo-Jo was dead, and since he was paired up with Catfish, the outlaw would wonder why Jo-Jo hadn't come back before now. Might be Catfish would ride out to have himself a look around Ross's place, hoping to find a sign of Jo-Jo—or Lark at an inopportune moment.

Ross disliked leaving the two women home alone. Best he could do was to make sure they were armed and ready to defend themselves if they had to. He'd get back as soon as he could.

He took his gloves from the saddle bag and pulled them on.

"Go on in," he said, gesturing with his chin at the house. "Lock up when you do."

Chat hooked her arm through Lark's. His kid sister would do all she could to protect Lark, he knew. Same as he would.

"We'll be fine, Ross. Try not to worry."

He took the reins to Jo-Jo's horse, climbed into the saddle of his own. Chat couldn't know how much he *would* worry.

"Ross."

He turned back toward the porch. Toward Lark. He heard the concern in her tone, the distress. She made a valiant effort to keep both from showing in her expression.

"Be careful," she said quietly.

It was all he could do to keep from getting back down and taking her hard against him. Console her with a heated kiss. Hell, at the moment, he could use some consoling himself.

"First sign of trouble, you know what to do," he said instead.

"Yes."

Taking one of the lanterns, leaving the other for Chat, she opened the door. Once they were inside, Ross waited for the bolt to slide into place before he turned the horses and headed toward town.

Ida Grove had settled in for the night. The boardwalks were quiet, the streets empty, each business establishment closed until morning. Except for the steady *clomp-clomp-clomp* of the horses' hooves, not a sound broke through the veil of darkness.

The advantage of waiting until nightfall to come into town. No one would get curious. Still, Ross avoided Main Street and used the side roads to get where he needed to go.

He pulled up in front of Sheriff Sternberg's office and dismounted. He swept a slow glance around him, noticed Mrs. Kelley's boardinghouse down the block. Noticed the row of windows on the second floor, too, and how lights shone through the curtains, an indication her boarders were still awake in their rooms.

Only one remained dark. Lark's. It struck him, that lone dark window. Made him think how it symbolized her life, how Catfish Jack was a dark place in it, and how alone she must feel, having to fight him because of her past.

Except she wasn't alone. She had Ross to help. Chat, too. And the sheriff, if Ross could convince him of her side of things.

Further down, the Hungry Horse Saloon stood silent, like the rest of the businesses on the block. Sunday night was the only night of the week the place closed early. That's how the upright and God-fearing folks in Ida Grove wanted it, and Ross was glad there wasn't a crowd around.

Wouldn't be easy telling Eb Sumner about his boy. As far as Ross knew, Eb ran a respectable establishment. Had he known his only son had taken up with a known outlaw? If he did, well, he'd have to live with the repercussions from it.

Which brought Ross's thoughts back to the purpose of his being here, at the jailhouse. He looped the reins from both horses securely to the hitching post and strode toward the door. A dim light burned in the window, but no sign of movement showed through the glass, and he guessed the sheriff had turned in for the night. Sternberg, a widower, kept a small apartment in the back, and it took Ross several firm knocks before he heard footsteps inside. The door opened, and the gray-haired lawman, a score of years older than Ross, peered out.

Ross had clearly roused the man from his bed. He stood in his stockinged feet with suspenders hanging past his hips. His trousers appeared hastily buttoned, since not all of them were, and he wore only his knit undershirt over his portly belly.

"Santana?" He blinked in surprised recognition. "What're you doing here this time of night?"

"Mind if I come in, Sheriff?" Ross asked.

"You wouldn't be here if you didn't have good reason. Hell, yes, you can come in."

Sternberg stepped aside, and Ross went in, taking care to close the door behind him.

The lawman had been one of the first to welcome Ross

and Chat to Ida Grove. Of course, since Sternberg got wind of Ross's former employment as a bounty hunter, he'd been quick to introduce himself, had even tried to hire Ross for a job now and again, but Ross always refused. Eventually, Sternberg learned to accept the fact Ross had hung up his guns for good. Learned to respect his privacy, too.

It'd been a while since Ross was in the lawman's office, and he took a minute to look the place over.

The small room contained only a desk, a couple of chairs, a wood-burning stove. Main thing he noted was the pair of empty jail cells. Sternberg took enforcing the law seriously, and folks in Ida Grove knew it. He'd been the only sheriff the town ever had. He knew everyone, and everyone knew him. If a stranger rode into town, Sternberg knew about it, one way or the other. If a man took an inclination to get rowdy or break the law—didn't matter if it was big or small—he knew he'd pay the price eventually if he didn't have the sense to go into someone else's jurisdiction.

Sternberg was one hell of a good sheriff. Call it a bounty hunter's intuition, but Ross trusted him.

The lawman padded over to his desk, pulled out a chair. "Have a seat, Santana. You want coffee? Pot's cold, but I'll make a fresh one if you're in need of it."

"No, thanks. I'm not staying long."

The chair remained empty. Sternberg studied him. "Saw Chat yesterday. At Doc Seeber's."

"So I heard."

"Everything all right out your way?"

"Been better."

But then, he'd never had Lark with him before. If he didn't include the trouble she was in, she'd be the most "right" thing that had happened to him in a good long while.

"I'm listening." Sternberg took the chair and sat himself in it, then leaned his elbows on the desk. The top, Ross noticed, was polished and cleared of clutter. Sternberg kept the peace in Ida Grove. No crime meant no paperwork to do.

"I've got Jo-Jo Sumner outside," Ross said. "He's dead."

Sternberg's attention sharpened. "What happened?"

"I killed him. Self-defense."

Thick brows shot up. "He came at you first?"

Ross nodded grimly. "Drunk and shooting wild."

"What the hell for? He wouldn't have had a rat's ass chance with you." The lawman stared hard at him. Ross could almost see his mind churn to determine the motive. "This have something to do with Chat? She's about his age, isn't she? Did he get too forward with her?"

"Chat has nothing to do with it. He was working with Catfish Jack."

"Catfish Jack!" Ross figured it took a lot to stun the sheriff. The news did a fair job of it. "You know that for sure?"

"He told me. Before he passed on."

Sternberg angled his head away with an oath. "Which means the son-of-a-gun is still around."

"Right under your nose, it seems."

The gray head whipped back. "I've already turned over every damned stone I thought he might be hiding under, Santana. I've got my feelers out, don't think I don't."

Ross held up a hand. "Easy. I'm not implying you're not doing your job. He's a sly cuss. Slyer than most."

The lawman seemed appeased by that. He crossed his

arms over his chest and eased back in the chair. "What do you know about him?"

"His name's Jack Friday. I tracked him clear to Canada a while back, but the arrest went bad." Ross hesitated. He didn't like drawing attention to himself, but the truth helped make his point. He tapped his eye patch with a finger. "His shotgun was responsible for this."

Sternberg let out a low whistle. "I'll be damned."

"He got away right after. Far as I know, he's been on the run ever since."

"You think he found out you were here, wanted to settle the score between you and used Jo-Jo to help him do it?"

"I know he did."

Ross kept his features impassive. He had no intention of revealing Lark's secret—her association with the outlaw and why he'd hunted her down.

He preferred instead to let Sternberg think it was Ross Catfish wanted. There was truth in it, besides. More important, it would help distract the lawman's thinking and keep him off her trail.

"Hell of a story, Santana." The sheriff scratched his chin. "Strangest thing about that Renault woman, though. You heard he attacked her in her sleeping room? Without provocation?"

Ross's mouth curved into a cold smile. "Hasn't everyone?"

"Now she's gone. Not a sign of her since. It just don't fit." The sheriff locked his gaze on Ross. "Any idea why Catfish would do that to her?"

"I want to find him. Bad." Ross held that gaze, saw the shrewdness in it. "When I do, we'll find out, won't we?"

"There's still reward money out for him."

"It's not about the money."

Sternberg continued to regard him for a long moment. "No, I don't suppose it would be." He sighed, got to his feet. "We'll work together on it. I won't have it any other way."

"Of course." Ross couldn't ask for anything more than that. "But if I get to him first, I'll handle him...as circumstances warrant. Agreed?"

For the first time, the lawman appeared amused. "Just keep it within the line of the law, Santana."

Ross had no intention of making a promise he might not want to honor. "I'll try to remember that."

He glanced out the window, to the pair of horses tied to the post. He had a job left to do. An unpleasant one, for sure. Dreading it, he frowned.

"Jo-Jo Sumner was trouble from the day he was born," Sternberg said, seeming to know Ross's thoughts. "But Eb's going to take it hard to hear he's dead anyways." He padded out from around the desk, headed toward his apartment. "Let me get my boots on. I'll go with you to tell him."

The distant clomping of horses' hooves alerted Catfish Jack he wasn't alone.

His ears pricked at the sound. Strained to figure its location.

He didn't move. The sound grew louder and with it, his sense of dread.

He'd gotten to know this part of Ida Grove since he started hiding out in the back of the Hungry Horse. Knew folks' comings and goings. Knew the routine of the businesses in the district, too. When they opened in the morning. When they closed at night.

Real unusual for someone to ride down the street this late.

His mind worked through the possibilities. Only one person it might be, but even then, it just didn't figure right.

He'd wanted Jo-Jo to stir up a little trouble for Wild Red today. Catfish decided to lay low, keep his watch on the boardinghouse, just in case she came back. The kid had been quick to oblige, but he should've been back by now. Hours ago. From sunup to sundown, the kid hung on Catfish like black on a spade flush. Wasn't like Jo-Jo to stay away so long. Besides, he kept his horse in the livery, the opposite side of town. Wouldn't make sense for him to go from this direction.

Whoever was out there, and their reason, meant trouble. No other explanation for it. Sheer willpower kept Catfish from creeping out from his favorite spot here beside the saloon to have himself a good look-see.

Wasn't long before he could tell those horses were coming toward the Hungry Horse. Two of them, far as he could tell. They weren't in no hurry, either.

Real odd they'd come this way. Eb Sumner closed up a while ago. Place was dark as a lobo's cave. Anyone could see that it was.

Catfish hurriedly crouched behind a wooden barrel. The thing was near overflowing with a week's worth of trash. Stank to high heaven, but at least the horses wouldn't pick up his scent.

He dared a glimpse around it. They showed up then. Silhouettes in the street. Two men walked alongside, reins in their hands. They talked low, too low for him to hear what they were saying. The shadows made it hard to see who they were, though, and he stared hard to figure—

Catfish went cold.

Ross Santana.

It'd been five long years since Catfish had been this close to him. Still tall, still lean, just like Catfish remembered. Still moved real easy, too. Deceiving a man like himself about how fast he could be, especially with a gun in his hand.

The bounty hunter came close to arresting him that day back at the Turf Club. Catfish would never forget how close. Even now, he could smell the cunning on him.

Catfish recognized Sheriff Sternberg, too. The lawman had been nosing around, asking questions about him, and now the two of them together like this—if Catfish could have squeezed into the bottom of that stinking barrel, he would have.

Both men tied their reins to the post, stepped up to the boardwalk. Their boot heels on the wooden planks sounded loud. Hollow.

Ominous.

One of them pounded on the saloon's door. Took a while before Eb Sumner shuffled out to see who was there. Santana said something, and Sumner let them in, then closed the door. The silence returned.

Catfish licked lips gone dry. He'd give his best shooting iron to know what Santana and the sheriff were saying about now. He dragged his gaze back to the horses and noticed the wrapped bundle hanging over one of the saddles. Damned if those weren't legs hanging down the side with boots attached to 'em.

Jo-Jo.

Catfish broke into a cold sweat. Stupid kid went and got himself killed. And that explained everything. Catfish didn't bother to think what fool thing Jo-Jo did to get Santana to shoot him for it. One thing had to be, though.

The kid had gotten too close to Wild Red. Santana had made him pay the price for it.

She was hiding out with the bounty hunter. Why, Catfish couldn't figure, but he'd seen her there himself. Yesterday. Sitting on Santana's porch and drinking lemonade.

Lemonade.

Just as free as you please. Like the Muscatine heist was the farthest thing from her mind. The red-haired witch didn't believe what ol' Catfish had told her—split the loot with him or else.

His lip curled. She didn't think the money was worth fighting for, either.

But he did.

And he intended to fight dirty to get it.

A night like this one reminded Ross of why "home" had come to mean just about everything to him.

Jo-Jo would never know it, but he'd shown Ross how complacent he'd gotten of late. He'd taken his blessings for granted. Blessings like freedom to live his life the way he wanted. Peace, hard-won at first, that let him sleep at night. And a deep-seated ability to know right from wrong.

Jo-Jo reminded him of how lucky he was to have Chat, too, and how she'd grown into a fine upstanding young woman. He'd have to tell her so the first chance he got. She deserved to hear it.

He unlocked the door and slipped quietly into the house. A single lamp burned in the front room. The bedroom doors stood open, their interiors dark, like the kitchen.

His glance swung to the couch and found Chat and Lark in their nightgowns, dozing, each with a Colt in their lap. Waiting for him.

The two women in his life. One by birth, the other by chance. Both of them claimed a part of him.

And both of them safe. The worry lifted from him, and

he pushed the door closed, turned the lock. The metal clicked, and Chat's eyes flew open. She sat up with a start.

He put a finger to his lips. He didn't want to disturb Lark if they could help it. Chat visibly relaxed, her eyes wide as he hung his Stetson on its hook and approached her.

"Everything all right tonight?" he whispered, squatting in front of her. He took the revolver and set it aside.

"Nothing happened," she whispered back.

"Good." He took her hand, pulled her up, walked with her toward her bedroom.

"Did you see Mr. Sumner?" she asked.

"I did."

"How is he doing?"

Ross hesitated, thought of the man's reaction. "He's hurting like any father would, under the circumstances."

The man's grief had turned ugly at Ross's part in those circumstances, but with Sheriff Sternberg there as witness, he couldn't act on it. At least, not then. Ross didn't know what to expect from him; time would tell if he had more sense than his son.

Chat didn't need to hear the details. She was distraught enough over Jo-Jo's death. To keep her from asking questions, Ross pressed a kiss to her forehead.

"We'll talk more in the morning, sweet. Go in to bed. And thanks for taking care of Lark while I was gone."

"She's a cool one." Chat peeped at him wryly from beneath her lashes. "I think she took care of *me*. She didn't act scared at all. Not like I was."

His heart twisted, hearing of her fear. "This will all be over soon. I promise."

"I hope so. I'm glad you're home." She leaned closer and gave him a quick hug. "Good night. I love you."

"Love you, too."

She yawned and entered her room, shutting the door. She seemed more like herself now that he was here, and he felt better, too, knowing it.

He turned and discovered Lark watching him. He strode closer, his boot steps silent on the thick rug, and hunkered down beside her.

"Did we wake you?" he asked in a low voice. The late hour seemed to call for talking hushed. Or maybe the solitude of the shadowed room did.

"I wasn't sleeping. Not really."

The arm of the couch cushioned her head, and wild curls spilled over the brocade fabric. A fine pillow they'd make, those curls. Silky, soft. Thick. Made him want to lay his head on them, too.

"You fooled me, then. Playing 'possum," he said, and his mouth curved.

Hers did the same. She looked relaxed half lying there, her bare feet on the floor, but the rest of her body reclined. Did she know how sultry she looked? How seductive?

"I learned to sleep that way a long time ago," she said. "Too many times, it was necessary."

He understood. He'd done the same, when he'd been on the hunt for a man who didn't want to be hunted, who resented him for it and intended to retaliate. Ross had taken a liking to waking up each morning. Sleeping half-awake allowed him the privilege.

Her smile faded. "What happened tonight?"

Unlike Chat, Lark needed to know the truth. "Eb took the news hard. Blamed me for Jo-Jo's death."

Dismay furrowed her brows. "Did you tell him it was self-defense?"

"I told him, but he wasn't hearing it."

"What do you think he'll do?"

She appeared more worried for him than anything. Appeared to have forgotten, too, that she had a worse problem with Catfish Jack, who'd be a more formidable enemy than Eb Sumner ever would.

"No way to know. If Eb turns against me, I'll deal with it then." Ross eased the Colt away from her, set it next to the first, further down the couch. "I had a talk with Sheriff Sternberg."

Her eyes widened a little. "And?"

"He's real frustrated that he's had no word about your whereabouts."

"Thanks to you and Chat."

"He's concerned."

She glanced away, as if the inconvenience she'd caused everyone troubled her. "I'm sure."

"He's had no sign of Catfish Jack, either, though he's done his best to find one. Demanded that Eb tell us what he knew about the man." Ross frowned. "Eb admitted Catfish had been staying in the back room of the Hungry Horse all along."

She drew back in surprise. "The Hungry Horse!"

The news had stirred up Ross's suspicions plenty. Questions about a man who'd knowingly hide someone like Catfish in his place of business. And why.

"But when we went back there, he was gone," Ross continued. "He'd grabbed his gear and disappeared."

She paled in the dim lantern light. "Maybe he knows Jo-Jo is dead."

"I'm figuring so, for him to up and leave like he did."

Despite Ross's efforts otherwise, Catfish had likely seen him ride in tonight with Jo-Jo's body. Which, in turn, would leave him feeling real desperate.

"That's all the news I have," Ross said, slipping an arm

beneath her head, the other under her knees. He lifted her from the couch.

Her arms came around his neck, as if she'd done it a hundred times. "That was plenty, I think."

He grunted. It wasn't near enough.

But he pushed the thought from his mind. He filled it, instead, with her clean scent and how it wrapped around him, refreshed him. How she felt cradled against him, too, her body soft and female through the thin cotton of her nightgown.

Thinking of nothing else, he turned and carried her to the bedroom.

Chapter Thirteen

He laid her gently on his bed, and Lark sank into the cool sheets. Heavy shadows veiled the room, attesting to the lateness of the hour. He found a match on the bedside table and lit the lamp's wick, keeping, she noted, the kerosene burning at its lowest vantage.

She expected him to leave for his bed on the couch. She was glad he didn't. She had her decision to tell him, and it couldn't wait until morning.

Still, she delayed shattering the awareness-charged mood which had arisen between them, an intimacy she found herself relishing. He stood over her, his hands on his lean hips, warming her blood with the very sight of him. His hair hung recklessly against his collar, his strength a powerful thing.

He seemed reluctant to leave, and she took courage from it. Her arm lifted. She twined her fingers through his and thought how easy it'd become to touch him. A gentle tug brought him down to sit next to her.

Neither pulled away. He watched her. Waited. As if he knew she had something to say.

Her gaze dropped to their joined hands. His, roughened by work, darkened by the sun. Capable of killing a man. Or gentling a woman. Her own...smaller, softer, not quite steady. And guilty of stealing what they shouldn't.

"Might as well get it off your chest, Lark," he said quietly. "I'm staying right here until you do."

Her gaze rose. "You must promise to hear me out."

His nod of agreement came slow, as if he measured the seriousness of what she was about to reveal. "You know I will."

"I'm leaving tomorrow."

Like a gathering storm, his expression darkened. "And where are you going?"

"Home."

"Home." His eye narrowed. "As easy as that."

"My job, too. The bank, I mean. My *life,* Ross."

"The hell you are."

She pulled her fingers from his and sat up. "Mr. Templeton expects me to be at my desk, as I always am on Monday mornings."

"He does, does he?"

"I *will* be there. Promptly, in fact."

Abruptly, Ross stood. "Templeton has no idea of the risk. If he did—"

"I intend to tell him."

Ross stared at her. "Tell him what? That you're Wild Red?"

She swallowed. Hard. "He deserves to know the truth, because if I don't tell him—"

"Listen to me, Lark."

"—Catfish will."

He opened his mouth as if to argue further, swore instead and left the room. The lamplight in the front of the house went out. He returned and pushed the door shut behind him—privacy from Chat overhearing.

"So you think I should just let you go," he said.

"I insist that you do."

"And if I don't?"

She stiffened. She knew he'd react like this. "You have no right to keep me here. Not really."

"Don't I?"

"I'm not running away. Please understand that. I'll be right—"

"—where Catfish can get you."

She pushed a mass of curls behind her ear in frustration. "What would you have me do? Stay with you forever?"

He strode closer, his gaze fierce upon her. "If I thought you could, yes."

She blinked. "That's impossible. You know it is."

"I don't have the perfect answer, but I've been thinking on one."

"Hide like a frightened rabbit, only to be shot like one when either of us least expects it, perhaps?" she taunted, brow raised.

How could he think it'd be any other way if she stayed? Jo-Jo was proof of how underhanded Catfish Jack could be. Believing she could outwit the outlaw time and time again was the thinking of a fool.

Better to come out of hiding. Meet him head-on and wide open if he came after her. Catfish had far more at stake than she did, with his list of crimes gone unpunished. She, at least, had atoned for hers.

Except for one…

Ross halted at the mattress's edge. How fierce he was, looking down at her. How intense. And strangely desperate.

"We can leave," he said. "I'll take you someplace. Anywhere you want to go."

In stunned confusion, she stared up at him. "Leave Ida Grove? With you?"

"We can head to Colorado. Or Arizona. California, maybe."

Her breath quickened. Abandon her job? Her life in this peaceful little town she'd grown to love? Who would care for Chat? Or Ross's thriving furniture-building business?

"No," she said firmly. "No."

He reached an arm toward her, but she eluded his grasp, sliding off the bed from the opposite side.

"Just until Catfish is caught," Ross said, watching her.

"Absolutely not." She shook her head for emphasis, and endured the first stirring of panic. Never had she seen Ross this determined. This driven to have matters done his way. "I can't."

"Sternberg has a posse organized. They're ready to ride. Now that he knows Catfish is close, they'll comb through every square inch of dirt around to find him."

"They can do that with me here."

"I won't let you be their bait."

A nasty word, *bait*. She folded her arms and shivered. "I'm willing, if it helps. I'll do anything to see him caught."

"So will I." Ross took a slow step toward her.

"He's eluded posses for years. What makes you think Sternberg's will find him?"

"Catfish is stone broke. He admitted as much to Eb Sumner when he asked to bunk in the back of the Hungry Horse. He needs you as his bankroll to get him out of the country." He paused. "Sternberg and his men will find him. I'll protect you until they do."

"By whisking me away halfway across the country?"

"Yes." He kept moving toward her, slow. Sure. "It's the safest way to keep you alive."

"The sheriff doesn't know I'm with you. He'll wonder why you've up and left. Just like he's wondering about me now. He'll do some digging. Wouldn't be long before he started putting two and two together." A new thought intruded into her logic. "He wanted you on the posse, too, didn't he?"

Ross halted. "Yes."

"But you told him no."

"Asking me to ride with the posse was a waste of his breath. He knew it. I'd hung up my guns before ever coming to Ida Grove."

"You're wearing them for me, though."

His gaze, dark and dangerous, glittered over her.

"Yes," he rumbled.

Hot emotion chafed her throat. She angled her head away, hiding it from him.

These damned feelings he kept stirring up inside her. They softened her too much, gave her an unfamiliar troublesome *ache* that burned deep in her belly.

He'd put the ache in her heart, too, with his soul-destroying kisses and dark, smoldering looks. Kept it there, whenever he held her in his strong arms. And he fired it up by making her believe he wanted to keep her safe— because she wanted to be safe more than anything.

Anything.

But she had to be strong. Focused. She'd survived her entire life by making her own decisions. She couldn't let Ross make decisions for her now, no matter how honorable they appeared to be.

A sudden memory of the Muscatine heist cooled the ache like a dousing of mountain river water.

Of course, Ross wanted her safe. He intended to hold her accountable for the crime.

That hadn't changed. It wouldn't, either. Catfish was just an irritating diversion to keep him from getting the job done.

Lark's shoulders squared, and she turned toward Ross. He stood unexpectedly close in front of her, so close she could smell the saddle leather on him.

She couldn't help taking a quick step backward. The man stole the very air she needed to breathe. Took the space she needed to keep her resolve, too.

"Lark," he said, a slight frown tugging at his dark brows.

She suspected he recognized the shift in her thoughts, and she moved back another step to bolster her will. The heel of her foot bumped a wooden chair, and the clink of the leg iron's chain links reminded her they were there, heaped on the seat.

How she despised them. The wall stopped her from going farther. Before she could slink past Ross from the side, his arms bracketed her head, caging her in front of him.

"Lark," he said, insistent.

She tilted her chin up. A lock of thick hair had fallen over his eye patch, and it was all she could do keep from reaching up and smoothing it away.

"I know what's going on in that stubborn brain of yours," he ground out.

Did he truly know the war she battled? The one she must win at all costs?

"Then you know what I intend to do," she said.

His jaw lowered to her temple. The shadowed bristle of a night's growth of beard scraped against her hair. The tension shimmered in him. The frustration.

"I can't let you go back to the bank. It'll destroy you. Why can't you see that?" he murmured roughly.

She focused on the sun-bronzed column of his throat. The urge to close her eyes, to savor his warmth, his nearness, ran strong within her. She had to concentrate. Had to convince him she saw everything with appalling clarity.

"I refuse to sit out here and wait for Catfish Jack to find me. He'll kill me if—"

She bit her lip. *...if I don't tell him where the money is.*

"Let Sternberg take care of him," Ross said. His head lifted, and he gently knuckled her chin up. "Let me take you somewhere safe until he does."

Her resolve cracked, just a little. Lark hastily shored it up again. She met his gaze without wavering.

"No," she said.

The thunder returned in his expression, and he pushed away from the wall with an oath. He unbuttoned his shirt with short, savage movements. Yanked the hem free from the waistband of his Levi's the same way.

"Then I'm going with you," he snapped. He hurled the shirt toward a hamper in the corner.

"To the bank?" she asked, taken aback.

He swung toward her. "Yes. So I can keep watch over you."

Her mind struggled to comprehend just how he would manage it. And failed. She had duties to perform, customers to attend to. Did he intend to watch her the whole day through?

Surely not.

"From the minute the place opens in the morning—" he jabbed a finger at her, showing her he meant every word "—until it closes up in the afternoon, I'm going to be there."

An image of him standing guard, looking imposing and dangerous and ready to shoot Catfish Jack down the minute he showed up—*if* he showed up—positively mortified her. He'd be like a glaring beacon to the townspeople, illuminating her troubles with Catfish Jack.

She moved toward him. "That's ridiculous, Ross. And completely unnecessary."

"No other way to save your fool neck when Catfish pays you a call." He hooked a boot heel on the bootjack, slid his foot free and proceeded to do the same with the other.

"But Mr. Templeton would never approve. It would be most inappropriate, besides. What would the bank's patrons say?"

"They're going to say plenty once they catch wind you're Wild Red. And just how do you think Templeton is going to take the news when you tell him?"

She stiffened. "If I thought it would be easy, we wouldn't be having this discussion, would we?"

He dropped his boots and socks next to the hamper. "I'm not letting you out of my sight, Lark. No telling what could happen when my back is turned. And that's my last word on it."

"You're overreacting," she said nevertheless. "Catfish is too smart to come to the bank in broad daylight. I'm sure he knows the sheriff is looking for him."

"Has nothing to do with being smart. Has to do with being desperate. He's in a real hurry to get to South America. That means he'll do just about anything to get himself there."

Lark conceded Ross the point on that, and, defeated, she fell silent. His ability to see the cold hard facts and lay them flat out on the table said it all.

Ross clearly considered the subject closed. He poured water into the washstand basin and lathered a cloth with soap. Lark's gaze strayed to the play of muscles in his back as he cleaned up for the night. Despite her somber thoughts, they fascinated her, the power in those muscles. The way the breadth of his shoulders tapered in perfect symmetry to lean hips, too, and reminded her yet again Ross Santana was as fine a piece of masculinity as any she'd ever seen.

Persistent and shrewd and a whole lot more besides. A man to be reckoned with, certainly, and how could she possibly win over his fervent need for justice?

"You're looking mighty serious, woman."

His low voice dissipated her musings. He'd finished washing and held the towel in one hand while the other finger-combed his hair back from his face.

"Am I?" she asked coolly.

"You are." He reached out, hooked the towel around the back of her neck. With an end in each hand, he tugged her up against him. "Scared, too."

Words leapt onto her tongue to deny it, but why bother? It was the truth.

"Wouldn't you be if you were me?" Her mouth curved into a pout. She didn't care how self-pitying she sounded.

He made a grim, guttural sound of agreement. "You have a lot at stake right now. No doubt about it."

If only he wouldn't be so brutally blunt. Couldn't he have given her something to hope for?

She heaved a weary sigh. Her head sank onto his chest, and he let go of the towel to enfold her in his arms. The heat of his skin soothed her, and oh, how she would miss him when she was gone.

Her eyes closed, and she allowed herself to treasure the

feel of him without questioning why. Her arms curled to his back and clung.

"Let me help you, Lark," he said. "Tell me where the Muscatine money is. Hard to do, I know. Real hard. But you have to trust me."

Her eyes shut tight. If she could just shut off the reality of what he was asking the same way.

"It's the only thing that'll save you from him, if the posse doesn't find him first," he continued, his tone grave. Darkly urgent. His hand slid up her spine and back down, over and over again. Melting her defenses. Making her want to weep. "Turn the money in, and you'll be rid of him for good. I promise."

"I can't bear to think of it," she whispered, tormented.

Yet his words circled harsh and relentless in her head. He was right. Deep down, in the blackest part of her soul, she knew he was right.

She had to tell him where the money was. She couldn't keep living like this, afraid for her future. Of going back to prison. Of being a convicted criminal all over again.

She had to tell him.

But she couldn't. Oh, God, she couldn't.

He breathed a curse, as if he'd opened up her mind and read her agony. And hurt right along with her.

"I wish I could take you out of this hell you're living in," he said huskily. His hands lifted to her face and gently nudged her to look at him. "I wish I could make it all go away for you."

No one had seen this hidden, ugly side of her except for him. No one else had protected her, worried for her. What would she have done, alone, without him to help shoulder the burden of her past?

After tomorrow, everything between them would change.

But she had tonight.

She wanted a part of him to tuck away into the memories of her heart. A treasure she would forever have, no matter where she was or what happened to her. She wanted Ross Santana, and it didn't even matter that he was a bounty hunter, because God help her, she'd fallen in love with him.

Her hands slid upward across his chest and wrapped around his neck. She pulled his head down to hers.

"You can," she said simply. "For a little while."

She heard his slight intake of breath moments before she brushed her mouth against his, a provocative invitation that teased as lightly as the flutter of butterfly wings. She angled her head, and brushed his lips again, one side, then the other and sealed the invitation by tracing their shape with the tip of her tongue.

Ross drew back. His gaze smoldered; she could feel the desire in him, desire he held in check with the control so much a part of him.

"You're feeling pretty low right now, Lark. You don't know what you're asking," he murmured.

"I want you to make love to me."

The barest of trembles went through him, a sign the hold he kept on his control was precarious.

"You might want it now," he said. "But things will look different in the morning. Might be you'll regret then what you're feeling now."

"I don't want to think of the morning, Ross." She speared her fingers into the ebony thickness of his hair. "I'll have to, soon, but not now. I want you. Tonight."

In the pale golden lamplight, his gaze glittered down at her, worry and fiery lust and understanding, all rolled together. "Yes." His hand fisted in her hair. "Yes, damn it, I want you, too."

His control shattered, and his mouth took hers with none of the gentleness that she'd given him before. Her own fire leapt through nerve endings already alive and pulsing. If not for the muscled arm he held at her back, her knees would have given way, and she'd have fallen boneless at his feet.

The hot, wet thrust of his tongue between her lips demanded she open for him. She was beyond denial when he delved deep, and the erotic game he played in the recesses of her mouth left them breathing hard and needing more.

"I'm going to make love to you all right." He dragged fevered kisses along her jaw, and her skin tingled from the restrained savagery in him. "The likes neither of us have been made love to before."

But his husky avowal intruded into the sensations rushing through her. Her eyes opened.

"I've never been with a man before you," she admitted softly.

He stilled. Lifted his head. Stared at her with a surprise she wasn't sure she should find amusing or offensive.

His brows furrowed. "I'm sorry. I assumed—"

"—that when I was an outlaw I would have been promiscuous?" She shrugged. "Hardly. For all their lawless ways, my cousins were protective of me. They would've shot anyone who tried to violate my virtue. For that, I'll always be grateful."

"I'll be the first." He sounded bemused, a little hesitant.

And made Lark wonder if he thought she was some naïve schoolgirl that would only fumble her way through lovemaking.

"I know how a man can pleasure a woman," she said.

"Do I look worried?" He kissed her, long and slow before lifting his head again, leaving her lips wet and swollen. "I'm just humbled by what you're giving me." He found the end of the white satin ribbon which held the front of her nightgown together. He pulled, undoing the bow, in no hurry to see the job done. "And I'll enjoy the gift all the more."

He unfastened her gown, button by button, his fingers charmingly out of place amongst the dainty tucks and lace against her bosom. He nudged the pristine fabric off one shoulder, then the other, until it drifted to the floor.

She stood naked before him and drew in a flustered breath. He chuckled softly, slid a bold knuckle down the swell of her breast and across the rosy-hued peak. The nipple pearled, and a slow heat pooled in her belly.

Sweet anticipation.

"No need to be shy, darlin', when you're as beautiful as this."

She gave him a taunting lift of her brow. "You think I'm shy?"

She'd know his body as well as her own by the time the night was gone, and she reached to unfasten the denim riding on his hips. After he stepped out of them, she had a pretty good idea this man would give her the most exhilarating ride of her life.

His beauty stole her breath away. That pure male part of him, thick and glorious and pulsating with life. She took him into her hand, stroked the velvet length, savored his manly feel. He sucked in a breath and covered her hand with his, an invitation for her to linger on him, that he was hers to take and pleasure. She marveled at his heat, at how he quivered beneath her touch and that she had the power to affect him like this, most of all.

Ross groaned and tumbled with her onto the bed. He

buried his fingers in her hair, holding her mouth to his. The feel of his skin, hardened and sculpted with muscle, of his big bounty-hunter body against her smaller, softer one, was unlike anything she'd ever imagined. She purred and twined her legs through his. Took his rough kisses eagerly. Hungrily. Matched them with a wildness of her own.

Her hands skimmed down his back, feeding the desire to touch all of him. She cupped his taut buttocks, pulled him closer against her, kneaded the strong flesh in her palms. He breathed her name again and again between frenzied kisses, heating her blood and her need. He shifted against her, but only to splay his hand across her breast and mold its fullness. Lark moaned in pleasure, her mind attuned to what he was doing, how he made her feel. He shifted again, lower, and licked at her nipple, again and again, before opening his mouth wide to suckle her deep.

She rasped his name on both a gasp and a moan. Her hands slid into his hair, keeping him against her. Every pull, every caress of his tongue across the sensitive tip sent her higher toward a crescendo somewhere deep inside.

Her hips moved beneath him in search of it, needing him to take her higher still. And when he rose above her, when her legs untangled and opened, when his male length probed her female folds to find his place, gently at first, she took him inside her, took him deep and fast, thrust for mind-numbing thrust, until that crescendo finally, and ecstatically, exploded inside her.

Ross heaved a throaty groan, eased down on top of Lark and lay there. He didn't have a single working muscle left in his body.

Never would he have thought himself worthy to receive what she had given him. That all-consummate female part of her that she'd shared with no one. Knowing she trusted him enough—that she *chose* him—was an honor in itself.

An honor that went beyond pure physical satisfaction. A distraction from her troubles. Or even the innocence of her virginity.

Lark had lifted him to a new level, a higher plane of trust and vulnerability and *feelings* that up to now she'd kept closed up tight inside her in one prim, respectable, red-haired package.

She showed him she was all woman. Lush and silky-skinned and without inhibition. And she made him feel things he wasn't sure he wanted to feel. Things she made him want to want. Impossible things, like being with her, like this, every night for the rest of his life.

"Got to be getting heavy on you," Ross muttered, his voice muffled in her neck and hair.

"Mmm. You're not."

He moved anyway, but only a little bit off her. He wasn't ready to let her go just yet, not when he hadn't had his fill, and maybe he never would. His hand skimmed her hip, dipped into the curve of her waist, and discovered an imperfection in her warm, smooth flesh.

His head came up to inspect it. A coin-sized scar, slightly puckered, pale pink and telling him exactly what put it there.

"That's where you shot me," she said, vaguely amused.

His horror melded into regret. "Looks like it hurt."

"It did, at the time." The hate was gone now, he realized. She could talk it about with no animosity. "The bullet went clean through, so I healed quickly."

He exhaled in disgust. The violence from that day. The ugliness neither of them could forget. "I'm sorry for putting you through it."

"Don't be. I had it coming, I suppose. I would've done the same to you, if the tables were turned."

She would have, yes. He would've understood, too. Accepted it as the price for justice each had to pay.

Her finger traced the narrow lacing that held his eye patch in place.

"You hurt back then, just like I did. But more, I think." She braced his head in her hands and tugged him closer to press a gentle kiss against the patch's black leather.

Her compassion moved him. He thought of the pain and fury he'd endured from Catfish Jack's shotgun. He'd felt plenty sorry for himself back then. Some days he still did. But Lark had always made him feel whole, despite his half-blindness.

"As long as we're tracking our injuries, we can't forget this one." He indicated the thin bandage on her shoulder, the knife wound Catfish had given her.

She sighed. "Yes."

As if his mention of the injury reminded her that reckoning with the ruthless outlaw loomed ever closer, her glance darted to the small clock on his bedside table. The slender hands read three hours after midnight. Dawn would arrive soon, and the worry returned to her expression.

Ross knew of ways to make her forget until it did, and he rolled to his back, bringing her with him. Without another word between them, he made love her to her again, slow and easy and thorough, until the sun peeked golden over the horizon.

Chapter Fourteen

"**I**'ll be out shortly, Lark," Chat said, hurrying from the kitchen to her room, drying her hands on a towel as she went. "I forgot my hat."

"Is there anything I can do to help you before we leave?" Lark asked.

"No, but thank you." The armoire door slammed closed. A dresser drawer clattered open. "Ross has already loaded the butter and eggs. I won't be but a minute."

"All right." Lark picked up the wicker basket holding her possessions, few that they were, and hooked the handle over her arm. She'd already pinned her hair securely in its usual bun. She wore her best dress, her sensible shoes and she carried the key to the bank's front door in her pocket. She'd been ready to go for the better part of an hour, but now that it was time to leave, she could hardly force herself out the door.

She cast a final sweeping glance around her. Ross's house. The home she'd come to love.

She wouldn't be back. If Mr. Templeton fired her this morning, she'd leave Ida Grove for good. If he didn't, well, she'd return to her sleeping room and show Catfish Jack he couldn't scare her away, no matter what.

Yet her gaze lingered through the open door of Ross's room. Sunlight beamed on the quilt spread neatly over his bed and brightened the rows of cheery blue squares. The furniture gleamed with its high polish. She'd always remember the magnificence of his bed and the time she'd spent with him there.

An incredible longing surged through her for those things that could never be. That damnable emotion, too, and she resolutely stepped outside before she crumpled from the weight of it.

She found Ross waiting by the buckboard wagon, one booted foot propped on the wheel. He appeared deep in thought as he put a cigarette to his lips and inhaled. His Stetson hung low on his forehead, and he'd rolled his shirtsleeves up his forearms. No one could miss the pair of Colts strapped snug to his hips.

He heated her blood. Excited her like none other. But she refused to let him deter her from her mission—to live her life in Ida Grove.

His gaze lifted. Found her. Watched her come toward him as he lazily exhaled a thin cloud of smoke.

She halted in front of him with her chin held high and her resolve firmly in place. His scrutiny burned hot down the length of her and back up again.

"You look pretty," he murmured. "Efficient and professional, too."

"Thank you."

"But then—" he studied the glowing tip of his cigarette "—I prefer you like you were earlier, wearing nothing at all."

"Ross." She drew in an unsteady breath. "Please, just don't say anything."

A tiny muscle leapt in his jaw. He straightened, sent his cigarette arcing into the grass before he took the basket from her and set it in the back of the wagon.

"You don't have to do this," he said.

"Yes, I do."

"They'll make you bleed for the whole world to see."

"I'm hoping they'll understand that I was an outlaw a long time ago, and that I'm an honest citizen now."

He made a sound of disgust. "Then you're a fool."

Wounded impatience spiked through her. "This is my decision, Ross. Not yours." She managed to keep her voice cool, even. Chat would be coming out any moment. "And let me remind you that it is at your insistence you accompany me to the bank this morning. Not mine."

"I won't have you go through it alone," he said, his mouth a grim line.

"Then you must accept what I have to do and not quarrel with me about it."

But she regretted the words as soon as they left her mouth. He was worried for her, nothing more. Wasn't she worried, too? She sighed and touched his cheek, roughened by the stubble he hadn't yet shaved. They'd lingered too long in bed for him to have time.

"We've had precious little sleep, and our tempers are showing it, I'm afraid," she said quietly.

"I'm not so tired that I couldn't make love to you all over again," he said, his voice a low rumble. "And I could fight the whole town for you, too, if I had to. Which I probably will." Still, he pressed a quick conciliatory kiss to her mouth. "Now, climb up. Let's get it over with."

The front door flew open. Chat lifted her skirts and rushed down the steps toward them. By the time she reached the rig, Lark was already in the wagon seat.

"I'm sorry, you two," Chat said, hustling around to the far side. Ross swung into place on the other, leaving Lark in the middle. "I never expected you'd insist upon going to work this morning. Of all things, Lark! And with Catfish Jack still on the loose, too."

"I've already had this discussion with your brother," she said, scooting closer to him to give Chat room. "It's something I need to do."

"Well, you have more courage than I would," Chat said. Ross slapped the reins against the horses' backs, and the rig lurched forward. She gripped the seat for balance. "Ross, you're not going to just let her fend for herself, are you? What if Catfish attacks her again?"

"I'll be staying at the bank with her," he said. "She needs watching, for sure."

Lark rolled her eyes at Chat. "And I don't want him there. Try to talk some sense into him, won't you?"

Jaw agape, Chat leaned around Lark toward Ross. "You're staying at the bank? The whole day through?" She turned her surprise back to Lark. "Oh, my."

"Preposterous, isn't it?" Lark asked.

"He must be really worried about you." Chat's voice had lowered. "He despises banks."

Lark recalled he'd declared as much that afternoon in his workshop, a couple of days previous. She found it as perplexing now as she did then.

He sat with his knees spread, his elbows propped on his broad thighs while he kept a hold on the reins. The butt of his Colt pressed into her hip, a cold reminder of why it was there.

"I'll take you to Sarah's first," he said to Chat, perusing the outskirts of Ida Grove sprawled straight ahead. "I want you to stay there after you tend to your business at the dairy. I'll pick you up as soon as the bank closes."

"All right," she said.

"I prefer to walk to work from the boardinghouse," Lark said, firm. "It's what I always do. I'm sure Mrs. Kelley won't mind if you park the wagon there for the day."

Ross glanced at her with a nod. "If that's what you want."

She took comfort in her small victory and sat quietly beside him as they drew ever closer to the township. Never once since she'd arrived in Ida Grove had she left its boundaries, and it seemed like forever ago that Father Baxter had spirited her away to Ross's for safekeeping.

So much in her life had changed since then.

And yet, so much remained the same, she mused, her gaze taking in the rolling farmland that sprawled around her. Acres of corn, wheat and oats thrived, as they always did, under the indulgent Iowa sun. Cows and horses grazed, chickens squawked, children played. Life went on around her, oblivious to her troubles with Catfish Jack. The thought left her feeling small and unimportant.

The buckboard rumbled into town and turned onto Main Street. Businesses were just beginning to open for the day. Only a scattering of people populated the boardwalks, and they glanced toward the rig with unabashed curiosity.

That would change as the morning wore on. Her sudden reappearance after her attack, with the Santanas, no less, would set speculation afire, which made her need to speak to Mr. Templeton before the gossip did all the more imperative.

As if she read Lark's thoughts, Chat took her hand and squeezed in encouragement.

"Try not to worry," she said. "This will all blow over soon. You'll be old news in no time."

"Old news," Lark said with a faint smile and slid her

palm onto Ross's muscled thigh for extra reassurance. "Not hardly, I'm afraid, but I'll hope anyway."

If Chat was surprised at the boldness of Lark's touch, she didn't show it. Ross had left his bedroom this morning before Chat rose. She wouldn't know of the intimacies he'd shared with Lark, but even if she did, it wouldn't matter. Lark already felt like she belonged with him.

Which was foolish and hopeless and made leaving him all the more difficult.

Ross pulled up in front of Kelley's Boardinghouse and set the brake. He dismounted from the driver's seat and assisted Lark down. Chat fended for herself from the other side.

"Do you want to go in?" he asked Lark quietly. "Mrs. Kelley will want to know where you've been."

"No," Lark said. She'd have to face her eventually, but the dear woman would fuss and ask an endless list of questions. Besides, she'd be serving breakfast to the rest of her boarders about now. Lark had no desire to face them all. "I don't want to be late in arriving at the bank."

"I'll tell her you're safe and that you'll explain later," Chat said, reaching into the wagon bed for her basket of eggs and butter crocks. "She'll be so relieved, you know, but she'll just have to wait to find out what happened."

"Thank you."

"Be discreet, Chat," Ross warned.

"I will, I will." Chat hugged him with one arm, did the same to Lark. "Everything will turn out fine. You'll see. Ross is the absolute best. He won't let anything happen to you."

"I know."

But he'd be powerless against Mr. Templeton's disappointment in her. Nor would he be able to save her job if she was fired. And since she was absolutely certain Catfish Jack wouldn't show his homely face in the bank, Ross's presence there was moot.

Chat bounded up the stairs and disappeared inside the boardinghouse, giving Lark one last chance to convince him to return home without her.

"I know you hate banks," she began. "So, really, there's no point in you accompanying me this morning."

He took her elbow, turned her firmly toward Main Street. The Ida Grove Bank was located several blocks down. "My opinion of them doesn't matter in your situation, and you know it."

"But if it makes you uncomfortable to be there, then why go?"

They stepped off the boardwalk into the dirt street. "You know that, too."

She heaved an ungracious sigh and gave up. "If you embarrass me today, Ross Santana, I shall never forgive you."

His dark brows pulled together. "Is that what you're worried about? That I'll embarrass you?"

"You can be quite gruff at times."

"Yeah?" But he didn't sound concerned by it.

They strode onto the next block's walkway. Their footsteps scuffed against the wooden planks.

"I don't want you to scare away the bank's patrons," she said.

"Long as they don't need scaring, I won't."

The door to Al Asher's Broom Shop stood open, and she noticed him already at work inside. He grew his own broomcorn, and the quality of the bristles was excellent. Al was blind, however, and appeared absorbed in what he was doing. She refrained from calling out her usual greeting.

"Just try to look as if you're not there," she said with a definite plea in her voice. They walked past the bicycle repair shop, still closed from the weekend.

"I'm the only one-eyed bounty hunter in town," he said drily. "Folks can't help but notice me."

"That's not what I meant. Find a dark corner somewhere and don't come out."

He had the audacity to look amused. "Now you've gone and hurt my feelings, Lark, darlin'."

She barely heard him. Her attention snagged on two women just ahead, waiting for Harrington's Clothing and Furnishing Goods to open for the day.

And they were staring with clearly-surprised expressions at Lark and Ross.

His amusement faded. "Looks like the hen fest has begun. Who are they?"

A shiny, late-model runabout turned in front of them. Ross took advantage of the diversion to cross to the other side of Main Street. She quickened her step to keep up with his long-legged stride.

"The tall one is Rachael Brannan. Her husband, Thomas, is an attorney-at-law," Lark said. Was it just her imagination or could she feel those ladies boring holes at her back? "The other is Georgiana Schwartz. J.T. Schwartz is the Secretary of the School Board." And instrumental in the building of a half-dozen schools in the area.

Prominent wives of prominent townsmen. Her pulse dipped at the wealth and power they wielded in their little town, and they would most certainly want to know who had attacked Lark in her sleeping room. And why.

"I've heard of them. Nothing but a couple of starched-up Presbyterians," Ross muttered.

"Unfortunately, yes," she said, thinking of the time Mrs.

Schwartz threw a full-blown tantrum when Mrs. Pankonin made an error on her account. Mr. Templeton had fallen all over himself trying to soothe her outraged feathers and made the correction himself. Afterward, he'd scolded Mrs. Pankonin soundly for her mistake.

"Ignore 'em."

One more block until they reached the Ida Grove Bank. Ross and Lark stepped onto the boardwalk that ran in front of the Hungry Horse.

The saloon stood starkly silent. A black wreath hung on the door, announcing Eb Sumner's loss. Lark's heart constricted. If folks hadn't already heard of Jo-Jo's killing, the wreath would spread the word in a hurry.

They passed the cigar store, crossed the street, and met the delicate aroma of baking pies and pastries from Nell's Bakery. Another day, Lark would have stopped in for a slice of molasses gingerbread or a fried apple fritter to savor with a hot cup of coffee, but not this morning. She didn't have the stomach for it.

The bank was right next door. She retrieved the key from her dress pocket and fumbled the metal against the lock. It refused to give. Ross's fingers closed over hers, and she stopped trying.

"Your hand is shaking," he said, leaning toward her. He maneuvered the thing just fine, and the door swung open.

"I'm not normally such a coward." She frowned and soaked in the comfort of his nearness.

"You're nervous," he said. He nudged her inside and closed the door behind them, then turned the lock, immersing them in the silence of the lobby's cool, dim interior. He pulled her against him, one strong arm at her waist, inadvertently pressing the buckle of his holster into her belly. "Just say the word, and I'll talk to Templeton for you."

His offer moved her. Made her wish it could be that easy. "Don't ask me twice, Santana."

"I will, if it'll make you feel better," he insisted.

His mouth hovered over hers, their breaths mingling. How strange to be here with him, just the two of them, on the verge of a stolen kiss. He suspended her in time, helped her forget, if only for a moment…

The sudden, persistent banging on the window sent Lark leaping away with a startled cry. Her gaze jerked to the door.

"See who it is," Ross ordered. He stepped back into the shadows, one hand on the butt of his Colt.

She peeked through the blinds. "It's Mrs. Pankonin."

"Who's she?"

"Our head cashier. She's not usually this early."

Lark dreaded having to deal with the woman's jealous antagonism, but she had little recourse but to let her in. Mrs. Pankonin burst through the doors, a whirlwind of curiosity and indignation.

"It's true! It *is* you!" she exclaimed, jaw agape, staring at Lark as if she'd sprouted a second head.

Lark secured the lock again.

"Yes," she said carefully. "It's me."

"I just talked with Georgiana Schwartz and Rachael Brannan. They said it was. I didn't believe it."

"Well, now you can." Lark forced a smile and pivoted to step around her, but Mrs. Pankonin would have none of it. She grasped Lark's arm firmly.

"Is it true you were attacked in your sleeping room and then you *escaped?*" she demanded.

Lark drew in a breath. "I'm afraid so."

"Why?" Mrs. Pankonin demanded. "Who attacked you? *Why* did he attack you? And where have you *been?*"

Ross stepped out of the shadows, and Mrs. Pankonin whirled with a shriek, as if she thought Ross intended to attack *her*. Or intended to rob them clean.

"What are you doing in here?" Her skin had paled to chalk-white. Recognition dropped her jaw again. "You're Ross Santana, aren't you? Chat Santana's brother. You're the—" aghast, she whirled back toward Lark "—bounty hunter. He's a *bounty hunter*, Miss Renault!"

"I know," she said.

He looked frightening, she had to admit. Dark and shadowed. Armed and dangerous, and in spite of everything, she was *glad* he'd given Mrs. Pankonin a good scare.

The woman took a quick step toward Lark and clutched her arm, as if to use her as a shield if Ross should decide to inflict bodily harm upon her person.

"You shouldn't be in here, Mr. Santana," she said. "It's highly irregular. Mr. Templeton would be most upset if he knew you were, so, please, if you will. Leave."

"I don't believe he'll go," Lark said.

Mrs. Pankonin pinched her lips together and glared at her in disapproval. "We'll be opening the bank in a few minutes time. He must step outside until we are prepared to accept customers. You are aware of the rules, Miss Renault."

"Rules are meant to be broken," Ross said amiably. "I assure you I won't bother you as you go about your duties."

Mrs. Pankonin let go of Lark's arm, but she eyed him with beady-eyed suspicion. "Why are you here?"

"Mr. Santana is a friend—" Lark hastily began.

"—and my being with her is none of your business," Ross finished.

Delicate blue veins bulged in Mrs. Pankonin's throat. "In that, you are wrong, Mr. Santana. As head cashier for this fine institution, it is, indeed, my business." She drew herself up in imperious disdain. "Very well, then. You may stay. But Mr. Templeton will be informed that his perfect little employee was entertaining a male friend of questionable reputation before bank hours in his absence."

"'Entertaining'?" Lark repeated with growing pique. "'Questionable reputation'?"

"You heard me correctly, Miss Renault." Mrs. Pankonin spun on her heel and strode across the lobby, her heels a brisk staccato of righteousness against the polished marble floor.

Lark glowered at the woman's narrow back. It'd be a cold day in hell before she'd give the old shrew the satisfaction of talking to Mr. Templeton first. He valued honesty and forthrightness, and she vowed that he'd learn the truth from her first before hearing it sullied from Mrs. Pankonin.

"Go on about your work, darlin'," Ross said quietly. "If she harasses you, just tell her to shut up. I'll make sure she does."

Exasperated, Lark turned toward him. "She's my superior, Ross," she whispered, to keep her voice from carrying. "I'll do no such thing. And neither will you."

"The offer's there." He tapped the tip of her nose with his finger. "Don't fret over her. She's not worth it."

Easy for him to say, Lark worried as she hurried toward her desk to put her lunch in its usual place in the drawer. *He* didn't have to work with her every day.

Lark would just have to make the best of the situation. Mrs. Pankonin would get over her peevishness eventually, just like she always did when Lark made her jealous about something. It wouldn't be the first time the old witch tattled on her, either.

All that mattered was Mr. Templeton and his opinion of her.

And he expected her to have his bank open for business within minutes. Mrs. Pankonin already had the vault and strong boxes unlocked and a stack of bills ready to sort into trays. Lark busied herself by readying a pot of coffee for him, so that it'd be fresh and hot by the time he arrived. She watered the plants in his office, opened the blinds and cracked the window. He'd appreciate the cool breeze as he sat at his desk throughout the day.

She'd already tidied the lobby before leaving on Friday. All that remained was to turn on the overhead lights, part the drapes on the tall windows and unlock the door. At Mrs. Pankonin's nod, signaling the teller's cash drawers were ready, Lark headed toward the front of the bank to do all those things, glancing at the clock along the way.

Ten o'clock, straight up.

In that regard, at least, the morning had started out just as it should.

With the place bright and ready for business, Lark returned her key for safekeeping in Mr. Templeton's office. Ross, she noted, sat in a chair on the far side of the lobby, one ankle crossed on his knee, absorbed in last week's edition of the *Ida County Pioneer.*

He looked like any other bank patron catching up on the local news. Not even Mrs. Pankonin could complain he looked conspicuous, and vastly relieved, Lark strode to her desk, picked up her pencil and opened the daily ledger.

The front door opened. Automatically, she glanced up, anticipating the first bank patron of the day.

Her pulse leapt.

Mr. Templeton had arrived.

Chapter Fifteen

"Good morning, Miss Renault," he said. He walked with a definite snap in his step, a sign he was in a hurry to get to his office.

"Good morning, sir." Lark half rose in her chair, her mouth open to tell him she'd like to speak with him at his earliest convenience, but he was past her before she could.

She sat back down again.

"Good morning, Mrs. Pankonin." Courteous to a fault, he duplicated the greeting without quite looking at her, which is how he tended to look at her most days, even when he wasn't rushed.

"Mr. Templeton." The woman gave him a tight smile, which of course, he didn't see. "If I could have a moment of—"

His hand lifted in acknowledgement. "Certainly, Mrs. Pankonin, but later, if you will. I'm expecting an important client shortly, and I've some papers to prepare before he arrives."

"Yes, sir."

He entered his glass-enclosed office. She, like Lark,

watched him remove his black felt bowler, hang it on the brass coat rack positioned at a perfect angle in the corner, then walk straight to his desk. He sat down and went right to work.

Mrs. Pankonin's frosty gaze slid to Lark with an unspoken promise that she'd not be deterred in her quest to enlighten their employer to all Lark's faults. His polite but firm refusal to talk simply delayed the inevitable a little.

Lark glanced away with a sinking sense of worry. She, too, had no choice but to respect his command to wait. But what if the old shrew managed to get to him before she did?

Over the top of his newspaper, Lark caught Ross's dark glance upon her, as if he willed her silent reassurance across the width of the bank's lobby. He'd heard the exchange, of course. She'd just have to bide her time, watch for the precise opportunity and take advantage of it.

Thank goodness no customers had arrived yet, but Lark was certain when one did, distracting her, then Mrs. Pankonin would make her move.

She sighed and dated a new page in the ledger. At least, Mr. Templeton hadn't heard of her ordeal with Catfish yet. He would've questioned her about it if he had. He'd be concerned, too, and offer to help any way he could.

Until he learned the truth.

She shook off a stubborn sense of doom and dragged her index finger along a pale blue line on her ledger page. With the tip of her pencil, she met that same line in a row of columns on the far side and wrote down the day's opening balances at the top of each.

"Miss Renault!"

Lark started. The pencil lead snapped. Her gaze jumped to Mr. Templeton's office.

He stood in the doorway. "Bring me last year's Accounts Receivable ledger, won't you?"

It took her a moment to find her voice. "Of course."

She tossed aside the useless pencil and bolted to her feet. All the bank's records were kept in the vault, right there in his office. He could certainly have found this one himself, but Lark suspected he was in too much of a rush to take the time.

The task could provide her with an unexpected opportunity to speak with him after all, and she hurried to comply, making a pointed effort to ignore Mrs. Pankonin's antagonistic stare along the way.

Lark found the book quickly. She handed him the tome, and he laid it on top of the report he'd been working on.

"Thank you, Miss Renault," he said and gave her an absent smile.

She dared to linger. "You're welcome."

Deft and efficient, his fingers maneuvered through the stack of pages in search of the information he needed. Why hadn't she noticed how pale his hands were before now?

Or that she preferred a man's hands lean and blunt-tipped? Calloused from work, too, and tanned from the sun.

Her gaze lifted again to Ross. She felt the strength of his protection, even with the distance between them.

"I trust all went well here at the bank while I was gone?" Mr. Templeton asked.

She managed to smile, though her stomach was tied in knots. "Fine, sir. No problems whatsoever."

"I thought not," he said, pleased.

The knowledge gave her courage. "Did you have a pleasant weekend in Omaha?"

"We did." He stopped flipping through the ledger and regarded her with a measure of amusement. "Phillip missed you."

"Me?" she asked, taken aback.

"I do believe he's smitten with you. He talked of little else."

Lark blinked. What had she done to affect the child so?

"You and outlaws," Mr. Templeton went on with a bemused shake of his head. "His mother and I don't know what to do about his peculiar obsession with them."

Irrational panic stirred inside her. Phillip couldn't know the truth of who she once was. He couldn't. He was only a child, still in diapers when she rode with the Reno gang.

"Well, he's a sweet little boy." She shook off the panic and drew in a breath. "Mr. Templeton, there is a matter I really must discuss with you."

"A bank matter?"

She hesitated. "No. It's more personal, I'm afraid."

"Let's wait, then, shall we?"

"But—"

"Miss Renault." It was rare that Mr. Templeton became short with her, but unfortunately, now was one of those times. "Later."

Her resolve crumpled, but she had to persist. "After your appointment with your client perhaps?"

"Fine, fine."

But already his attention had returned to the numbered columns in front of him. Would he even remember he'd agreed to speak with her after he completed his report?

Lark squared her shoulders and left. She didn't think to ask who he'd be meeting with, but it didn't matter. Whoever it was would be coming soon. She just had to be patient a little while longer.

Al Asher stood at Mrs. Pankonin's teller window. He needed a bank draft written, payment for an order of wire and twine he was expecting to arrive at his broom shop this morning. The details of the transaction engrossed them both, and Lark passed by without acknowledging him.

She sat at her desk again. She didn't want to be aware of Ross across the lobby, didn't want to be thinking of Mr. Templeton and her impending conversation with him, either. She especially didn't want to worry about Mrs. Pankonin's animosity, and she'd have to be sure to tell Al Asher hello before he left the bank, because she always greeted him when he came in, and he'd feel rebuffed if she didn't.

Holy hellfire. No wonder she was beginning to feel frazzled.

The front door opened again. Ollie Rand marched in with a pile of newspapers under his arm. He strode right past her without stopping at her desk to chat.

Ollie *always* stopped to chat.

Lark stared after him as he headed straight to Mr. Templeton's office. It wasn't like him to be in such a hurry, but perhaps he was the client Mr. Templeton was expecting. Or maybe he was simply bringing Mr. Templeton copies of the latest edition of the *Ida County Pioneer,* as he often did, since the newspaper office was just across the street, and Mr. Templeton enjoyed being one of the first to receive the local news and—

Lark's tumbling thoughts came to a screeching halt.

Today was Monday.

Ollie always printed his newspaper on *Wednesdays*.

Her heart began a slow, hard pound.

She shot a worried glance across the lobby. She'd become in dire need of feeling Ross's silent reassurance again.

Except he wasn't looking at her this time. Ollie and Mr. Templeton occupied his complete attention, and by the hard, grim set to his jaw, she knew—she *knew*—he suspected something was wrong.

Like she did.

Nothing was wrong. Nothing was wrong. Nothing was wrong.

She recited the silent mantra while forcing herself to find a different pencil and resume her work. Ollie was only here to inform Mr. Templeton about Jo-Jo's death, that's all. A killing just didn't happen in Ida Grove, even if it was self-defense, as it'd been in Ross and Lark's situation, and, oh, God.

She dared another glance into the office. Ollie stood with his back to the glass, but she could see Mr. Templeton clearly. He listened with rapt attention to whatever Ollie spoke with him about. Then, as if he'd pulled a plug, the color drained straight away from his smooth cheeks.

Lark forgot to breathe.

Mr. Templeton stood, and his leather chair clattered on its back legs from the suddenness of it. He hastened out of his office, and his brisk footsteps tattooed wrath against the marble floor.

Mortified that he might catch her staring, she jerked her glance back to the ledger page, and hoped, *prayed,* those footsteps would keep on going and head right on out the door. But each one grew louder than the last, past Mrs. Pankonin's teller window, past her own, until to her complete and absolute horror they came to an abrupt stop.

Right in front of her desk.

"*Miss* Renault!"

Never had she heard him speak with such fury, and if

she could've escaped to the moon to save herself from what would come next, she would have.

Her head lifted. With all the courage she had left in her pathetic, guilty body, she steeled herself to meet his gaze.

He said nothing. Merely flung the newspaper in front of her with such scathing, burning contempt, she could have burst into flame.

Bank Teller is Infamous Outlaw!

The words screamed across the top half of the *Ida County Pioneer* in a headline so bold, so damning, they could've been heard clear in the next county.

Lark Renault once rode with the Reno Gang.

The sub-headline blurred into the rest of the story below it. Lark couldn't have read more if she wanted, which she didn't, and she swayed with the faint that threatened to pull her under.

Catfish had done this. Somehow, he'd gotten to Ollie and convinced him to print the truth of her past, just as she feared he would, and she grappled for the last shred of dignity she had left to look at Mr. Templeton again.

"What do you have to say for yourself, Miss Renault?" His lip curled. "Or should I say Wild Red?"

"Please understand. I had every intention of telling you the truth."

"When? Six months ago when I hired you?"

Words stuck in her throat. How could she admit she'd had no intention of *ever* telling him who she once was? That it'd been Catfish's greed that had thrown her back into the world she'd hoped to leave behind forever?

"I trusted you," Mr. Templeton said. "I gave you the key to this bank." His voice shook with the outrage he could barely contain. "I gave you the combination to the *vault,* for God's sake."

"And I have done *nothing* to betray that trust!"

"You could've been stealing me blind."

"I wasn't." Desperate to make him believe, she stood, met his accusations head-on. "I never took a single cent. I swear it. All the bank's finances and those of our patrons are in perfect balance, sir."

"An outlaw! I hired an outlaw to work in my bank!" He sounded appalled at himself. He drew up straighter. "I intend to call for an audit. If there is the slightest irregularity, I'll have you make restitution tenfold!"

"Go right ahead." Ross's low voice rumbled between them. "You'll find she's telling you the truth."

Mr. Templeton jerked. Clearly, he hadn't been aware of Ross's presence. Seeing him, several inches taller, dark and rugged and fearsome with his black patch and the Colts against his hips, her employer took a sudden step backward, as if Ross had just exposed him to a plague.

"Who are you?" he sputtered. "One of her kind?"

A muscle leapt in Ross's jaw. "Name's Santana. Ross Santana."

"A friend," Lark said, sending him a beseeching look to behave. To let her handle Mr. Templeton without him.

"The bounty hunter. I've heard of you." Mr. Templeton turned a scornful gaze on her. "Does she have a price on her head, Mr. Santana? Perhaps you're here to arrest her?"

Ross made a sound in his throat, similar to an angry tiger's growl, and grasped her elbow.

"She doesn't deserve this," he snapped. "I'm taking her away from all of you."

"No, Ross." Lark resisted. "Not yet."

"She can't leave, Mr. Templeton." Mrs. Pankonin's voice sounded authoritative. "Don't let her escape!"

Lark whirled. The woman vacated her teller window

and rushed toward them, her clawed fingers on a copy of Ollie's newspaper.

"Call Sheriff Sternberg." Mrs. Pankonin drew on all her years as head cashier to issue the order to her employer with stern-faced resolve. "She should be held in jail until the audit is completed. If any bank funds are missing, she'll be held accountable."

"I didn't steal anything!" Lark insisted, devastated that anyone would think she did, and horrified at the prospect of going to jail again.

"I'm withdrawing my money, Templeton!" Al's cane tapped the floor. "Every dime. Give it to me now."

"Mr. Asher." Mr. Templeton scrambled to soothe his worry. "That won't be necessary. I assure you your money is safe, now that we know of Miss Renault's past tendencies."

"I heard about them Renos!" the blind man scoffed. "Not a tougher gang rode these parts. No, sir! She might be in cahoots with them still."

Lark gaped at him. "No! Not for a long time."

"They're dead, besides," Ross said.

"Except John Reno," Al shot back.

"And he's locked away in prison," Ross snapped.

"Don't matter, not if she's workin' with him on the outside! I want my money!"

Suddenly, the bank's door opened, and John H. Moorehead stormed in with a copy of the *Pioneer.* He was the most influential man in town, the wealthiest, too, having been one of the first settlers in the area. Indeed, Ida Grove wouldn't be the town it was if not for him, and not a finer public servant could be found.

Mr. Templeton paled at his approach. "Good morning, Mr. Moorehead."

"What's this?" the townsman demanded, giving his newspaper a shake. "Some kind of sick joke?"

"No joke, sir. I just received the news about Miss Renault myself. And I'm rectifying the situation. You can be sure of that."

"Ida County will be the laughingstock of the state of Iowa. An outlaw—*a bank robber*—of her caliber working here? What were you thinking, Templeton?"

Mr. Templeton's cheeks bloomed red spots. "I'm well aware of the scandal which is likely to ensue, but if I'd had any idea of her true nature, I *never* would have let her set foot inside this institution's doors."

The avowal whipped through Lark like rawhide. She couldn't breathe from the pain. She'd known it wouldn't be easy, but this…this was unlike any hurt or humiliation she'd ever imagined.

Ross had been right. She should've run away while she had the chance. She'd been a fool to expect Mr. Templeton's understanding, his forgiveness and, holy hellfire, she wanted to get out of here and never come back.

Ross would help her. She trusted no one else, but before she could appeal to him, before he could snatch her to someplace far away…she heard the voices.

She swung toward the bank's front windows. On the boardwalk outside, a crowd had gathered. Ollie moved among them, distributing his newspaper to each, and the shock and fear on their faces turned Lark's blood cold.

"Damn," Ross muttered, seeing them, too.

The door burst open. Thomas Brannan strode in, looking every bit like a shrewd, successful attorney in his expensive black suit and polished leather shoes. He handled the legal affairs for the Ida Grove Bank, few that there were, and his account balances, both personal and business, were sizable. His wife, Rachael, clung to his arm, having wasted no time in informing him of the latest news. Neither spared Lark so much as a cursory glance.

"This is an outrage, Templeton," Brannan said. He threw his newspaper to the floor in disgust. "A bank robber in your employ?"

Mr. Templeton blanched. "Unfortunately, I was not aware of her profession when I hired her. You must understand!"

"Do you think your patrons will understand? I certainly don't." He pointed toward the crowd and their growing restlessness. "You'll soon have a riot on your hands."

A riot?

Lark pressed trembling fingers to her lips.

Mr. Templeton broke into an unflattering sweat. "You're exaggerating, Tom. Only a simple explanation is needed, and they'll calm down. I'm sure of it."

"Explain away, then. While you do, my wife and I will withdraw our funds for safekeeping elsewhere until this matter is settled in every legal sense. Mrs. Pankonin? Your window, please."

Al Asher sputtered. "I'm getting my money before you do. I already told 'em." His cane tap-tapped against the marble as he hastened to be first in line.

Mr. Moorehead shook his head sadly. "I hate to admit it, Templeton, but I agree with them. I'm closing out my accounts, too. I have several businesses to run. I can't afford to find out my money's been stolen. Best to get it now while I still can."

"Gentlemen!" Mr. Templeton appeared on the verge of dropping to his knees to beg them to reconsider. "Your money is completely safe with us!"

Brannan's chest puffed in indignant superiority. He ignored the plea.

"Mrs. Pankonin," he barked. "Your window. Now."

Faced with the dilemma of seeing to an influential customer's demands or obeying the wishes of her employer, the woman wavered with indecision, and she cast a helpless look at Mr. Templeton. The vault contained limited funds. Once the money was gone, the bank would likely go under, and in all Lark's nightmares, her very *worst,* she never dreamed it would end like this.

"I'm sorry." Raw anguish coursed through her. She grasped Mr. Templeton's arm in an appeal for the forgiveness she didn't deserve. "I'm so very sorry."

He yanked away, as if her touch revolted him. "It's too late for that, isn't it, Miss Renault?"

Stricken at the contempt in his voice, she jerked back. A part of her choked and died from that contempt. Her respectability, too. Hope for happiness and a normal life.

Acceptance.

Never would she be accepted for the woman she'd tried so hard to be, and why had she wasted the time trying? To all the judgmental eyes in the world, she was an outlaw. She'd always be an outlaw, no matter how law-abiding she'd become.

"Lark, darlin'," Ross grated in a rough tone.

No one understood the pain like he did. His arm curled around her waist and took her against him, right there in front of Mr. Templeton and the rest.

Lark lifted her face to him, knowing he'd see the torment, the agony of what she'd done, of what was happening now. He'd read her need to escape, too, and understand why.

His arm tightened to pull her away with him. The door crashed open, and a flood of townspeople rushed in, each carrying a newspaper, each rushing toward a teller window and demanding his money.

In the crush, a chair overturned, the same one Ross had been sitting in only a short time ago. He swore at the escalating chaos. The lobby filled with a wall of frantic people, caring less about Lark than the money they'd feared she'd stolen. They pushed shoulder-to-shoulder against one another, their voices raised in panic. Mr. Templeton's was the loudest of all, though, as he tried to calm the frenzy.

"Lark, Lark!"

Amazingly, Phillip Templeton's call reached her through the bedlam. His mother clung to his hand, her porcelain features aghast at the turmoil. She searched for her husband, rising on tiptoe to see past the Stetsons and bowlers on the heads of his patrons, calling his name, again and again.

Someone knocked her hat askew. She no sooner righted it when another's shoulder rammed her from the side. She lost her balance and screamed. Mr. Templeton whirled, just as she went down.

"Amelia!" he cried out and rushed toward her.

In the pandemonium, she lost her hold on Phillip's hand. His frail size was no match for the thoughtless adults who towered over him, and Ross scooped the boy up to keep him from being trampled underfoot.

He set him on top of Lark's desk. His perfectly-parted hair had become mussed, and Lark automatically smoothed it into place again.

"Phillip! Are you all right?" If he'd been hurt because of the trouble she caused, she'd never forgive herself, and impulsively, she gave him a quick hug.

"Yeah." He looked only a little overwhelmed by the chaos going on around him. After adjusting his tiny gold-rimmed spectacles on the bridge of his nose, he grinned up at her. "You're an outlaw, aren't you, Lark?"

"No, I'm not," she said. "But I used to be."

Triumph shone in his expression. "I knowed you were! I knowed it! You're Wild Red, and you knowed the Reno gang, too, huh?"

Lark hated being honest. "Yes."

"How did you figure that out?" Ross asked.

"'Cuz I knowed all about 'em." He held up the stereoscope Lark only now noticed, kept tight against his chest. "I have a picture of the Renos, and you're in it, too, and I wanted to show you, 'cept I didn't tell Mama I wanted to, 'cuz she'd get mad."

"Good thinking," Ross said, his troubled gaze sweeping the crowd.

Phillip blinked up at him. "Are you an outlaw, too?"

"No." Ross's dark glance touched on him. "But I used to be a bounty hunter."

"A bounty hunter!" His eyes rounded behind his spectacles. "Is that how you got your black patch?"

Ross's mouth quirked. "Something like that."

"Phillip, baby!" Amelia Templeton, frantic, on the verge of tears, appeared out of the crowd.

"Are you hurt, son?" Mr. Templeton asked, snatching him into his arms.

"No." He clutched the stereoscope against him again. "Me and Lark was just talking. She's an outlaw, did you knowed that?"

Mr. Templeton's mouth tightened. Without another word, he elbowed his way toward his office to deposit his son and wife there for safekeeping.

But Amelia held back.

She glared at Lark. "If you've so much as stolen a single cent from my husband, Miss Ree-no, I shall personally see to it that you are arrested and thrown into jail for the rest of your life. Do you understand me?"

Lark despaired of trying to defend herself. "Yes."

"And stay away from my son, too. You're a horrible influence for him."

Lark could've bled from the pain slicing through her. Amelia spun and hurried after her husband.

"Let's get out of here," Ross muttered, pulling her from around her desk.

"Ross!" Chat shoved her way through the crowd with Mrs. Kelley and Sarah on her heels. "We heard what happened. Oh, my God. Lark, you poor thing."

Her pity was nearly Lark's undoing, and she choked back a sob of abject humiliation. Of everyone, having Chat see her like this, disgraced and hated, her dignity gone... how could Lark ever face her again?

"Sheriff Sternberg is coming." Chat pushed at Ross's arm. "Go. The back door is that way. Hurry!"

Instinct kicked in. With everyone's attention fixed on withdrawing their money, he took Lark's hand, and together, they escaped the bedlam in the Ida Grove Bank.

Chapter Sixteen

It'd been ridiculously easy getting her out.

Ross thought of how the hysteria had consumed the bank's customers. Made them forget she was there. Once outside, he'd discovered the alleys and streets all but empty. No one saw him take Lark back to her room here at the boardinghouse.

She needed her things. They both knew she couldn't stay in Ida Grove anymore. Folks wouldn't give her any peace if she did. So what had to come next tied his belly in knots.

She hadn't said a word since they arrived. Just sat on her chair, staring out the window, far enough back from the parted curtains that no one would notice.

She was hurting. Made him hurt right along with her, too. It'd be easier if she yelled and screamed about how she'd been treated. But this god-awful silence…

Words to console her were lost on him. He had no encouragement to offer. Nothing positive to give.

She'd reached the end of the line.

His gaze made a slow sweep of her room. Clean. Orderly.

Starkly simple. Not a single picture hung on the wall. No family keepsake on the dresser top. Nothing from her past life to keep her happy in the present one.

Except her respectability.

And now, she'd lost that.

But she had him, for what it was worth. She had to know he'd fight hard for her, too. Do all he could to keep her safe and alive.

If not for the Muscatine heist…

"Ollie's coming."

Lark's subdued voice scattered Ross's thoughts. He strode toward the window, flicked aside the curtain, and scanned the street below. The boardwalks had begun to fill again, which meant the uproar at the Ida Grove Bank had ended. And yeah, there was Ollie, heading toward Kelley's Boardinghouse.

"What the hell does he want?" Ross muttered.

"To talk to me, I suspect."

"I'll send him away." Ross let the curtain drop.

"No."

He halted. "You *want* to talk to him?"

"He's my friend, Ross."

"Not anymore." He hunkered down to her level and tamped down his impatience. "Friends don't do what he did to you."

"No." Lark returned her haunted, pensive gaze to the window. "That's why I want to hear what he has to say."

She sat straight-backed and proud. Took a lot of courage to face the newspaper editor, and Ross admired her for it.

"Reckon we both do," he said. "The man has some explaining to do."

Some of her hair had fallen from the pins, and he fingered an auburn coil dangling against her ear. Time was ticking fast. Too fast. And there was still so much between them.

"We have to talk, Lark," he said quietly. "After Ollie leaves, we're going to make some decisions."

He'd tried before, but she'd have none of it. Now, she didn't have a choice. He wouldn't let her leave this room until she did.

"We?"

The delicate arch to her brow rankled. Why would she question it? Did she think he'd let her fight the world alone?

"Yes, we," he growled.

"My problems are my own," she said. "So are the decisions that must come with them. I'm not going to let you influence me, no matter how I feel about you."

"What the hell's that supposed to mean?"

His mind worked over the words. Over the possibility she might have some covert plan he hadn't suspected. Or did she, even now, despise the justice that ran in his blood?

"Surely you know I've fallen in love with you," she said, her tone almost sad. She laid her palm gently against his cheek. "Haven't I made it so very obvious?"

The admission rocked him. Left him humbled. But before he could begin to fathom the repercussions, a knock sounded on the door.

"Ollie's here." She roused herself, tucked the loose curls behind her ear and gave them an absent pat. "Let him in, won't you?"

"He can wait. We're not through talking yet."

How could she dismiss her admission of loving him so easily…when he was still reeling from it?

"Yes, we are." Her chin lifted. "I think whatever he has

to say is more important. I doubt he'll take long, under the circumstances."

Reluctantly, he rose. "I'll make sure he doesn't. And what you've just told me is damned important."

He headed toward the door and opened it with guarded caution, just in case it wasn't Ollie standing on the other side.

It was, but only a shadow of him. Ross had done work for him in the past—a fine-looking seating bench for his newspaper office—and knew his cheerful nature. Now, the man could barely look him in the eye. Guilt, Ross knew, from what he'd done.

"Hello, Ross."

Ollie shifted uncomfortably. He looked disheveled in his dark suit and white cotton shirt. Wrung out. Easy to tell he'd been up half the night writing his news story about Lark, setting the type and running the whole thing through the presses.

"Ollie."

"Saw you in the bank with Miss Lark today," he said.

"Saw you, too. I'm guessing just about everyone did."

The man grimaced. "Had a hunch you might've come here. To keep watch over her, I suppose."

To protect her from the likes of you.

He glared the thought. "That's right."

Ollie cleared his throat. "I'd like to talk to her, if you please."

Ross leaned a shoulder against the jamb. Took his time complying. Let the man squirm.

"Hell of a thing you did, Ollie. Playing dirty with a woman. I'd bet my good eye she's never done an unkind thing to you or anyone else in this town."

"No, Ross. I don't reckon she has. That's why I'm here. To explain myself. I mean, if she'll listen."

"A little late for that, don't you think?"

Ross gave serious thought to throwing the man out on his cowering ass. But the bounty hunter in him suspected Ollie's actions had been prompted by Catfish Jack. If that was true, Lark needed to hear him out, same as Ross did.

"Let him in, Ross."

She'd moved from the window, close enough to hear the conversation. Ross stepped aside with a glower, let him pass and locked the door.

Ollie paled a little, seeing her, then took off his bowler and clutched it with both hands against his chest. Looked to Ross like he might break into tears any minute.

"Miss Lark. I didn't want to do it. You've got to believe me," he said.

She gave him a cool smile. "Oh, but, Ollie, everyone knows how you love to put the town's gossip in your newspaper. You thrive on it." She cocked her head, her lack of emotion chilling. "Tell me. Have you ever had a story more newsworthy than mine?"

"Never known one to sell more copies, that's for sure." Ross added his sarcasm to hers. "She was good for business, wasn't she, Ollie?"

His glance darted between them. "It wasn't like that at all. I knew what printing the story would do to her. It's just that—"

He halted. Ross could've sworn the man's chin trembled.

"Just what?" Lark asked, her face bloodless. "Are you going to tell me folks deserved to know the truth about me? That it was your job to keep them informed? So you decided to start your own witch-hunt to get the story out?"

"No, Miss Lark!"

"The least you could've done is come to me first. To let

me know what you were going to do." She drew herself up taller, holding on to what little dignity she had left. "Couldn't you have done at *least* that, Ollie'?"

His face crumpled. "You're a fine upstanding woman, Miss Lark. I consider you my friend. Always have, right from the day you came to Ida Grove, and it broke my heart to do it." He sniffled. "Plumb *broke* it!"

"So why did you?" Ross demanded.

Ollie needed a moment to find his voice. "Because of this."

He whipped off his string tie. Yanked open his shirt collar. Parted it wide.

A thin red line decorated his neck, the blood only recently dried.

Lark's fingers flew to her lips. "Oh, my God."

"He told me he'd kill me if I didn't print the story," Ollie said in a dull voice. "He showed me how he'd do it."

"Who did?" Ross and Lark asked in unison.

But they already knew.

"He didn't tell me his name. Under the circumstances, I didn't ask." His fingers dropped from his collar. "All I can tell you is he had the strangest eyes. Not quite matched up. Spooked me, I have to tell you." Ollie swayed a little, the memory obviously horrifying.

Lark hastened for a chair. "Here you are. Sit. Would you like some water?"

"No, Miss Lark." But he sat with a miserable sigh and hung his head.

"His name is Jack Friday. Goes by Catfish Jack," Ross said, grim. "He was acquainted with Lark a while back."

"So he said." Ollie accepted the glass she handed him, and despite his earlier refusal, downed the water in a few long gulps.

"What else did he say?" Ross demanded. "Start from the beginning. We have to know everything."

"All right." The man seemed to feel better for his drink. Took a breath, then let it out again. "Catfish Jack paid me a call in the middle of the night. Woke me from a dead sleep with his knife against my throat."

Lark made a small sound of dismay.

"Almost sent the missus into palpitations, I tell you." He shuddered. "He tied her up to keep her quiet. Then he dragged me down to my newspaper office. Told me all about you once being an outlaw with the Reno gang. That's when he said if I didn't print the story he'd kill me and the missus both." Ollie met her gaze. "I believed him, Miss Lark. I *believed* him."

She crossed her arms under her breasts and shivered. "It's good that you did."

"Anything else?" Ross asked.

Ollie rubbed a hand over his forehead, as if to erase the memory of his ordeal. "He said Miss Lark was staying with you and that the truth would draw her out because she had one robbery left to answer for." He appealed to Lark. "I don't care one whit about what you did or didn't do. I swear I don't. All I care about is keeping me and my wife alive." He stood, as if by doing so, he could make Lark understand. "I had to print your story. He would've killed me if I didn't."

Tears shimmered in her eyes. "Yes."

"You could've gone to the sheriff first," Ross said. "Catfish Jack has a long string of crimes. He's been running from the law for years. Sternberg's posse is itching to get their hands on him."

"I had to keep quiet. Don't you see? He would've killed me!"

"Where's Catfish now?" he asked.

"You think I'd know? I don't. But he's out there. I can feel him. Like he's breathing down my neck." He faced Lark again. "I'm sorry, Miss Lark. I feel real terrible about what I did to you. You don't know how terrible."

"Yes, I do." She stepped forward and embraced him. "Catfish Jack won't bother you again. I promise."

Ollie eyed her dubiously. "Quite a vendetta he has against you. What're you going to do now?"

"I'll do what I must, that's all."

Another time, for sure, Ollie's curiosity would have pressed her to expound on the vow, but at the moment, he was too despondent to care. He pushed his bowler back onto his head.

"Good luck to you, Miss Lark." He headed toward the door, as if he couldn't leave fast enough. "I have a feeling you're going to need all you can get from here on out."

He was gone before Lark could respond.

She stood unmoving. Just stared at the closed door, like she'd been shut off from the rest of the world.

Which she had, Ross knew with a twisting in his gut.

Shut off from her life in Ida Grove.

Abruptly, she strode to her bed, got down on her knees and pulled out a small valise stored beneath it. She laid the case on the mattress, went to her bureau and scooped up the contents in the drawers—stockings, nightclothes, day clothes—and dropped them into the case.

"Lark."

She gathered her toiletries on the washstand. Dumped them in, too.

"Lark," Ross said again.

"I'm leaving." She added a pair of shoes, pushed them deep into the disorderly pile.

"I see that," he said carefully. "Where to?"

"I'm not sure yet. North, maybe. Canada. It's safer there."

Safe, yes. But so damn far.

"We'll leave right away," he said.

She tossed him a cold look. "I'm going alone. You have Chat to care for. Your business. They need you more than I do."

"We'll only be gone until the sheriff and his posse find Catfish. Not long." His brain clicked through details. "Chat can stay here with the Kelleys. My furniture can wait."

And she needed him more than she wanted to admit.

But he refrained from telling her so. He had to get her out of town before Sternberg put Wild Red and the Muscatine heist together—and came up with jail time. And did she really think she could defend herself against Catfish Jack?

The brass catches on her valise snapped into place. Her fingers quickly slipped the leather straps into the buckles and secured them tight. Finally, she stood the case on end and faced him.

"You may as well head on home. I'll be fine from here on out."

He regarded her. "You have no weapon to protect yourself. And your money is sitting in its account at the bank."

She frowned slightly.

"I have both," he said.

"My funds can be wired to me. A simple matter. As for protecting myself?" She shrugged. "I'll buy a gun if—if it comes to that."

"You'll wire your money so that your location can be traced?" A corner of his mouth lifted in a cold smile. "Given Templeton's current opinion of you, he'd be quick to enlighten the law to your whereabouts."

"I'll find a way, Ross." Frustration laced through her words. "You've been more than kind to me, and I shall be eternally grateful for all you've done, keeping me safe and everything, but, please. Leave."

Anger flickered through him that she thought she could dismiss him so easily.

"Is that what you think? That I've been *kind* to you all this time?" He drew closer, until he stood an arm's reach away. "Was making love to you this morning being kind? Or being scared out of my head for what the people in this town would do to you? Or Catfish or the sheriff?" He grasped her shoulders and pulled her against him. "Damned if I know what to call it, but it sure as hell isn't that."

He was incapable of defining the awful fear of letting her go, of what might happen once she was out of his sight. He had a deep, unshakable need to protect her any way he could, no matter the cost, because if anything happened to her…

His mouth took hers with a desperation he didn't bother to control. Her breasts pressed into his chest, proclaiming her femininity. That she was all woman, goodhearted, soft and beautiful, not an outlaw to be despised and condemned. Her arms curled around his back, clung tight. She felt small in his arms. Vulnerable. And, by God, she inspired in him a possessiveness so keen and fierce, he shook from the power of it.

She hung on to him as if she couldn't let go, as if she used the hunger in her kisses to tell him she didn't want him to leave no matter what her words declared, that she needed him, her warrior in the fight against the sins of her past.

His head lifted. Her eyes opened, slow and languid,

and he relished the look of her mouth, wet and swollen and ready to be kissed again.

"I'm coming with you," he said, just in case she needed to hear it said.

"Yes," she sighed.

They'd lost too much time already, and reluctantly, he released her. He carried her valise and followed her to the door. She took his hand, for courage maybe, strength for sure, but paused to cast one final glance around the sleeping room—the blue-flowered curtains at her window, the potted geraniums growing on the sill, her narrow bed, and simple bureau—all those things that had once made the place her home.

Then, as if she feared she'd change her mind, she turned away and hurried with him out the door.

Seeing them, a slow, satisfied smile formed on Catfish Jack's mouth.

He kept himself tight in the shadows behind the blind man's broom shop, the best place he could find to lie low since he'd had to leave his favorite spot by the Hungry Horse. He couldn't see the front of the boardinghouse as well here. Not like he could there.

But he could see the back of the place just fine.

And that's where Santana had taken Wild Red, to keep her hidden while he unhitched his horses from his buckboard rig and saddled them up right quick. Meant he was fixing to leave town with her. Didn't want folks knowing about it, neither.

Wild Red was running scared. Paying a visit to that yellow-bellied newspaperman had done the trick, just like ol' Catfish had known it would. All she'd had to do was tell him where she hid the Muscatine money to save herself some trouble. Now, folks were spittin' mad about her. Got her lily-white reputation ruined, too.

His smile faded. Only thing he couldn't figure was Santana's part in her leaving. He was stickin' to her like sweet on sugar, hardly letting her out of his sight and being real careful to keep her safe.

Why?

He'd know about the money, one way or the other. That's why he'd tracked her clear to Canada all those years ago. But the way them two was acting now, like a couple of pups in a basket…

Hell, it just didn't figure.

One thing was sure. Santana didn't have a hankering to turn her in just yet. He'd had plenty of chances by now, what with him being friends with the sheriff and all. Besides, the jail was just a stone's throw away from the boardinghouse. Would've taken him but a blink of his one good eye to throw her in.

Didn't figure one bit.

The back door opened, and his thoughts scattered. Santana's kid sister came out, carrying what looked like a bag of food. Santana took the bundle and tied it to the back of one of the saddles. Then Wild Red handed him a valise, and he tied that on, too.

The valise showed she planned on being gone a spell. And the way all three were hugging and saying goodbye like they'd never see each other again, well, that pretty much confirmed it.

Wild Red climbed onto her horse, a real pretty piebald. Santana gave his sister a kiss, said something quick and climbed onto his sorrel after.

Catfish eased himself out of the shadows and sprinted toward his own mount, hitched to a shed behind the broom shop. He couldn't shake the unease that Santana had something shady up his sleeve. The bounty hunter wouldn't be leaving his only kin behind if he didn't have good reason, unless—

Catfish nearly tripped.

Unless Wild Red told him where she hid the Muscatine heist and promised him a cut if he didn't turn her in, and that's where they were headin' now.

To get the money.

That had to be it, and infuriated rage arced through him. He yanked the reins loose and leapt into the saddle.

Wild Red thought she could pull a fast one on him, did she? Thought she'd get back at him for blowing her secret wide open for everyone in Ida Grove to know?

She had another think coming. Ol' Catfish wouldn't be fooled so easy. And he'd follow her into the fires of hell to get that money.

Then kill her and Santana both when he did.

Chapter Seventeen

By sunset, Lark was exhausted.

After riding hard all day, they pulled up along the tree-lined banks of the Missouri River to rest the horses and let them drink their fill. Too tired to even dismount, she stared broodingly into the green-brown water—hundreds of miles of it, stretched out across the belly of the country. Powerful and beautiful, the river. Unstoppable by man or beast.

Unlike her own life, which had become dangerously narrow and boxed-in, and on the verge of coming to a shuddering halt.

Spending these long hours on the back of a horse proved a brutal reminder of how she'd once lived—on the run and in the elements. Reminded her, too, of how soft she'd become. How easy her life in Ida Grove had been. How civilized and respected, so why did she feel like an outlaw all over again?

As the day dragged on, she'd grown weary of looking over her shoulder for anyone in pursuit. Each snap of a twig, every sound from an unseen bird or wild animal stirred her worries up, until they ate at her from the inside out.

Her bones and muscles ached. The sun had burned her nose, and the wind tangled her hair. She felt adrift. Lost. Alone.

And yet Ross never left her side. He'd asked nothing of her but that she accept his protection and give him her trust. She'd done both.

But for how long?

Already, she'd begun to see the wrong in her decision to flee Ida Grove. The hopelessness. When would the running end?

She'd considered the consequences of her actions a hundred times over throughout the day. The alternatives, especially, but none more often than the somber reminder that gratification came with restitution. A slate wiped clean, a debt paid in full for the crime she'd committed.

But, holy hellfire, the fear of doing it.

A fear so strong, so crippling, she couldn't help but cling to the belief that running away was the answer, after all. That it would save her from every possible alternative and its consequences, however right and honest they might be.

Yes, she had to keep moving. As far and as long as she could. For today, certainly, toward Omaha.

It'd been Ross's idea that they go there. A smart one, too. The city was heavily populated. Even better, it headquartered the Union Pacific Railroad. She intended to take a train west and lose herself in the vast territory beyond the Nebraska state lines.

He didn't know she'd be going alone, of course. She knew better than to tell him. For all the trouble she'd caused him and Chat both, he was better off without her.

But more than that, she feared the stubborn streak of justice that ran strong within him.

"Lark, darlin'."

She dragged her gaze toward him. He sat on his horse beside her, his face shadowed by his Stetson. She'd always remember the way he said her name, all deep and husky and just a little rough. And whenever he added the endearment, well, he just about made her toes curl from the sound of it.

"You need to eat something." He produced an apple from his saddle bag. "Here."

She considered the fruit, held in his palm. Chat's thoughtfulness. His, too. "Thank you."

She refrained from telling him she wasn't hungry. He'd insist she eat anyway. She polished the apple against her thigh, and the red skin gleamed, but she didn't take a bite.

"Take a drink, too," he said.

He held out his canteen, the cap already unscrewed and hanging from its chain. It wasn't easy meeting his glance, given her plan to escape him once they reached Omaha. He was an intuitive man, uncannily shrewd, and she kept her lashes lowered.

The water tasted cold and refreshing. The dust from their ride had parched her throat more than she realized, and she took several long swallows before handing the flask back.

"It's going to be dark soon. We have to keep moving," he said and drank, too.

"Yes." She perused the sky and the sun sagging closer toward the horizon. A longing to stay right where she was warred inside her.

"We'll get a room as soon as we get to Omaha." Saddle leather creaked as he returned his canteen to its place. "You'll feel better after a hot bath."

She closed her mind to the appeal of sharing a room, a bed, with him. And spending the night warm and safe in his arms.

He tucked an unlit cigarette into the corner of his mouth. "I'm going to wire Sheriff Sternberg when we get there."

The image of sleeping with him shattered. Alarm took its place. "Why?"

"We left town in one hell of a hurry. Someone needs to know our whereabouts in case we run into trouble."

"Sternberg is the last person who should know where I am."

"I know you think so." He made a grim sweep of the cottonwoods and willow trees around them. "But Catfish is tailing us, for sure. He isn't going to let you get away. He wants the Muscatine money too much. When he catches up with us and tries to force you to tell him where it is, I want him arrested." Ross's expression turned hard. "Unless I kill him first."

Lark's resolve to escape wobbled. Oh, God. He'd do it. He'd kill Catfish just like he'd killed Jo-Jo if that's what it took to defend her.

She didn't want Ross killing anyone ever again.

The sick feeling of hopelessness edged back.

"Then we shouldn't be just sitting here, waiting for him to find us," she said. "We shouldn't even stop in Omaha. We should keep running—"

She nearly gagged on her own words.

At what she'd become.

"Holy hellfire. Listen to me." She drew in a bitter breath. "Have you ever heard anyone who sounded more pathetic? Or more desperate?"

He took the cigarette out of his mouth. "Desperate, yes," he said slowly. "Reckon circumstances warrant—"

Something inside her snapped. "Damn the circumstances, Ross! What good will it do to run away? What kind of life is that, for either of us? And yes, you're right. Catfish Jack is sure to be tailing us. We're only prolonging the inevitable before he gets to me, aren't we?" She fought the overwhelming urge to burst into tears. "This is all so ridiculous!"

Ross's brow arched. "Ridiculous? To want to save your life?"

She didn't even try to make him understand.

"Once Catfish finds me, and the sheriff arrests him, or you kill him—it doesn't matter which—then your revenge against him is done, isn't it? An eye for an eye, so to speak."

Ross's jaw tautened. "He's been dodging the law for years. He's got crimes to pay for."

"What about me?" she asked.

He took so long to answer that Lark figured the answer on her own.

"Are you just going to let me go, Santana?" she asked, calmer now that her blood had all but gone cold.

"Lark." Ross sighed heavily.

"You're not, are you?"

He lifted his hat, raked his fingers through his hair, squinted into the setting sun.

Still, he said nothing.

"There's something about the Muscatine heist that's eating at you." The dread built inside her, higher and higher. But she had to know the truth. "After all these years, you still want justice done against me. Why?"

He looked at her then. Square in the eye.

"You took Santana money that night, Lark," he said, his voice quiet, devoid of emotion. "Every dime my father ever saved in his life was in that treasury. You and your gang stole it all."

Her world tilted. The apple rolled to the ground. "Oh, my God."

"He was a master carpenter in Muscatine," Ross went on. "Had a small cabinetry shop going, but he faced bankruptcy when he couldn't keep up the payments. And with no sign of that money or the Reno gang, he drank himself into an early death."

The anguish rolled through her in waves, so thick and heavy Lark pressed her fist to her mouth to keep from choking on it. How he must have hated her back then. He probably still did, deep down.

"My mother had passed on a few years previous. About then, I tracked you and Frank to the Turf Club. After Catfish shot me and you went to prison, I came back, sold what was left of my father's assets and moved to Ida Grove with Chat."

She hugged herself against the pain, her body hunched and miserable in the saddle. The devastation from what she'd done, of all she was responsible for, was almost more than she could bear.

"You helped steal an entire *community's* money, Lark."

"Yes," she whispered and closed her eyes tight against an avalanche of ugly guilt.

"I'm figuring folks are entitled to get back what's theirs," he finished.

They were, of course. For five long years, she'd kept the knowledge suppressed inside her. Now, the truth of his words seared through her like a branding iron to cowhide, leaving her raw and aching.

How could she have been so selfish? So utterly close-minded to the consequences? She'd never even been to

Muscatine, Iowa, before that wintry night. Neither had John or Frank. The citizens, victims of the gang's cold-blooded greed, had done nothing to deserve getting their life's savings taken from them.

If only she knew then what she knew now. She'd change everything about what happened that night. Spare all those people their loss and heartache. Spare herself her own.

But she couldn't. No one could. Not now or ever.

It was much too late.

"I'm sorry for what I've done to you and your family." She fought hard to get the words out. It seemed useless to say them, but she had to. "I don't deserve forgiveness, so I won't even ask, but please know how very sorry I am."

"Telling me where you hid the money will go a long way in proving it," Ross said.

The fear kicked inside her again. She teetered on the edge of succumbing to its power.

"I'll go to prison if I do," she said hoarsely.

"I'll do everything I can to keep you out. I swear I will."

He nudged his horse closer, his arm extended toward her, as if he needed to console her. Himself, too. But she jerked back, so abruptly the piebald flinched. If she allowed Ross to touch her, even in comfort, even with both of them sitting their mounts, she'd lose her ability to reason.

Instead, her lip curled with renewed bitterness. "Keep me out of prison? It's impossible. So please save your breath and don't even pretend it's not."

Thunder brewed in his expression. "You think this isn't tearing me up inside, too?"

"That sounds very gallant, doesn't it? But the truth is, I've done a terrible thing. I must deal with the consequences myself."

"I'm not letting you go through it alone."

"Yes, you are." She grasped the reins, turned her horse before Ross could grab the bridle to stop her. "I need some time away from you. I have to think."

"Damn it, Lark!" he said.

She flinched at the vehemence in his tone and dug her heels into the piebald's ribs, her need to run surging strong within her. But too quick, Ross angled his sorrel in front of her, leaving the riverbank as her only means of escape.

"Please, Ross." The piebald shied, and Lark did all she could do to keep her seat. A sob of frustration pushed into her throat. "Let me go."

"You need time to think?" He leaned forward, caught the chin strap, held on with an iron-fast grip. "Fine. I'll give you time. But you'll have it with me right beside you."

The tears spilled then. At his loyalty or his stubbornness, she couldn't be sure. "I don't want you with me anymore. Do you hear? Get away from me. Just let me *go!*"

"You're not going anywhere just yet, Wild Red," a voice boomed.

Lark's breath jerked. It took her only a split moment to realize the command hadn't come from Ross, but instead, somewhere beyond her range of vision.

Searching, she twisted in the saddle. Ross did, too, and spat out an oath.

Sheriff Sternberg had arrived, surrounded by his entire posse, and Lark knew, then, her time had just run out.

"Best that you back away from her, Santana," Sternberg said. "Reckon she's not going anywhere."

Neither of them were, Ross thought, grim. A half-dozen men, armed and smelling blood, flanked the lawman. One wrong move, and they'd shoot for sure.

Still, it was damned hard to let go of the bridle. He took his time doing it. He needed to stick close to Lark. Figured she might want him to, besides, considering she had six rifle barrels trained on her.

Seven, including Sternberg's.

Hell.

Ross's fingers loosened their grasp, and he eased back. He chanced a quick look at her, saw her wet cheeks, her pale skin, her haunted eyes. That look told him she knew as well as he did she was fresh out of hope.

"Going to ask you to throw down your weapons, Santana," Sternberg said. "The rifle in the scabbard first. Then the two you got strapped on you. Real easy, now."

Ross kept his irritation tamped. What did Sternberg think he'd do? Risk a damned shoot-out?

He pulled his Winchester from the leather, tossed it to the ground. The Colts followed. He felt all but naked not being armed, but he saw the sheriff's side of it. Ross would've done the same if the situation was reversed.

"Get down off your horse." Sternberg's own rifle lowered, now that Ross was unheeled. "You first, then Wild Red."

"Her name is Lark Renault," Ross said, swinging down from the sorrel.

"So she says."

"We'd both appreciate it if you'd address her proper."

"Ross, please." Her husky voice pleaded that he leave the issue alone. "It doesn't matter anymore."

He tossed her a hard glance, telling her it mattered to him. Telling her, too, he intended to lay a few ground rules up front. Sternberg was in charge, no doubt about it, but Ross refused to be bullied into submission.

Her throat moved, as if she understood and swallowed

down further protest. She sat motionless in the saddle with her skirts fanned out behind her. He recalled the time she took getting ready to go to the bank this morning. Chose her best dress, worked her hair up real pretty. Now, the dust had settled into the fabric, dulling its color, and the wind had blown those auburn curls wilder than ever.

She stirred his blood, even now. Fired up the need to protect her, too, and he stepped forward to help her off the horse. He wanted her on the ground with him, close, where it'd be easier to keep her safe.

"Stay right where you are, Santana," Sternberg barked. "She can get herself down without you."

Ross halted, though it grated on him to do it. "She's been riding most of the day. Won't hurt to give her a hand."

"I'm all right," she said and dismounted, quicker than she might have otherwise.

She swayed a mite once she was down, though. She had to be sore and stiff. But she held herself with grace and dignity, and damned if she didn't make him proud, just looking at her.

Only then, with both of them at the posse's mercy, did Sternberg sheath his rifle and dismount, too.

"Got a few matters to discuss with you," he said.

Ross nodded once. He had a grim feeling neither he nor Lark would like what he had to say. "We're listening."

The lawman's badge hung shiny and stern on his shirt pocket. He withdrew a folded paper tucked inside, shook it out. "Did some checking on Jack Friday this morning. Seems there's still a reward out for his capture."

"Not surprised," Ross said. "His justice is long overdue."

The lawman's attention shifted to Lark. He studied her long and hard, then produced a second piece of paper, folded like the first. "Got a wire from the folks at the Muscatine County Treasury, too. They caught wind of Ollie's story about you. Wanted me to know they've got a reward up for your capture and arrest."

Her composure slipped, but she shored it back up again and said nothing.

"Here's the details, if you care to read about them," he added and offered her the document.

She made no move to take it. "I don't, but thank you."

He shrugged. Refolded the message, returned it to his pocket. "Two wires in one day about a couple of outlaws hiding out in my town, right under my nose." He shook his head in disgust before leveling Ross with a disapproving scowl. "You packed up and left town with her mighty fast, Santana. Wouldn't have thought it of you, under the circumstances."

"Had my reasons, Sheriff."

"You knew who she was. What she'd done."

Ross hesitated. Considered the implications of what he was about to admit. "Yes."

"You knew about Catfish Jack, too."

"I did."

Sternberg's scowl went deeper. "You never let on she's been holing up with you all this time, either. Or why. Makes me think you're in cahoots with her somehow."

"She's a good woman, Sheriff. Turned her life around since her time in prison. Ask Templeton how honest she's been. Ask anyone."

Sternberg glowered. "Doesn't matter. Not anymore."

"She's a model citizen. Finer than most."

"She's got a price on her head. That changes things."

Ross clenched his teeth. The lawman was past listening. Eb Sumner, looking full of piss and vinegar, walked his horse out of the group of riders, and Ross realized he had yet another fight on his hands. He tensed at the hostility in the saloonkeeper's expression.

"You're wastin' your breath defending' her, Santana," Sumner snarled. "We don't want her and her lawless friends in our town."

"That's right, Ross." Joe Rinehart spit a dark stream of Skoal into the weeds. He owned the Bowman Lumber Company, and Ross had given him a fair share of business over the years. "That's why we're here. To keep her and her kind out. For good."

Lark stood still as stone. Ross could feel the hurt cutting through her from the prejudice and hate simmering inside these men. Made him hurt, too.

He raked a condemning glance over each of them. Eb and Joe. Tom Bassett, the contractor who built most of the businesses in Ida Grove, including the bank. Sam Allison, a local stockman. William Fourney, who owned the boot and shoe store right across from Al Asher's broom shop. And Gil Usher, a tough-as-nails Civil War veteran who farmed just outside of town.

Sheriff Sternberg's handpicked posse. Each had conducted their financial affairs at the Ida Grove Bank. Each had once stood at Lark's teller window and trusted her with their money and their accounts.

And now each one burned with a hemp fever that turned Ross's stomach sour.

"All her fault my boy is dead," Eb said. "Her caboodling with Catfish Jack makes her responsible."

Mumbled grunts of agreement went up among the posse.

"Jo-Jo took up with Catfish on his own," Ross snapped. "She had nothing to do with it. I was the one who killed him, besides. Self-defense, just like I told you last night."

"She's guilty of stealing that money in Muscatine, too, ain't she?" Joe argued. "The sheriff's wire is proof she is."

Sumner unhooked a coil of rope from his saddle horn, held it up for the group to see. "I say we take care of matters right here and now. Save ourselves a heap of time and trouble later."

"That's enough!" Sheriff Sternberg slashed a glare over the men with a ferocity that kept even the saloonkeeper's mouth shut. He set his hands on his hips and singled the man out. "Understandable you're still grieving about Jo-Jo, Eb, but you're not thinking straight. We're not judge and jury here. If you're finding it hard to be fair, then it's best you head on home right now. You hear me?"

Sumner scowled, but he put the lariat away. "I hear you."

"Anyone else having trouble obeying the law tonight?" he demanded.

One by one, the men shook their heads. After a long moment, the sheriff appeared satisfied and turned back toward Lark.

"All right, then, young lady." He produced a set of handcuffs, and for a fleeting moment, regret flared in his expression. "I suspect you know what's got to come next."

Lark darted a panicked glance at Ross. Just about dropped him to his knees, knowing what she was feeling, and a sick panic of his own wedged in his gut.

But she recovered faster than he did. She stood taller, straighter, and held out both fists toward the lawman.

"Yes," she said quietly. "I do."

Ross had always held a deep respect for the workings of the law. Lived it to the letter most all his life. Profited by it, too.

But in this case, justice fell short. He had to keep Lark from going to jail. To do that, the law needed some twisting.

"Wait," Ross said.

Sternberg did, his thick brow lifted in question.

Now that Lark had come into his life, Ross couldn't let her out. He had to find a way to keep her with him. A part of him. If he failed now, in the next five minutes, he'd never have another chance.

He took a deep breath. "I'll make you a deal."

Chapter Eighteen

He hunkered with Sternberg on the narrow stretch of beach lining the riverbank. The water lapped onto the sand, rushing in, then fading back, making a peaceful, serene sound. Ross doubted Lark took much comfort from it, but the way she stared hard out into the Missouri made him think she tried at least.

She sat on a fallen log, close by where he could keep watch over her, and out of the posse's earshot. Out of his own, for that matter. She didn't seem to much care what deal he worked out for her. Or that he even tried. Considering all the men who had tracked her out here, she'd think it wouldn't do any good anyway.

She'd given up.

But he hadn't.

She needed him more than she'd ever needed anyone right now. From here on out, he was going to make her decisions for her, whether she appreciated it or not.

Someone in the posse had lighted a torch against the nightfall. The men waited, talking, having a smoke. Leaving Lark's fate in the sheriff's hands for the time being.

Ross offered him a rolled cigarette, but he declined. Ross took it to his own lips and lit the tobacco, then inhaled deep, taking the time he needed to sort through the plan jelling in his brain.

"Long ride back to Ida Grove, Santana," Sternberg said, cutting to the chase. "What kind of deal are you thinking of?"

"One that'll help us both get what we want." Ross studied the glowing end of the cigarette. "I figure we've got two problems that need solving. Capturing Catfish Jack and recovering the money taken from the Muscatine County Treasury."

Sternberg shook his head. "You're forgetting Wild Red—" his lips thinned "—Miss Renault, I mean. Her arrest makes three."

"No." Ross's hard gaze didn't waver. "She's the solution."

"How so?"

"She knows where the loot is. Catfish will follow her to the devil to get his hands on it."

"I suspect so. But she won't want to tell us where it is, considering the consequences she'll be stuck with."

Ross's silence showed his agreement. She didn't want to go back to prison. Who would? She had to know that by cooperating with the law, she'd up her chances to stay out.

He slid a glance toward her. Noted the way her hand trembled when she tucked a breeze-tossed curl behind her ear. How incredibly weary she looked. He turned his attention back to the lawman.

"Fact is, Sheriff, you're not going to arrest Catfish Jack without her help."

"Won't be easy, true, but it's not impossible, either."

"Not much you can do that a score of other lawmen before you haven't tried. Myself, included."

Sternberg appeared to consider that. "What do you have in mind?"

"I'm asking that you trust me with her custody. I'll do what I can to recover the money from Muscatine and bring Catfish in for you."

Gray brows shot up. "Alone?"

"That's right. Take your posse and head on home."

The lawman's expression turned defiant. "I can't do that, Santana. Can't believe you'd think I would."

Ross leaned forward. "Spare her the indignity of being arrested by the same men who were once her bank customers."

"She's guilty of a crime—"

"—that she committed when she was a kid running with lawless cousins who messed up her thinking on what was right and wrong. She's turned herself around since then. She's paid the price demanded by a court of law. She's *respectable*, Sheriff!"

Sternberg rubbed his chin, took so long to answer that Ross began to hope he'd agree to the deal.

"How do I know you're not scheming with her to run off with the treasury money?" the lawman demanded.

The accusation stung. Ross let his resentment show. "I left my sister back in Ida Grove, remember? Chat still needs some raising yet. I've no intention of abandoning her, and damn you for thinking I would."

Sternberg gave him a curt nod, conceding the point. "The possibility crossed my mind, and I had to ask, that's all." Sighing heavy, he lifted his Stetson, smoothed the gray hair on his head, and pushed the hat back on again. "I think you're in love with her."

Startled, Ross sent his half-smoked cigarette sailing into the Missouri. The stub landed with a tiny plop.

In love with Lark? Where would *that* get him?

She'd never return to Ida Grove again, not with her reputation ruined. And Ross had responsibilities there. Once he took care of Catfish and the Muscatine money, he'd have to go back. For good.

"You're wrong," he said.

"No other reason I can think of why you're so hell-bent on protecting her." Sternberg's mouth curved in a ghost of a smile.

Ross thought of his time with her. The kisses they'd shared. Making love. Hearing her laughter, husky and intoxicating. Even her cooking, and how all those things had wound their way through into his heart.

He frowned, resisting the possibility. "I've seen the good in her, that's all."

Sternberg grunted and rose to his feet with a grimace, as if his bones had gone stiff.

"Helluva lot of reward money riding on these two cases," he said. "If things pan out like you think they will, you'll be a rich man."

Ross followed him up. "It's not about the money. Never has been."

Sternberg shrugged, as if the denial didn't matter.

"It's about Lark's cooperation with the law and getting her sentence commuted," Ross persisted, driving his point home. "Leniency."

Their gazes met. He read the shrewdness in the lawman's eyes. The need for justice so much like his own.

"Not making any promises, Santana. The deal can be done, I suppose, but I'm just a sheriff, not a judge and jury." He bent, lifted Ross's confiscated holster with one hand, his rifle in the other, then handed them all over. "In the meantime, I'm hiring you. You're a damned fine bounty hunter. If anyone can bring Catfish Jack in, recover that money and keep Wild Red alive and agreeable, you can."

Ross took the weapons.

"I want to be kept informed," Sternberg continued, looking stern again. "I'll be expecting a wire from you every day."

Ross nodded, tried not to hope for more than what the man gave. The worst of the job still lay ahead. He buckled on the Colts. "Consider it done."

"As for Chat, well, I'll be watching her close for you. Just to make sure you haven't abandoned her."

Ross wasn't sure if he should be annoyed or amused at the implication. "Fair enough."

The lawman's gaze lingered on Lark. "I'll let her know what the plan is." He took a step toward her. "She needs to understand her part in it."

"No." Ross laid a hand on his arm, halting him. "I'll tell her."

He wanted to do the talking when the sheriff wasn't around, just in case she refused to cooperate. Ross would have his hands full trying to convince her to reveal the money's location, something the sheriff didn't need to witness. He'd pull the whole deal, for sure, and Ross couldn't risk it.

Sternberg reluctantly gave agreement. "Good luck to you, then."

He headed toward his men, his stride purposeful now that decisions had been made. Like he'd said, they had a long ride back to Ida Grove.

Lark rose slowly from her perch on the log, her gaze riveted to the departing lawman. She strode closer, to better see in the torchlight. "Ross? What's going on?"

"Sternberg cut us some slack, that's all."

The sheriff said something to Eb Sumner, and the other men listened. Mumbles of protest rose up among them, Eb's loudest of all, but Sternberg barked a command, and they quieted. It wasn't long before they mounted up, all sending frowns of reluctance in Lark's direction.

"They're leaving." She turned incredulous eyes on Ross. "Why?"

"The sheriff put you in my custody."

She blinked, her expression gradually showing suspicion. He preferred that over the gut-wrenching despair he'd seen on her most of the day.

"You're using me, aren't you? As bait. You and the sheriff. To get Catfish and the Muscatine loot."

He grimaced at how cold she made him sound. "I'm buying you time, Lark. Trying to get you in the good graces of the law."

"Sure, you are."

"You want to be a guest at your own necktie party?"

"Don't be cynical with me." Her eyes narrowed. "Is Sternberg paying you a decent bounty for my arrest?"

"Not if I can help it."

"What's that supposed to mean?"

"It means—" He blew out a breath. "You have to cooperate with me."

The blood had fused back into her cheeks. "And if I don't?"

"Lark." He considered getting down on his knees. Would she quit fighting him then? "You know what'll happen if you refuse."

She stood still, so still he wished he could see inside her brain to know what she was thinking.

"Fine. *Fine.*" She lifted her skirt hems with a resigned swish and strode toward her horse.

"Fine what?" Ross demanded.

She halted. Swung toward him. Bitterness shone in her features. That god-awful despair, too.

"You win, Santana," she said. "I'll take you to the money."

From a tree-covered ridge above the riverbank, Catfish Jack watched Sheriff Sternberg and his men mount up.

"I'll be damned," he whispered, stunned. "They're leavin'."

Pure relief rushed through him. He could track Wild Red for sure easier without an entire posse breathing down his neck. Santana had been jawin' with the sheriff for a spell. What plan had he hatched to convince them to go?

Even more strange, why was Sternberg letting Wild Red stay with Santana when he'd had the perfect chance to arrest her?

Not that ol' Catfish was disappointed. No, sirree. He needed Wild Red to lead him to the money, all right. She couldn't do that when she was holed up in a jail cell.

Might be a trap to catch ol' Catfish, he thought suddenly. The hairs on his scalp rose. He'd have to watch his back even more careful from here on out.

He couldn't figure why they'd been heading toward Omaha, though. Far as he knew, Wild Red never rode with the Renos this far west, so why would Santana take her?

They were climbing into their saddles, and Catfish hurried for the reins of his own mount. He kept his gaze glued onto their horses, illuminated by the golden glow of torchlight. They turned away from the riverbank and took off in a whole new direction.

Understanding dawned, and a slow grin of delight spread on Catfish Jack's mouth.

December 19, 1867

The three riders rode hard into the black, wintry night, as if Lucifer himself was hot on their trail.

Which would've been fitting after what they'd just done.

It was Wild Red's idea to head to Illinois after busting into the county treasury in Iowa. Farlow's Grove Cemetery southeast of Matherville, not far from the state line, would be the safest place to hide the loot.

Not that she wanted to hide it at all. She wanted to go to South America, but John would have none of it.

He'd gotten real jittery from the string of heists they'd pulled. Folks in a half-dozen states were talking about the Reno gang. Which meant the law just about everywhere was looking for them, thirsting for justice.

Might be they were right to come out here after all. How far would they get with three canvas bags heavy with thousands of dollars in gold, bank notes and greenbacks strapped to their horses?

Holy hellfire, the risk. Wild Red shivered, but she blamed it on the cold. She was glad to see the small plot of land appear on the horizon. A few trees and a thin wire fence marked off the place, and their horses slowed in approach.

She knew where to go, even in the dark, and she led Frank and John through the entrance. Only a scattering of headstones poked up from the ground. Uncle Wil had been dead since the spring past. The loot would rest easy, right along with him.

She pulled up in front of the plain marker bearing the Reno name; Frank and John did the same. Puffs of air billowed from the horses' nostrils. Their muscles twitched.

"Queer feelin' to use the old man's burial pit like this," Frank muttered.

"You hear him complaining?" John yanked up his collar against the wind and ran a nervous glance around them, but the bone orchard sat alone in the Illinois countryside, and this time of night, no one was around.

Wild Red ignored a bite of grief for the man who'd taken her in as his own. "He wouldn't want us getting lynched. He'd understand why we're doing it."

"He'd think we'd gone plumb crazy to leave the loot behind," Frank shot back.

Red secretly agreed. Planning the heist, pulling it off, had taken plenty of raw nerve and guts. Now, they'd just ride away and have nothing to show for their trouble.

"We got to lay low for awhile," John said. "You want to hightail it south, don't you? The money will get us there. We just can't go yet. Not with them Pinks and money-hungry bounty hunters after us." He swung down from the saddle. "Now quit your whinin' and let's set to work. We got to haul out of here before the sun comes up."

Red and Frank exchanged a look, but dismounted. In grim silence, they took their shovels and began to dig.

Lark remembered as if it were yesterday.

Farlow's Grove Cemetery brought the heist alive with appalling realism. But instead of riding out with Frank and John in a frenzied race against time, Ross rode with her, close and protective, one hand on the Winchester he rested against his thigh. No cold December wind blew; rather, summer stars twinkled in the sky. Far from being a notorious gang leader, Ross planned their destination with care, acutely aware of the risks involved, a plan that insisted they ride out well after the midnight hour for the darkness that would shield them from curious eyes.

And now, as she'd done then, she rode through the wire

gate and straight to Uncle Wil's marker. In the silver-gray moonlight, Ross studied the Reno name etched in the stone.

"You hid the money in the old man's grave," he said and shook his head, as if he still couldn't believe it.

"I'm afraid so."

He frowned. "Well, it was clever, if nothing else."

She bit her lip and said nothing.

"Let's see if he's kept your secret all these years, shall we?"

"I'd rather not."

"I know." His low voice revealed his understanding. "But we have to." He swung out of the saddle and rolled up his shirt sleeves, never relinquishing the hold on his rifle. "This is going to take awhile. Might as well get down and keep me company."

Did he think she intended anything else? Holy hellfire, she was more than a little spooked about the whole thing. Was there a task more irreverent? Her imagination had kicked in, too, making the headstones look like stubby fingers pushing through the grass. The breeze slid through the leaves with an eerie whistling sound, and oh, those deep, dark shadows could hide anything.

Or anyone.

She hastily dismounted to get the deed done. Ross lit a lantern and laid it next to the grave, then did the same with his rifle. The flickering light added to their macabre surroundings, but he seemed unaffected by it.

His shovel scooped dirt again and again, the scraping of metal against earth the only sound in the night. For the hundredth time, she regretted doing what she'd done. She regretted, too, that Ross was thrust back into a bounty hunter's world, leaving the peace of his own to track a man who'd rather see her dead except for the riches he craved.

Throughout their journey east, they'd seen nothing of Catfish Jack. Not even a *hint* of a glimpse, and a sense of urgency swept through her, the possibility that they might, after all, beat him at his own game.

She and Ross were almost there. Hours from turning the money back over to the county treasury. Restitution. Deeper and deeper Ross dug, just like she'd dug with Frank and John, until the anticipation, the *need* to free herself of the guilt dropped her to her knees to scrape up mounds of dirt with her bare hands.

Suddenly, the digging took on a different sound, and Ross halted. He stood thigh-deep in the hole. Sweat glistened on his brow, and his glance met hers.

"It's here," he said.

"Yes."

She sat back on her heels. She'd known it would be. There wasn't a better place to stash the loot. None more bizarre, certainly, and no one in their wildest imaginings would think to look in a Reno's grave.

She held the lantern over the pit. Ross scraped away the last layers of dirt with the tip of the shovel, and then, finally, the lamplight caught on a brass latch.

The first of the canvas bags. Lark herself had laid them on top of her uncle's pine casket, neatly, side by side.

"Two more after this one," she said, suppressing a shiver. "Hurry, Ross, so we can get out of here."

He bent, grasped the handle and lifted. Dirt fell away, and he hefted the bag up to the ground, and seeing it now, exactly as she remembered, made her crime more awful than ever.

The cavity revealed the presence of the second, and in moments, he had all three out.

"Get the rope off my horse," he ordered. Clods of earth fell back onto the casket, rushed along by broad sweeps of his shovel. "We'll tie two bags to my saddle, the other to yours."

The sorrel whinnied low at her approach, and she patted his neck to calm his skittish nature while she unhooked the lariat. She freed one end and returned to the bags.

Her fingers moved swiftly forming the same knot around the leather-covered handle that she'd made all those years ago. Tonight, however, she needed both hands to lift the case aside to repeat the process on the second. How had she managed to hoist the thing out of the treasury and onto her horse? Sheer adrenaline?

The sorrel whinnied again, but this time, Lark froze. A faint noise, hauntingly like the clink of a bridle bit, threw her pulse into a jerky rhythm. Or had the sound only been Ross's shovel working the dirt?

Her senses screamed alarm. The rope fell from her grasp. She shot a glance into the deepest, darkest corner of the cemetery.

And there he was. Catfish Jack, riding toward them with his rifle to his shoulder and his finger steady on the trigger. The lantern's light cast him into a spine-chilling glow.

Or maybe it was the greed that did.

"Now, don't you two go and do anything stupid, y'hear?" He halted, only a few yards away from the money. "You just do what ol' Catfish tells you to do, and no one's going to get hurt."

She straightened slow and easy. Forced herself to breathe the same way.

The barrel jabbed in Ross's direction. "Set that shovel down, Santana. Over there a spell. You ain't going to be needing it anymore, are you?"

"Reckon not," Ross said and tossed the tool aside without looking where it landed. He waited. Let Catfish make the next move.

Lark marveled at Ross's control. They'd suspected the outlaw would be tailing them. Had known he would. But to have him show up now, when they'd been so close to taking the money...

The rifle lowered with the barrel aimed right at Ross's chest. "Take off your hardware next." Ross complied, and the holster and Colts landed in the grass with a soft thud. The rifle jerked again. "Now, get your hands up. Both of you."

Lark obeyed, despairing that she wasn't armed, and now Ross wasn't, either. Catfish eased his hold on his weapon, but only a little. "All right, then, Red, honey. Long as you're getting them bags ready to ride, you might as well give 'em a throw right here in ol' Catfish's direction."

She shook her head, stalling, giving herself and Ross time to think their way out. "I can't. They're too heavy."

The rifle cocked. "Do it!"

She flinched but gave the nearest one a kick with the toe of her shoe. The case didn't budge. "See? Heavy."

"She's right, Catfish," Ross said. "Took three horses to haul this loot out of Muscatine. You think you're going to do it with one?"

The outlaw dropped his gaze to the canvas. Lifted it back up to Ross. Swung it sideways to Lark.

Those shifty eyes unnerved her. She had to concentrate to figure which one was looking where.

Catfish smiled, showing the stain of tobacco on his teeth. "Well, hell, Red, honey, you're coming with me, ain't you? To South America? We'll split the loot, just like we talked about. You can help me carry it out of here, just the two of us."

Lark shook her head. "I didn't agree to go there with you. Don't say that I did."

The smile vanished. "Never took you for a fool, Red, but I guess you are. You're going to rot in prison, y'know that? I'm giving you a chance to save yourself."

A detestable word, rot. Lark had the sick feeling it'd be true one day. "The money belongs to the lawful owners. You've no more right to it than I do. You don't really think you're going to get away with this, do you?"

Those crazy eyes turned a little wild. "If it's the last thing I do."

She cocked her head and kept talking. "Ross is an expert bounty hunter. You know that he is. He tracked you all the way to Canada, remember? He'll find you in South America, too."

Ross appeared amused. "And if I don't, well, I guess the sheriff and his posse will stop you before you get there."

A full heartbeat passed before Lark realized what he meant. Only then did she hear the thunder of hooves in the distance.

Chapter Nineteen

Armed with rifles cocked and leveled, they pulled up in a grim circle around Wilkinson Reno's grave, holding Ross captive in the middle with Lark and Catfish Jack.

They were all there. The same six men who had tracked her to the Missouri River with Sheriff Sternberg.

The same men who should've returned to their homes in Ida Grove.

But hadn't.

Satisfaction rolled through Ross. Soon, the covert plan he'd devised with the sheriff would be complete.

The idea had come to him the night Jo-Jo was killed. Ross needed a way to set Catfish up for arrest. The wires he sent every morning on the trip east and the wires waiting for him when he did had fine-tuned the plan.

Justice, in all its glory.

Sternberg was as determined to arrest Catfish as Ross. They both wanted the money recovered in full, too. Made sense to work together to close the cases for good. Making Catfish believe the posse had gone home helped get the job done.

Sternberg had already ordered the outlaw down from his horse and to stand a short distance away with his hands in the air, his rifle out of reach in the grass. The lawman shucked his own weapon and swung a leg over the saddle. He moved a little slow once he was down; Ross figured too many days on the back of a horse tightened up the man's muscles.

"Reckon you know what charges I'm bringing against you, Catfish, but I'm going to tell you, anyway." Sternberg walked closer, pulling a sheet of folded paper out of his pocket as he went. "There's a whole list of 'em. Assault and battery, burglary, swindling, grand larceny and so on." Sternberg halted. "Anything you don't understand that needs explaining?"

"Not a damn thing," the outlaw scowled.

"Plenty of reward money out for you, too."

"So I've heard."

"You'll be going to jail for a long time."

"That so?" Catfish taunted.

"I got six men here that are going to take you there."

The outlaw slashed a contemptuous gaze around the circle holding him trapped, one man after the other, letting them see his hate for what they were about to do.

Until he got to Eb Sumner.

Those shifty fish eyes lingered, and Ross saw trouble.

He moved closer to Lark, thought of his rifle lying in the dirt on the other side of the Reno grave, his holster by another. Eb fidgeted, as if Catfish made him uneasy.

But then the look ended. Catfish snatched the arrest papers from Sternberg.

"Let me see that," he snapped and angled his body slightly, to see better in the lantern light.

Ross chanced another glance at Eb while the outlaw

read the charges. The man was nervous about something all right, but before Ross could put his finger on the reason, Lark suddenly screamed.

He whirled. Catfish whipped out a knife. The lawman reacted a split second too late, and the blade sank deep into his side. Catfish yanked it out again. Sternberg doubled over and went down with a moan.

Rage slammed through Ross. Before he could act on it, Catfish leapt toward Lark with a snarl and hauled her against him, pushing the blade against her throat and smearing Sternberg's blood on the creamy-smooth skin.

Ross's heart dropped to his toes.

The posse scrambled to aim their weapons.

"Nobody shoot!" he yelled. "Nobody *shoot!*"

"That's right." Catfish let loose with a slimy cackle. "Don't shoot if you don't want her dead."

Ross swallowed down a vehement curse for the half vision that handicapped him. For the crippling dark of the night, too. He had to think more than he could see. Had to know what could happen before it ever did to save Lark's life.

It was his fault she was at Catfish's mercy. If not for Ross's setup to get him arrested, she sure as blazes wouldn't be in a cemetery in the middle of the night with a blade at her throat.

She'd gone pale and held herself rigid against the outlaw. Only the hitch in her breathing revealed her terror, and if Ross did nothing else in his sorry, justice-seeking life, he couldn't fail her now.

"Throw your rifles down, boys," the outlaw commanded. "Way back into the dark, y'hear? Just like you made ol' Catfish do."

Nobody moved.

The rage built in the outlaw's features. "You want her dead? Drop 'em, I said!"

This time, the posse showed signs of wavering right along with Ross. Losing all those rifles, become defenseless, unable to protect Lark—

But to refuse would only force Catfish to see his threat through. He'd have nothing to lose.

"Eb!" Desperation grated in Catfish's voice. "You want a cut of the loot, don't you? I'll give you a cut. Make 'em drop the guns!"

Eb's glance dragged over the bags, stayed on them for a little too long.

Like a buzzard smelling raw meat, Catfish went in for the kill. "Lot of money sitting there, Eb. Yours and mine. We'll go to South America."

"Don't listen to him, Eb," Ross said. He had to keep the outlaw talking. Distract him a little. "He's not going to give you a dime."

"That's right," Joe Rinehart said. "He's just airin' his lungs at you is all."

"Think of Jo-Jo, Eb," Catfish bit out. "He was a fine boy. He'd still be here if not for her and her bounty hunter lover. You know that, don't you?"

Eb's expression contorted. "She's caused folks enough trouble. She's responsible for my son's killing for sure!"

Lark's eyes closed in despair. Ross knew how much she despised bloodshed. To be blamed for Jo-Jo's cut her deep.

"We don't owe her a damn thing, not after all she's done." Eb's fury was fired up, now that Catfish had given him a good stoking. "We've been at this long enough."

"You sure have. Tracking her clear into Illinois, tasting dust all day, well, you deserve a little reward, don't you?"

The saloonkeeper glanced at the money again.

"Make them drop their guns, Eb," Catfish said, giving

Lark a little shake in his frustration. "Else I'm going to kill her!"

Ross had heard enough.

"Do as he says, boys. Drop 'em," he snapped.

"Since when did we start taking orders from you?" Eb demanded.

"Since Sternberg gave me custody of this woman, that's when." Ross ran a harsh gaze over the men. "Drop your rifles, I said."

"Ross, are you crazy?" Sam Allison demanded.

Ross shot him a quelling glare, one that said he knew exactly what he was doing, and that he had the authority to do it. The man reluctantly obeyed. Another rifle dropped, another and another, until five weapons lay in the grass.

Only Eb Sumner kept hold on his.

"Now back off. Let me handle this without you," Ross said. Still, the posse hesitated. "Go on." After they complied, losing themselves in the cemetery shadows just beyond the range of lantern light, he turned back to Eb. "May as well get down off your horse and join us."

The saloonkeeper glanced at Catfish.

"Do what he says, Eb!" the outlaw snapped. "We ain't got all night to wait on you."

"He could be pulling a fast one." But he dismounted and moved closer to Catfish, his rifle in both hands.

Ross had each man in plain sight. Lark, too, most of all. "This woman means more to me than the money ever did." The words flowed from him of their own accord. "I'm going to let you have it."

"Ross!" Lark hissed and gave a tiny shake of her head. "Don't do it."

He ignored her. "The loot's been buried so long, folks aren't going to miss it anyway."

One of Catfish's mismatched eyes narrowed. "You bluffin' me, Santana?"

"On one condition," Ross went on. "You let Lark go. Once you do, you can load up the bags and leave."

Time ticked. Ross let it.

"I don't trust him, Catfish," Eb said finally.

"I'm not heeled, am I?" Ross held his arms out. "No one here is. What's not to trust?"

"You hand over the money. What then?" Catfish demanded. "You'll just send this here posse to get it back again."

"No." Ross shook his head. "I can get you to St. Louis. I'll make sure you get on that ship south."

"Yeah?"

The outlaw was tempted all right.

"She's no good to you. I am," Ross insisted.

"He's just colorin' his story to get you to believe him, Catfish," Eb warned. "You know he is."

Ross reined in his frustration. Leveled the saloonkeeper with a hard look. "It's me you want, even more than the money, isn't it? I was the one who killed Jo-Jo. Not her. So let her go."

"She got us to the money, that's all that matters. How long you going to keep arguing about it?" Seemed Catfish was feeling some frustration of his own with the man. "You want proper compensation for losing Jo-Jo or not? Here's your chance!"

"Just don't feel right, that's all."

"We'll even help you load up the loot," Ross said. "Lark knows how. She's done it before. Isn't that right, Lark?"

He willed her to understand what he needed her to do. Her eyes darted downward to the canvas bags, then back to him, and she nodded ever so faintly.

Just beyond her, Ross caught faint movement. Stirring from the sheriff. He needed medical attention, and the urgency in Ross increased tenfold.

"Take that knife from her throat, Catfish." The outlaw was on the verge of caving in. Ross had to keep talking to push him over the edge. "The bags are roped up and ready to tie to your saddle. Let's do it and get it over with. Posse'll be losing their patience soon."

"All right. All right." Catfish slid his tongue over his bottom lip, and at last, the blade eased off Lark's throat. He backed up with her to where his rifle lay in the grass, bent and scooped it into his hand. He straightened, let Lark go at the same time he pointed the barrel at her back.

"Start loading the loot, Red," he said, sheathing the bloody knife into the leather at his waist. "Never shot a woman before, but I'd be happy to make you the first if you try anything slick."

The light breeze played with the curls against her cheek. She dared to face him. Ross marveled at her courage, considering the firepower aimed her way.

"You were always fast on the trigger, Catfish," she said, cool as ice. "I remember that about you."

"Do you now?"

"You were strong, too. Stronger than me, for sure. Those bags are heavy. They'll be hard for me to lift, but I'll do it for you. Just so you know."

A faint smile appeared on the outlaw's mouth. The flattery she used to soften him up.

"Not too late to come with me, Red, honey," he purred.

She stepped back toward the money.

Ross gauged the distance to his Winchester, half-hidden in the dirt.

She tucked both hands around the first bag's handle.

"I don't think so," she murmured.

She swung the canvas hard against Catfish Jack's rifle and knocked the piece right out of his hands.

Ross dove for his Winchester, aimed and pumped the trigger, then rolled back onto his feet, shouldered Lark into her uncle's half-filled grave and fell in with her.

From somewhere, another shot exploded.

Men yelled. Startled horses whinnied. Hoofbeats pummeled the ground, the posse storming in to help.

And then, that quick, it was all over.

Sternberg held himself up on his elbow, his bloodied hand clutched to his ribs. The other held a revolver, and Eb Sumner lay writhing, his knee blasted useless.

"Damned if I've ever shot one of my own men before, Eb, but you had it coming," Sternberg declared in disgust.

"Sheriff, you all right?" Joe Rinehart rushed toward him. The rest of the men scrambled off their mounts.

"Hell, no, I'm not all right," he snapped. "Get me to a doctor."

Joe looked rattled. First time the Ida Grove lumberman had ever witnessed a shoot-out, for sure, and this one cost him his nerves.

"Give me a hand, Gil. Sam, you going to just stand there?" Joe called.

"Tom and William, keep an eye on them two hoodlums," Sternberg ordered and winced as he struggled to his feet with the help. "Not that they're going anywhere."

Ross had to agree. Catfish especially, dead with a pair of Ross's bullets locked deep in his chest.

"Holy hellfire," Lark breathed. She pushed against him, as if just realizing where she was. "Holy *hellfire!*" She bolted out of the grave and batted at the dirt clinging to her skirts. "Of all the places to throw me in, Ross!"

He followed her out. "Would you rather have gotten hit?"

Her glance swung to Catfish, and she shuddered.

"No. Of course not." She leveled him with a somber look. "The setup was flawless, wasn't it? You got everything you wanted. Catfish. The money." She cocked her chin up. "Me."

Ross braced himself against all that had to come next. "Yes."

"And now it's all over."

A raw ache began to form in his gut. There was no going back from here on out, but God, he wasn't ready to lose her. Even with all the planning, the need for his justice satisfied…he'd never be ready.

"Yes," he said again.

The sheriff shuffled toward them, one arm around Joe Rinehart's shoulder. The man bled justice. Despite his injury, he still had a job to do.

"I appreciate what you did to help us bring Catfish down, Miss Renault," he said.

"You sound as if you're surprised that I would."

He grimaced, from pain or from the bluntness of her words, Ross couldn't tell.

"A forked road, I'm afraid. You could've gone either way on it. I wasn't sure which one you'd choose."

Her brow arched. "Really?"

"You'll have to come with us, I'm afraid." He hesitated, sent Ross a weary glance. "I'll do all I can, of course, but…"

His words trailed off. He didn't need to say more.

"Certainly, Sheriff," she said with more courage than

Ross could muster for himself. "I'd like a few moments, though, to—to say goodbye."

He managed a nod through his pain. "We'll be waiting."

Boot steps scuffed the grass, then faded away. Ross ignored the muted voices of the men around them.

"I'm coming with you," he said. He hated feeling this desperate, but his world had turned upside down from his own doing. How would he survive without her?

"Why?" she asked coolly. "I'm going away. There's no place for you in my life anymore."

His fists clenched. "I'll hire the best lawyer this side of the Missouri. We'll get the robbery charge dropped. We'll—"

She shook her head sadly. "Don't you see? I have to take the consequences for what I've done. No one will ever be sure which road I'm on otherwise. Everyone must know I'll always take the straight one." She regarded him, again with that cool look he'd come to dislike. "Including you."

"Lark." He reached for her, to take her into his arms, but she jerked back.

"No. If you touch me, if I let you kiss me—oh, God. I couldn't bear it." She squared her shoulders, hung on tight to what was left of her composure. "Goodbye, Ross."

She pivoted away from him, took one step. Two. Unexpectedly, she turned back. "You did just fine tonight, you know. With one eye. Your aim was true." Her mouth softened. "You're still an expert bounty hunter, Santana."

And because she'd closed her heart to him, she disappeared into the night.

Epilogue

~~~~~~~~~~

Anamosa, Iowa, State Penitentiary
8 months, 11 days later

"Renault. Someone here to see you."

Matron Wood never called any of the female inmates by their first names. Lark had found it difficult to get used to the burly woman's brusque manner, but she hardly noticed it now, her surprise was so great.

"To see me?" she asked.

"Anyone else around here with your name?"

She hardly noticed the sarcasm, either. She couldn't imagine who'd come to visit her, or why, and she set down her paring knife, gave her hands a quick dip in the bowl of water and potato peelings, then dried them on her apron.

Rising from the table she shared with three other women, kitchen workers like herself, she tried not to speculate. Removing her apron and laying it beside the bowl, she tried not to hope.

Yet she did both.

She avoided the curious glances of the other inmates

and hurried after the matron, already departing the room. Lark did her best to tidy the wild wisps which had escaped their pins. She fanned her too-rosy cheeks, flushed from the hot ovens. By the time they reached the Visitors' Room, she'd straightened her collar and smoothed her skirt and tried to look *far* more composed than she felt.

She stopped short at the sight of the dark-suited man staring out the window. He was too well-dressed, not as tall, certainly not as broad, than the one she'd hoped to see. And when he turned to face her, confirming that he was who she thought he was, she still couldn't stop a flabbergasted gasp.

"Mr. Templeton!"

"He says you weren't expecting him. You want to talk to him?" Matron Wood demanded.

Lark's jaw had fallen. She closed it again.

"Yes," she said softly. "Yes, of course."

"I'll be watching through the window. You can have one hour with him. No more." With that, Matron Wood closed the door.

He hadn't changed since Lark saw him last. Every hair was still perfectly combed on his head, his suit was pressed and impeccable, his expensive shoes shining, without a speck of dust. She could even detect the faint scent of starch about him, as she always could.

But she'd never seen him so ill-at-ease.

"I wouldn't blame you if you refused to see me," he said quietly.

Lark was nearing the end of her term here in Anamosa. Throughout the long, lonely days of her incarceration, never once had she blamed him for his disappointment in her.

She only blamed herself.

She drew in a breath. "Mr. Templeton, please."

"My behavior that day at the bank was inexcusable. I never gave you a chance to explain yourself when I knew, I *knew,* your reputation was flawless. I saw it every day that you were in my employ."

"But I never told you about what I'd done, and I should have. It wasn't fair that you had to learn from Ollie. I mean, Catfish Jack. I could have spared you the shock if I'd only told you the truth."

"Can you find it in your heart to forgive me?"

Lark blinked. Had he heard anything she'd said? "It is I who must ask forgiveness of *you.*"

He smiled a little smile. "It seems we have a different perspective on who was wronged more, doesn't it?" His smile faded; admiration took its place. "We heard what you did to bring Jack Friday down."

She recalled the sordid details from that night in the cemetery. Could her reputation drop any lower?

"We all did," he said. "The whole town of Ida Grove. Ollie printed the story in the *Pioneer.* Several times, in fact. Mr. Santana insisted upon it."

Her surprise overpowered the tiny lurch in her heart from hearing his name. Ross? Who detested gossip? Used Ollie's newspaper to spread some of the most notorious gossip the little town ever had occasion to relish?

About *her?*

"You've become somewhat of a legend, Miss Renault. A heroine in the truest sense." His smile returned.

Lark regarded him with grave uncertainty. It was all more than she could comprehend.

"Which brings me to the true nature of my visit," he said, assuming the businesslike efficiency she'd always remember about him. "I've been in conference with Sheriff Sternberg. He told me you wished to make restitution to the victims of the Muscatine heist with compounded interest."

"Yes," she said carefully. "I discussed the matter with him at length."

After her arrest. Before her trial and sentencing. The lawman had promised to look into the matter.

"That's one of the reasons why I'm here. To assist you." He opened a leather case placed near the window. He retrieved a ledger from inside, laid it on the plain wooden table—the only piece of furniture in the Visitors' Room except for a pair of matching chairs—and opened it to a marked page, filled with rows of names that spilled onto the following page, and the one after that.

"This is a list of all the people who had funds in the county treasury the night of the robbery. Also, the amounts due them, which they were paid shortly after the money was confiscated."

Mr. Templeton dipped into the bag again and removed a stack of bank drafts. And finally, her shiny Victor adding machine, all the way from Ida Grove.

Lark tried not to look confused. "And what will we do with all this?"

Mr. Templeton tapped the names on the ledger page with a perfectly-groomed fingertip. "Pay them the interest."

Her glance skimmed the pages of names—oh, God, there were so many—and she endured the first stirrings of panic. "How could I possibly pay all these people interest? I have no money, except for my account at your bank, and that's a *fraction* of what I'd need."

"But you do have money." He showed her another page in the ledger, this one blank except for three posted deposits, made, she noted, by Ross Santana.

"Reward money," Mr. Templeton said in reply to her confused glance. "The bounty he received for capturing Catfish Jack, for recovering the Muscatine heist…and for your arrest."

Her brow knitted. "I don't understand. How can his money help *me* make restitution of the interest?"

"He refused to accept the rewards for himself. He claims the money is yours as much as it is his because you helped him close the cases. He has directed me to see that the funds in their entirety are given to the Muscatine Treasury depositors instead—as interest."

Her mind spun. From Ross's generosity. At the opportunity he'd given her—as well as the robbery victims.

"There won't be enough, however, to pay the full amount due," he said. "I'm prepared to offer you a loan so that you can."

Her spirits—just raised from what Ross had done—deflated again. "I'm not prepared to take out a loan. I have no means to repay you."

"Yes. You do." He leaned toward her. "By coming back to work for me as the best bank teller I've ever had. I'll simply deduct a portion of the loan out of your earnings each week. You'll have enough to live on afterward, not extravagantly, but comfortably. Please, Miss Renault."

Never in the days since her arrest did she think she'd hear the words Mr. Templeton was saying now, nor did she dream that he'd ever *want* her to work for him again, and holy hellfire, she was tempted to go back.

But there was Mrs. Pankonin's jealous animosity to consider. Georgiana Schwartz and Rachael Brannan and the rest of the Ida Grove gossipmongers who would only resent her return to their town.

Lark bit her lip. The words to refuse simply wouldn't form on her tongue.

The words to accept wouldn't, either.

A sound from somewhere beyond the Visitors' Room had Mr. Templeton straightening. His glance swung toward the door.

"I've brought someone to see you," he said with a faint smile. "He's grown tired of waiting, it seems."

Again, hope surged through her, anticipation, too, and when Matron Wood opened the door, her gaze lifted to see a tall, fierce bounty hunter striding through.

It dropped to find Phillip Templeton instead.

He gaped at her, his eyes owlish behind the lenses of his spectacles. Suddenly and acutely aware of how she must look, a convict in her black-and-white-striped calico dress, Lark's cheeks pinkened in embarrassment.

She didn't feel this way with Mr. Templeton. Perhaps the surprise at seeing him had overridden it. But this little boy, who had idolized her, *liked* her, from the time he'd come to recognize who she was...

He must be very disappointed in what she'd become.

Yet he bolted toward her and flung his arms up to hug her with all the strength his frail frame could give.

"Lark, Lark! I thought you were *dead!*"

He spoke with his face pressed into her skirt, and she was sure she misunderstood. Her confused gaze darted to his father.

He nodded. "With all the talk about Jo-Jo's killing, then Catfish Jack's and with you running away, well, he's believed the worst about you ever since, even though we tried to convince him otherwise. He's been quite distraught, in fact."

Though her heart melted, she tossed Mr. Templeton a

"so-you-brought-him-*here?*" look. She bent down and scooped Phillip into her arms. He shifted his grip to her neck, and Lark gave him a reassuring kiss on his cheek.

"I'm fine, Phillip. See? I'm not dead at all."

He lifted his head. "But you don't work at Papa's bank no more, and remember when everyone was mad at you?"

She pursed her lips. "I do."

"And then you left and didn't tell me goodbye, so I knowed you were dead. I just knowed it!"

Her mouth softened. Phillip had been worried for her welfare, and how could she not fall in love with him for it? "I think you knowed wrong, then."

His grasp loosened, but only a little. He looked with bold curiosity around him. "Is this where you live?"

She hesitated. "I'm afraid so."

"Do you like it better than your sleeping room in Ida Grove?"

"I do not."

"Then why do you stay here?"

"Because I must."

"Because you stole some money, huh?"

She sighed. "That's right." Phillip was far more astute than any six-year-old should be. But he needed to understand exactly where he was. "I want to show you something."

She carried him to the window. Together, they peered out into the bleak February day.

"This is where they send outlaws, Phillip. I'm staying in the women's department. Over there—" she pointed "—is where the men live. There are *hundreds* of them, all very bad." She shifted her stance. "See that fence? It's thirteen feet tall and stronger than any fence you've ever seen. Nobody can come in or leave unless you have special permission from Warden Heisey. You'd have to wear a striped uniform, eat the same food every day and no one would hardly ever visit. It's no fun to be here, Phillip. That's why you must never, *ever,* be an outlaw when you grow up."

Phillip shook his head. "But I don't want to be an outlaw anymore."

"You don't?" she asked, taken aback.

"I want to be a bounty hunter and *catch* outlaws. Just like Ross."

"Oh." Lark swallowed against a sudden welling of emotion. "Ross is a fine bounty hunter," she said softly. "You'd do well if you grew up like him."

Matron Wood opened the door. "Five minutes left."

"Thank you," Lark said and set Phillip down. She missed him already, now that it was time for him to leave.

Mr. Templeton took his son's hand. "I'll be returning later to assist you in calculating the interest payments and writing the drafts. I've already made arrangements with Warden Heisey. There's much work to be done."

Lark nodded. Excitement stirred within her, a renewal of her love for numbers. The opportunity, too, to right the wrong she'd done. "Yes. There is."

"Oh. And before I forget." He reached into his suit pocket and pulled out an envelope. "A one-way stagecoach ticket to Ida Grove. I'll expect you at your desk promptly, the first morning you're back."

She pressed her fingers to her mouth and fought tears. A chance to start over. One more time.

"I'll be there," she whispered.

Lark was all kinds of a fool for thinking he'd come. As the stagecoach rumbled to a stop at the Ida Grove station, the last leg of her journey from Anamosa, Lark searched the platform for Ross's tall form, for the dark eye patch that set him apart from other men.

He wasn't there.

Disappointed, she let the window curtain drop. It was her own doing, she supposed. That night in the cemetery. She'd pushed him out of her life, her pride unable to bear having him see her humiliated. A prisoner wearing stripes. Punished for what she'd done.

But where her words declared one thing, in truth, her fickle heart wanted another.

She'd missed him terribly. It was the worst part of her incarceration, being separated from him, stifling her love for a man she'd come to admire for his honor and devotion to justice, when what she really wanted was some sign that he'd missed her, too. A letter. A visit.

Or a few of his bone-melting kisses.

Evidently he didn't need her now that the justice had been done. He didn't want a woman with a blemished past. And God knew he had plenty to do with his time, building furniture and taking care of Chat. Maybe he had even found another woman to hold in his arms at night.

And wasn't *that* a depressing thought?

She had to quit thinking about him. She couldn't forget that this was the happiest day of her life. That she was truly free, her debt to society paid in full.

Yet, now that she was here, what if the citizens of Ida Grove didn't want her back?

She'd never know if they forgave her shame and guilt until she went in amongst them to find out. The stagecoach door opened, and taking a deep breath, Lark climbed down.

A light blanket of snow had fallen overnight, but the platform was swept clear, as were the boardwalks going in every direction. The cold February air filled her lungs, chased away her worry, left her invigorated and eager to begin her new life.

Mr. Templeton stepped forward with a broad smile. "Good morning, Miss Renault. Did you have a good trip?"

"Any trip away from a penitentiary is a good one, don't you think?"

He chuckled his understanding, the camaraderie that had built between them. The driver tossed her valise down, and Mr. Templeton took it upon himself to carry it for her.

"Shall we?" he asked.

He presented his arm, and she tucked her fingers in the crook of his elbow. The Ida Grove Bank was a short walk from the stagecoach station. Lark was both honored and relieved that he insisted upon escorting her there.

Their footsteps clomped on the wooden planks. Her gaze took in the businesses lined up side by side, just as she remembered. If not for the change of seasons, she could almost pretend she'd never been gone.

They rounded the corner. Scores of people lined the boardwalk in front of the bank. Men, women, children. All ages. All familiar. All so startling to see that she faltered in midstep.

But Mr. Templeton merely patted her arm. "Don't be alarmed, Miss Renault. These are your friends. They're here to welcome you back, that's all."

They kept walking. Closer. Someone called out her name, and a sudden cheer went up.

Mrs. Kelley appeared out of the crowd, her round face beaming. "Lark, dear. It's wonderful to see you again. I've saved your sleeping room, you know. I'll expect you for dinner this evening, too, just like always."

All her boarders were there. Sarah, too, smiling shyly,

and then there was Chat, who'd grown even prettier over the past year. She threw her arms around Lark in a quick, exuberant hug.

"I'm so happy you're back!" she said, laughing in delight. "We'll talk soon! I promise!"

Before Lark could answer, Nell, the plump owner of the bakery next door, moved in front of her. She thrust a fried apple fritter, wrapped in paper and still warm from the fryer, into Lark's hand.

"To eat with your morning coffee," she said. "Just like you used to."

Lark exclaimed her thanks, and Ollie elbowed his way to her. "Having you here in Ida Grove is great news, Lark I'll be by to do an interview. Folks from miles around will be happy to read that you've come back home."

Home. Lark loved the sound of it, and her mouth opened to reply, but Mr. Templeton kept her moving past scores of familiar faces—his wife, Amelia's, included, and little Phillip, grinning and waving madly, Father Baxter, too—until they reached the front doors. Sheriff Sternberg waited there, looking fit as ever after his knifing from Catfish Jack.

"A fine thing you did, helping the law and all, Miss Renault," he said. "You made Ida Grove a safer place to live. Folks are just showing their appreciation. We're proud to have you with us. Don't think we're not."

She didn't have time to make an appropriate response before Mr. Templeton ushered her into the bank and locked the doors again, keeping everyone out until the official opening time at ten o'clock.

In the sudden silence of the bank's cool, dim interior, she was positively speechless at what had just happened.

Mr. Templeton smiled, set her valise down by her desk

and removed his hat. "Do you remember the combination to the vault?"

Still holding her fritter, she began to unbutton her coat. "Yes, sir. I believe I do."

"Good. Very good." He gave her a broad wink before his bank-president demeanor returned. "We have a bank to open, Miss Renault. No time to waste."

He left for his office, and Lark hung up her coat, added her hat and hastened to her desk, skimming a quick glance about the lobby as she went. Everything seemed the same—the gleaming marble floor, the polished furniture, even the latest edition of Ollie's newspaper on the tables.

Oh, but it was wonderful to be back!

She sat in her chair and positioned the Victor so that it perched in its usual place. Impulsively, she gave the crank a quick shine. It wouldn't do to have her customers see a smudged adding machine, would it?

Mrs. Pankonin appeared, a cup and saucer in her hand. Lark tensed, but refused to let the pinch-nosed woman dampen what had so far been an almost perfect morning.

"Miss Renault," she greeted her in a stiff voice. "I brought you some fresh coffee." She set the steaming brew next to the Victor.

"Thank you," Lark said carefully and tried to recall when Mrs. Pankonin had done anything of the sort before.

She failed.

A moment passed. Mrs. Pankonin sniffed. "The audit we did after you left showed all accounts in perfect order," she admitted. "Not a single penny was missing."

"I know," Lark said coolly.

"It seems I judged you unfairly, and for that I apologize."

Perhaps the woman was human, after all. Lark smiled. "Your apology is accepted."

The lines around Mrs. Pankonin's mouth faded. Relief, perhaps?

"The bank hasn't been the same since you left. Welcome back, Miss Renault," she said in a rush, then hurried away, her heels brisk against the marble floor.

Lark watched her go with an amazed shake of her head.

By the time the lights had been turned on and the doors unlocked, Lark found herself running a little behind. She stood at her window, arranging the pencils she'd just sharpened in their tray. She still had to double-check the money in her drawer, but, unfortunately, a shadow appeared at her window.

Her first customer of the day. She was feeling a little harried not being ready, but she summoned her most courteous smile and lifted her glance.

Ross stood on the other side of the counter, tall and lean and devastatingly male with his hair a little too long and his eye patch a little too dangerous-looking. An instant pool of heat formed deep in her belly.

She'd not seen him in such a long time. She had to remember that he'd stayed away. That what happened between them was gone forever, and now he was only a bank customer, nothing more.

"Good morning, Mr. Santana," she said, appalled at how flustered she sounded.

He inclined his head and looked amused. Was he mocking her somehow? "Miss Renault."

"What can I do for you this morning?" she asked.

He slid a leather sheaf under her window. "I want to make a deposit."

"You do?" She hid her surprise. "Well, certainly. What is your account number?"

"Don't have one."

She eyed him. "Do you want to *open* an account with us?"

"Guess I need one to put money in one."

Clearly, he didn't hate banks so much anymore. He had, after all, entrusted Mr. Templeton with his sizable reward money, hadn't he? The thought pleased her.

"It won't take but a minute to prepare the papers." She opened the sheaf and blinked at the stack of bills. Holy hellfire, a small fortune. She glanced over at him again. "This is what you want to deposit?"

He frowned. "Just about every damn dime I own is inside that leather."

He looked so grave, she couldn't help giving him a gentle smile of reassurance. "We'll take good care of it, Mr. Santana. I promise you."

As soon as the words were out, she realized how trite they sounded. He knew as well as she did banks weren't impenetrable. Vaults could be blown wide open and stripped clean in minutes.

Still, robberies were the exception. Countless banks throughout the country kept hundreds of thousands of dollars safe every day. Up to now, the Ida Grove Bank had done the same. No reason to believe they wouldn't keep on doing it, too, for a long time to come.

To soothe his misgivings, however, she closed up the sheaf. "The bank is getting rather busy. If you don't mind, just to be safe, I'll count the money and prepare the deposit in the vault." She stepped away from her window with her best bank-teller smile. "I'll return shortly."

She strode into the small steel-encased room which protected the bank's funds and drew in a slow breath. The man still had the power to knock the wind right out of her.

She needed a little time to gather her wits so she could think. And count. Opening the sheaf again, she pulled out the hefty stack of bank notes. She'd be far more accurate if Ross wasn't watching and getting her all rattled—

A muscled arm banded her waist. "Quit playing games with me, Lark."

"Oh!" Startled at Ross's low growl in her ear, several bills slipped from her fingers.

"'Good morning, Mr. Santana'," he mimicked. "'Certainly, Mr. Santana'." He swore. "Is that what you think I am? Just an ordinary bank customer?"

The vault barely had room enough to hold one person, let alone two, and one of Ross's size, especially. She had to push to get herself turned around to face him.

"Well, aren't you? It's been so long since I've seen you, I've forgotten what you are to me."

He stared at her in disbelief. "You sent me away!"

"But I didn't want you to *stay* away!" she blurted.

Why hadn't he seen through her foolish heart? That she'd wanted to be with him no matter what she told him in the cemetery? That even a single, brief visit supervised by Matron Wood would have been better than the awful loneliness she endured believing she'd never see him again?

"What?" he asked, incredulous.

She felt ridiculously near tears. "I certainly couldn't come to *you*, could I?"

For a long moment, he just stared.

In the next, he hauled her against him with a roughness that sent a few more bills drifting to the floor. "I thought— I was sure—" His head lowered, and his mouth covered hers with a restrained savagery that told her she wasn't the only one who'd been miserable. "I've lived hell without you." His hands moved up and down her back, as if he couldn't touch her enough. "Knowing where you were, how you hated being there, what it cost you to go."

"It had to be done," she managed between frenzied kisses. "I *wanted* it done."

"But *I* had to stay behind. I don't know what was worse."

She curled her arms around him, still clutching his money, barely aware that he shouldn't be in the vault with her, that Mr. Templeton or Mrs. Pankonin could come upon them at any time.

"Got to where I couldn't stand being alone, even when Chat was around." At the admission, his head lifted. "I started finding excuses to go into town. When I did, folks would stop and want to talk about you." His hand fisted in her hair; his thumb stroked the auburn coils. "It helped that they missed you almost as much as I did. Admired you, too. I made some friends from it, I guess. They kept me from going crazy."

Lark wasn't sure what she'd done deserved anyone's admiration. But if it helped Ross bury his bitterness and reach out for companionship to the goodhearted townspeople eager to give it, then her ordeal had been worth it.

"You made Ollie write about me," she murmured.

"Because I've learned gossip is what folks do. Sometimes bad, but it can be good, too. I wanted to make sure when the gossip was about you, it was the truth."

"Well, I'm not the only one folks are talking about." She gently touched the smooth leather of his eye patch and smiled. "Little Phillip can't talk about you enough."

Ross grunted. "He's a cute kid."

"Smart, too. You've made quite an impression on him." As he had, she knew, on the rest of Ida Grove. In their time together, while working at the prison, Mr. Templeton always spoke of him with respect, as if he understood that Ross Santana wasn't a bounty hunter to be pitied and feared, but a man with strong ideals and a staunch sense of honor and justice.

She gazed up at Ross. Let her love shine in her eyes. And saw a man comfortable with who he was, what he'd become.

"I love you, Lark," Ross said. "From the time you showed up on my doorstep, hiding in Father Baxter's cape, I've needed to take care of you." His hands slid down to her hips, pulled her tight against him where she could feel the strength of his desire for her. "You're home now. Here, in Ida Grove, with all of us. But most of all, with me. And I'll take care of you forever."

Happiness soared through her.

"Marry me, Lark. Be my wife for always."

"Yes," she breathed. She was home to stay. "We'll take care of each other."

The last of his money drifted to the floor, but it didn't matter.

She had something far more valuable in her life.

Author's Note

I've always found it great fun to breathe life into fiction by weaving in bits of history about real people.

John Reno was a true outlaw. On October 6, 1866, he and two members of his gang committed the world's first train robbery just outside of Seymour, Indiana, a crime for which they were never charged. In 1868, John was sentenced to twenty-five years of hard labor at the Missouri State Penitentiary for robbing a courthouse treasury. John's gang included four of his brothers, Frank, Simeon, Clinton and William, as well as Charlie Anderson. A sister, Laura, never participated in law-breaking.

The Turf Club in Windsor, Canada, did indeed exist as a hideout for outlaws on the lam from the States. And it was there that Frank Reno, Charlie Anderson and Dick Barry plotted to kill Allan Pinkerton, as I'd depicted in the story. And yes, Jack Friday was hired to drive their rig while they hung out there.

By the time John was a free man again, he'd lost Frank, Simeon, William and Charlie to vigilante lynchings.

In truth, Wilkinson Reno died in 1877 and was buried in Seymour, Indiana.

I hope you've enjoyed Lark and Ross's story.

Pam Crooks

The next book in
THE BRIDES OF BELLA LUCIA *series*
is out next month!
Don't miss THE REBEL PRINCE
by Raye Morgan
Here's an exclusive sneak preview
of Emma Valentine's story!

"OH, NO!"

The reaction slipped out before Emma Valentine could stop it, for there stood the very man she most wanted to avoid seeing again.

He didn't look any happier to see her.

"Well, come on, get on board," he said gruffly. "I won't bite." One eyebrow rose. "Though I might nibble a little," he added, mostly to amuse himself.

But she wasn't paying any attention to what he was saying. She was staring at him, taking in the royal blue uniform he was wearing, with gold braid and glistening badges decorating the sleeves, epaulettes and an upright collar. Ribbons and medals covered the breast of the short, fitted jacket. A gold-encrusted sabre hung at his side. And suddenly it was clear to her who this man really was.

She gulped wordlessly. Reaching out, he took her elbow and pulled her aboard. The doors slid closed. And finally she found her tongue.

"You…you're the prince."

He nodded, barely glancing at her. "Yes. Of course."

She raised a hand and covered her mouth for a moment. "I should have known."

"Of course you should have. I don't know why you

didn't." He punched the ground-floor button to get the elevator moving again, then turned to look down at her. "A
relatively bright five-year-old child would have tumbled to
the truth right away."

Her shock faded as her indignation at his tone asserted
itself. He might be the prince, but he was still just as an-
noying as he had been earlier that day.

"A relatively bright five-year-old child without a bump
on the head from a badly thrown water polo ball, maybe,"
she said defensively. She wasn't feeling woozy any longer
and she wasn't about to let him bully her, no matter how
royal he was. "I was unconscious half the time."

"And just clueless the other half, I guess," he said, looking bemused.

The arrogance of the man was really galling.

"I suppose you think your 'royalness' is so obvious it
sort of shimmers around you for all to see?" she chal-
lenged. "Or better yet, oozes from your pores like…like
sweat on a hot day?"

"Something like that," he acknowledged calmly. "Most
people tumble to it pretty quickly. In fact, it's hard to hide
even when I want to avoid dealing with it."

"Poor baby," she said, still resenting his manner. "I
guess that works better with injured people who are half
asleep." Looking at him, she felt a strange emotion she
couldn't identify. It was as though she wanted to prove
something to him, but she wasn't sure what. "And anyway,
you know you did your best to fool me," she added.

His brows knit together as though he really didn't know
what she was talking about. "I didn't do a thing."

"You told me your name was Monty."

"It is." He shrugged. "I have a lot of names. Some of
them are too rude to be spoken to my face, I'm sure." He

glanced at her sideways, his hand on the hilt of his sabre. "Perhaps you're contemplating one of those right now."

You bet I am.

That was what she would like to say. But it suddenly occurred to her that she was supposed to be working for this man. If she wanted to keep the job of coronation chef, maybe she'd better keep her opinions to herself. So she clamped her mouth shut, took a deep breath and looked away, trying hard to calm down.

The elevator ground to a halt and the doors slid open laboriously. She moved to step forward, hoping to make her escape, but his hand shot out again and caught her elbow.

"Wait a minute. *You're* a woman," he said, as though that thought had just presented itself to him.

"That's a rare ability for insight you have there, Your Highness," she snapped before she could stop herself. And then she winced. She was going to have to do better than that if she was going to keep this relationship on an even keel.

But he was ignoring her dig. Nodding, he stared at her with a speculative gleam in his golden eyes. "I've been looking for a woman, but you'll do."

She blanched, stiffening. "I'll do for what?"

He made a head gesture in a direction she knew was opposite of where she was going and his grip tightened on her elbow.

"Come with me," he said abruptly, making it an order.

She dug in her heels, thinking fast. She didn't much like orders. "Wait! I can't. I have to get to the kitchen."

"Not yet. I need you."

"You what?" Her breathless gasp of surprise was soft, but she knew he'd heard it.

"I need you," he said firmly. "Oh, don't look so shocked. I'm not planning to throw you into the hay and have my way with you. I need you for something a bit more mundane than that."

She felt color rushing into her cheeks and she silently begged it to stop. Here she was, formless and stodgy in her chef's whites. No makeup, no stiletto heels. Hardly the picture of the femmes fatales he was undoubtedly used to. The likelihood that he would have any carnal interest in her was remote at best. To have him think she was hysterically defending her virtue was humiliating.

"Well, what if I don't want to go with you?" she said in hopes of deflecting his attention from her blush.

"Too bad."

"What?"

Amusement sparkled in his eyes. He was certainly enjoying this. And that only made her more determined to resist him.

"I'm the prince, remember? And we're in the castle. My orders take precedence. It's that old pesky divine rights thing."

Her jaw jutted out. Despite her embarrassment, she couldn't let that pass.

"Over my free will? Never!"

Exasperation filled his face.

"Hey, call out the historians. Someone will write a book about you and your courageous principles." His eyes glittered sardonically. "But in the meantime, Emma Valentine, you're coming with me."

If you enjoyed what you just read,
then we've got an offer you can't resist!

Take 2 bestselling love stories FREE!

Plus get a FREE surprise gift!

Clip this page and mail it to Harlequin Reader Service®

IN U.S.A.
3010 Walden Ave.
P.O. Box 1867
Buffalo, N.Y. 14240-1867

IN CANADA
P.O. Box 609
Fort Erie, Ontario
L2A 5X3

YES! Please send me 2 free Harlequin Historicals® novels and my free surprise gift. After receiving them, if I don't wish to receive anymore, I can return the shipping statement marked cancel. If I don't cancel, I will receive 6 brand-new novels every month, before they're available in stores! In the U.S.A., bill me at the bargain price of $4.69 plus 25¢ shipping and handling per book and applicable sales tax, if any*. In Canada, bill me at the bargain price of $5.24 plus 25¢ shipping and handling per book and applicable taxes**. That's the complete price and a savings of over 10% off the cover prices—what a great deal! I understand that accepting the 2 free books and gift places me under no obligation ever to buy any books. I can always return a shipment and cancel at any time. Even if I never buy another book from Harlequin, the 2 free books and gift are mine to keep forever.

246 HDN DZ7Q
349 HDN DZ7R

Name _____ (PLEASE PRINT)

Address _____ Apt.# _____

City _____ State/Prov. _____ Zip/Postal Code _____

Not valid to current Harlequin Historicals® subscribers.

Want to try two free books from another series?
Call 1-800-873-8635 or visit www.morefreebooks.com.

* Terms and prices subject to change without notice. Sales tax applicable in N.Y.
** Canadian residents will be charged applicable provincial taxes and GST.
  All orders subject to approval. Offer limited to one per household.
  ® are registered trademarks owned and used by the trademark owner and its licensee.

HIST04R   ©2004 Harlequin Enterprises Limited

**Introducing an exciting appearance
by legendary
New York Times bestselling author**

DIANA PALMER

HEARTBREAKER

He's the ultimate bachelor…
but he may have just met
the one woman to change his ways!

Join the drama in the story of a confirmed
bachelor, an amnesiac beauty and their
unexpected passionate romance.

**"Diana Palmer is a mesmerizing storyteller
who captures the essence of what
a romance should be."—*Affaire de Coeur***

**Heartbreaker *is available from Silhouette Desire
in September 2006.***